For Kelly

Wonderful to meet you!

Tabitha DeVilliers

for Kelly,

you have to think!

—Herman Melville

Tangled Roots Grow in Darkness

Talitha DeVilliers

All rights reserved. This book or any portion thereof may not be reproduced or used in any manner whatsoever without the express written permission of the publisher except for the use of brief quotations in a book review.

Print ISBN: 978-1-09837-799-1

eBook ISBN: 978-1-09837-800-4

Change your opinions, keep to your principles.
Change your leaves, keep intact your roots.

Victor Hugo

Apollonia, in a time reminiscent of the latter days of the Renaissance

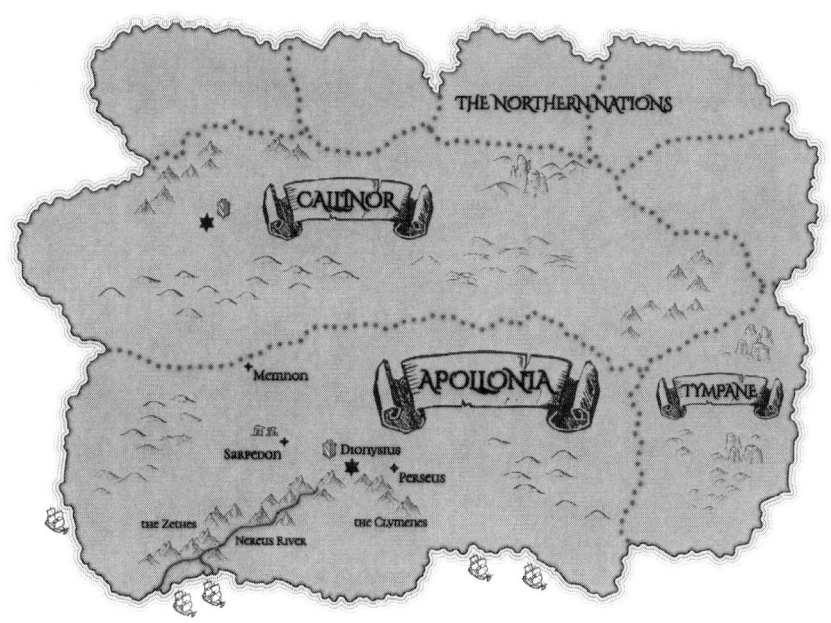

Cory

DUSK IS A MOST CHERISHED TIME OF DAY. THAT LIMINAL period – shorter or longer depending on the season – when the sun is ready to settle in. Having met its obligations, it takes a little time to relax and finally descends, gradually at first, and then seemingly all at once, slipping into the dormancy of nightfall. The transition is quiet. Peaceful. And you might miss it altogether if you aren't paying attention.

Not me. I notice every moment of dusk. Every time I walk home from work, I savor the time to myself, walking a barren path alone. I follow the sun's lead, merely trying to relax.

I can only imagine what a sight I must be to anyone who happens to pass by me – an undersized girl walking with a limp I can no longer hide after a long day on my feet, face marred by a scar on my right cheek, often inflamed after so many hours spent working outdoors. Both the limp and the scar came on after an accident in childhood that dually robbed me of my parents and sent me to live with my aunt and uncle, but it was so long ago I don't even remember it. In any case, I'm an oddity people either stare at or ignore, their eyes burrowing into my scar or gliding past, never settling on me. With my unsightly features, I think I prefer it this way. That is, being invisible.

I follow the same road leading away from the Martin family's modest manor where I have worked for six days out of every week for the past four years. When I was twelve, the family took me on as a mercy after my Aunt Trudy passed away. She had been a cook in their home for some fifteen years, and they felt my employment would show their gratitude for her enduring service to them. But rather than give me chores inside where my deformities could be seen close up, they sent me outdoors to toil under the hot sun. I spend my days tending to the sparse crops they grow, drawing water from the well, or mucking horse stalls and pigpens. It's just as well considering I don't share Aunt Trudy's proficiency for cooking. Not even close.

I enjoy my work, though. Outdoors, the other hands don't say much, but neither are they unkind. They mutter to each other in low conversation that I'm typically left out of, the only girl in this crew of drudges. Still, I see them peering at me from time to time, as put off by my defects as everyone else.

My feet ache as I make the long trek into town. Normally, I'd go left at the fork, which is the shorter path home. But today, I have to visit the apothecary. Uncle Penn's lung condition has worsened and he now struggles to walk across the room without gasping for air. I've had to double my hours ever since he reached the point that he could no longer work in the smithy. While the work is always there, the Martin family doesn't always like giving me more hours, so it's a constant battle to work enough to cover expenses for the both of us.

As the edge of town comes into view, I pat the pocket where my earnings for the day are tucked safely within. The streets are busier than normal because the Princess of Apollonia has traveled from the city. She takes biannual tours through the country, and our town, Perseus, is usually her first or last stop depending on the route she takes. She's set up in the town square, meeting the locals, accepting their gifts, and making empty promises about new policies sure to help the downtrodden here.

As I cross the square myself, I can see her move her hand to her nose over and over, trying to be surreptitious about it. I've lived here all my life, so the stench doesn't bother me. But she grew up in the castle in Dionysius, the capital city, which is the next town over. It's six hours away by foot and packed with shops, taverns, and pretty homes all in a row. I visited once with my uncle and thought it was nice enough, but I prefer the wide open space of the country to the crowded, boisterous climate of the city.

I close in on Princess Giselle's perch and pause a moment to watch. I don't know anyone in line waiting to talk to her. Then again, I hardly know anyone other than Uncle Penn, my neighbor Bethea, and the handful of people I work with.

Princess Giselle has a pretty face, but her eyebrows carve a strict line above her eyes. They give the impression that she does not want to be here, that she would prefer not to be approached. Moreover, her practiced smile does little to challenge the notion. Still, the people seem to fawn over her, the nation's only princess.

She has four guards, two on either side, all of them carrying swords at their hips. I would guess there are more guards stationed around the square keeping watch at all angles, but the crowd obscures them from my view. The guards wear helmets, but their faces are mostly exposed. Only a strip of metal covers their noses down to the tip. They all wear the same unyielding expressions. They are surely paying attention to everything, but it looks as though they see nothing at all.

I turn toward the apothecary. Uncle Penn is out of the ointment he uses for the pain in his joints, though he's been too proud to ask me to get more, knowing how tight our finances are these days. As I turn away from the princess, a body slams into me before taking off into the crowd. I hit the ground and land hard on my arm. I'm just getting my bearings when I feel a hand grab hold of my other arm, pulling me upright again. I immediately dig into my pocket and pull out my coins … or what's left of them.

"No," I mutter to myself, shaking my head in disappointment.

I had been paid twelve pieces for the day's work and I only have three left now. It's barely enough for the ointment. I look off in the direction of my swindler's escape, but he has disappeared.

"Are you all right?" The voice belongs to the man who had helped me up. He's one of the princess's guards. He fixes his gaze on me with an intent look that seems magnified by the dark shade of his eyes. *Like hickory*, I think. His concern seems genuine, but I'm more taken aback by the fact that his eyes don't stray to the scar on my cheek, which is what I've become accustomed to from strangers. At least when they bother to look at me at all.

I nod in response to his question, then drop my gaze to my coins again.

"How much did you lose?"

"Nine pieces," I tell him. I'm almost embarrassed to admit how little I make. Then again, he's a member of the Royal Guard and looks young at that. Guards don't earn much either. No need to pay them decent wages when their four years of service is required by the crown.

"Can you wait?" he asks, and I look at him inquisitively. "Maybe ten minutes." He glances back at the princess, who spies us out of the corner of her eye. "I'll get it for you," he clarifies.

"He's long gone," I say, shrugging. "Whoever he was." My eyes drift back across the square where the thief has long since vanished.

"I mean I can get you nine more pieces. To replace what you've lost." I narrow my eyes, suspicious of what such generosity is going to cost me. "Just wait here."

"I have to go into the apothecary before they close," I say. I can already see Mr. Barlow getting ready to shutter his shop.

The guard nods and steps back into place by the princess. I move toward the apothecary, wondering why on earth the princess's guard would bother helping me at all and never daring to hope that he actually will.

Mr. Barlow knows me because I'm in his shop every week, but he doesn't acknowledge me as anyone special or even likeable. He caters to the high-end clientele with effusive attention – as high-end as Perseus is likely to see, that is. Though he's happy to take my money, Mr. Barlow doesn't go out of his way to wait on me. Still, he knows why I'm here, so he shuffles to the back of his shop just as soon as he finishes adjusting his display.

Finally, he collects a small jar of the salve from behind the counter. It smells of mint and alcohol, a scent I've come to love because it reminds me of my Uncle Penn. I set my three pieces down and Mr. Barlow gives me a half-piece in change. He doesn't bother wrapping up the jar, though I could certainly make use of the cloth and string. He won't waste such things on me. So I wordlessly slip the jar into my pocket and step back outside.

The line to see the princess has dwindled, and she is speaking to the last woman, who keeps her head bowed ever so slightly. Others stand around, hoping for a minute of the princess's time, but the guards have interceded. It's time for her to move on to the next town. Even though it's getting late, Princess Giselle would never deign to stay in Perseus. There's not an inn or home in this town worthy of her presence. There's nothing until Agenor which is some ten miles away. It's a far more affluent town than Perseus with plenty of noble families eager to host the princess. With the poor condition of the roads that threaten to tear up any carriage wheel, I'm surprised she has stayed here as late as she has.

The guard who helped me up is nowhere in sight. I was right not to get my hopes up. So I take my half-piece and salve and turn in the direction of home knowing it will be dark before I make it back.

The roads are muddy from last night's rain, which stretched into the morning. The shower was just turning to a quickly evaporating mist as I made my way to work in the pre-dawn. Luckily it stayed dry all day for me to complete my chores outside. But the clouds above threaten another downpour, and I'm only hoping I can make it home before the torrent. I pick up my pace just a little. Even in the desolate country, it's dangerous to be walking alone at night.

I'm not on the road five minutes when a carriage passes by. It's ornate and golden and accompanied by several men on horseback. It's evidently the princess's carriage on the way to Agenor. The wheels hit a puddle and the muddy water splashes me, drenching my legs and stockings all the way down into my shoes. I curse under my breath.

Then one of the horses in the princess's entourage rears back and turns around. He trots up to me and the guard atop dismounts before me.

"You left," he said. I recognize his voice as belonging to the guard who helped me in town. I'm surprised he could identify me now that the sun has all but finally set.

As I don't know how to respond to his statement, I simply say nothing. I don't want to tell him I didn't think he would – or even could – get me the nine pieces he offered to procure.

He drops his horse's reins and digs a hand under the sash that crosses his torso. He pulls out a single coin and holds it out for me. By the size of it, I can tell it's a 20-piece coin. I'm flabbergasted at the sight of it, still unsure of what to say or do.

"Well?" He lifts my hand and places the coin in my palm.

Words continue to escape me, so I withdraw my half-piece and dumbly offer it to him by way of trying to make change.

His mouth turns up into a smile. "Keep it," he says. He glances up the road at the quickly disappearing carriage. "Where are you headed?"

I finally find my voice. "Home. Off of Tibus Track." I point in the general direction.

"I can take you part way," he offers, eyeing the path. "It might rain. And seeing as how you're already wet, you don't want to catch cold."

I nod my acceptance of his offer, and he helps me onto his horse. He climbs up behind me and we take off at a brisk trot. Mud and muck slosh under the horse's hooves, making a sucking noise with each step until we finally come to a stop at the road that will take me to Tibus Track. Home is just a quarter mile away now.

"I'm sorry I can't take you farther," he says once I'm back on solid ground. "But I need to catch up and fall back into rank before they get too far ahead."

I peer up at him. He has a stately appearance in his uniform atop his equally regal horse, both sumptuously outfitted in the nation's colors – red, white, and gold. I feel intimidated despite the kindness the guard has shown me. "I appreciate you taking me this far," I say. "I don't know how to thank you for the coin."

"No need. Just watch your pockets from now on."

He digs the heel of his boot into the horse's flank in a swift motion and just as quickly, the horse takes off down the road. I watch until his form fades into the blackness of the night before turning to walk the rest of the way home.

Uncle Penn is sitting on a straight-backed chair when I enter. He spends a lot of his time here, as he has difficulty moving from room to room. For him, the chair is conveniently positioned in the house, and he's padded it with a small hay sack for comfort. He has altogether abandoned the thicker sack he used to lie on at night, as it's easier for him to breath if he's sitting upright.

He hands me two apples. "Bethea brought some over today. I saved you a couple," he tells me.

Bethea is the neighbor to our south. She's in her mid-thirties, I think, and married to an older man, her second husband after she was widowed by her first. She had a child who was sickly from birth and now rests six feet under the oak tree closest to her home. She spends her days tending to the apple orchard in the field behind our homes and checking on the dozen hens in their coop. She often thinks to bring me and Uncle Penn a few apples or eggs. Sometimes she brings goods like extra blankets in the winter or a new belt when Uncle Penn's leather ones finally snap from overuse. She's been more generous with her gifts since Aunt Trudy passed away. I suspect she's as lonely without her little boy as Uncle Penn is without his wife. Although neither of them is really alone.

I exchange the salve for the apples, and Uncle Penn practically groans in relief at the sight of the ointment. He's been without any for days, and I know his joints must be paining him.

"I hate to pester," Uncle Penn starts, "but Vanders came by today."

I'm chomping down on a bite of apple when I hand the 20-piece and the half-piece over to him. We still need to pay *last* month's rent, and Mr. Vanders has been over every day this week trying to collect. Rent went up in the past year, and we've struggled more every month to get it paid. We keep falling further and further behind, and I can't seem to work enough to keep up. I just don't have a good enough job to pay rent for a place this size on my earnings alone. It was fine when Aunt Trudy was around and when Uncle Penn could still manage a bit of work, but we're way past that now. Since neither of us wants to abandon this home where I grew up, where Aunt Trudy's memory is everywhere, we tend to avoid the conversation altogether.

Uncle Penn stares at the money the way I did. "How did you …?"

"An angel of the gods," I tell him because I surely have no other answer. The kind of generosity the guard had shown simply isn't bestowed on someone like me. That he is an angel is as good an explanation as any. And one my uncle would understand. He taps the center of his forehead in thanks to the gods.

"It still doesn't mean …" I start.

Uncle Penn nods reluctantly. He knows I was going to say that the blessing of the 20-piece coin doesn't mean we can stay in this house. The coin will buy us some time but not forever. My wages are still what they are. Insufficient.

Uncle Penn pats my hand. Some of his salve sticks to me.

"It's about time I retire to bed. You don't mind, do you?"

I shake my head no and go back outside to collect some water for washing. I'm filthy and my stockings need a good scrubbing before work tomorrow, though I know they won't be dry by then. I expect it will be a long, uncomfortable day, and my toes will surely have blisters by day's end. It will be nice to have the day after that to rest, but I also rue the lost wages from the break.

ON MY DAY OFF, WE GO TO THE TEMPLE TO PAY OUR RESPECTS to the gods. We take Bethea's horse-drawn cart so that Uncle Penn doesn't have to walk. The journey should be faster than walking but the roads are in such need of repair, we have to travel slowly in order to avoid losing a wheel or getting stuck.

Bethea dutifully accompanies us to the temple every week, though she remains angry that the gods claimed her only son. Truthfully, I'm not sure she would go at all if not for Uncle Penn and me, so I'm doubly grateful to her for escorting us.

The temple is busy this day, but we stand in line patiently. Even Uncle Penn bears the wait until we reach the altar and offer our prayers and donations. I see him drop the half-piece into the pool of water before us. It will be collected as alms and used to feed the homeless, the infirm, and the hungry. My heart sinks a little at losing the precious coin, but I'm reassured that we may be blessed by the gods tenfold for this offering, no matter how small.

"Cory," I hear from behind me as I ritualistically tap my forehead and step away from the altar.

It's Leta. She works in the Martins' household. She's the only indoor domestic who doesn't treat me like an outcast. In fact, I've never seen her withhold kindness from anyone she encounters. She's disconcerted today, though, and clasps my hand in both of hers. As she's several inches taller than me, I peer up at her with a question in my eyes.

"I've heard talk from the Martins," she tells me. Leta isn't the gossiping type, and given her demeanor, I brace for whatever bad news she's about to impart. "Mrs. Martin has fallen ill, and they've decided to move closer to her family. They aren't planning to return."

I understand what she's telling me. Without the Martins here, it's only a matter of time before I'm out of a job.

"What will happen to you?" I ask her. Leta serves as lady's maid to the Martins' daughter, and she confirms that she will be relocating with the family and staying on in her current role.

I never really had friends, but Leta has come closest. I'm about to lose her and my source of income. I squeeze her hand and thank her for the warning. At least now I'll have time to look for another position before I'm cast out of the Martins' employ.

"Good luck, Cory," Leta says, the concern on her face never fading as she bids me farewell.

On the ride home, I sit in front with Bethea. No stranger to remorse, she asks me what's wrong and I quietly tell her the news. I don't want Uncle Penn behind us to hear.

"Hmm," she sighs, but that's all the response I get from her. The rest of the way home is traversed in silence.

It doesn't take long for Leta's news to be proven valid. The very next day at work, Mr. Martin's steward summons me and hands me my earnings for the day with the added message that my services are no longer needed. I think I see pity on his face, but when I look again, no such sympathy is evident. He turns his back, signaling that he's through with me.

I leave forlorn. I didn't expect to be let go so quickly. I look hopelessly at the coins in my hand, my final wages. I'm astounded to see only eight pieces there, and I turn immediately to report the mistake.

The steward reluctantly opens the door at my incessant knocking. When I tell him what's happened, he simply apologizes, denies any error, and informs me that eight pieces is all I've earned.

"But I worked a whole day!" I insist. "I should have twelve!"

"We regret you were not notified that a full day's service was unnecessary. The Martins send their appreciation for your work and wish you the very best in your future endeavors." The steward closes the door on me again.

I'm aghast, but there's nothing I can do. He doesn't care what happens to me. I'm no longer of concern to the family. Frankly, I'm not sure I ever was.

The sun's descent is already well underway by the time I stumble home, tears wetting my face. I try to remind myself that the guard's generosity has put us ahead, but without a new job – and fast – it won't last long.

Despite the hour, I head into town. I stop by the apothecary first to inquire if Mr. Barlow needs any help manning the store or tidying up. He looks down his nose at me and ushers me out of the store. If I'm not there to make a purchase, my presence isn't wanted.

I knock on each and every shop – the ones that are still open anyway – and ask the same question. But no one can afford to hire me. Or, they simply don't want a girl like me working in their place of business.

I release a deep and exhausted sigh. It's pitch black when I give up and start the walk back home, which takes longer than normal. Being cheated the full sum of my last day's earnings and finding no work in town has left me feeling particularly weary.

When I finally step inside, I find Uncle Penn already asleep on his chair. Good. I'm not up for rehashing the day's events just now. I drop the eight pieces on the table, then cursorily scrub down in the washroom before crawling onto my hay sack. I want to sleep for ten hours, though I know I'll be up at the crack of dawn to look once more for work.

For several days, my search for employment continues. In town, I find time and again that every shop or tavern I enter has no need of me.

"You might try Satine's," the proprietor of the last tavern I enter suggests. He wipes down a mug with a dirty rag, drawing his eyes up and down my body.

Satine's is the last resort for girls without other options. But I'm not prepared to give up looking for work, nor do I have any intention of ever selling my body. I don't think I'll ever fall that low. I can't imagine the degradation.

I then decide to go house to house. Surely somebody could make use of a housemaid or stable girl. I may not be too good in the kitchen, but I do know how to clean until things sparkle, tend to crops and animals, and make a variety of repairs. If necessity is the mother of invention, I should be able to fashion myself a whole new life.

Alas, I am out of luck. This is a poor little town. No one has anything they can part with for the luxury of a little help. I return home exhausted, desperate, and empty-handed. I'm sure we'll be out on the street before the month is out.

AT THE END OF THE WEEK, I TAKE THE TIME TO BRING IN enough water to fill the washbasin and strip myself down for a full soak. It's been days since my last bath. At least the water isn't bad. A bit chilly perhaps, but it's been warmed some by the sun. I dunk my head underwater and scrub my scalp. I make sure to rub behind my ears and scrape under my fingernails. The blisters on my toes have either healed or torn, the serum inside washed away, flaps of dead skin still hanging on. I carefully tear them away, leaving the fresh layer of skin beneath exposed. I take the soap and run it over my entire body until there isn't a speck of dirt left on me. It feels good to be so clean. I don't usually have the time for luxuries such as baths. And I don't want to waste the soap if it's not necessary. It takes too much time to make more.

Once I've dressed, I look for something to eat. In the kitchen, I find Bethea sitting at our rickety table with Uncle Penn. She's brought a basket with a half-dozen eggs to gift us. Even though I'm starving, I resist the temptation to snatch them up, remembering my manners.

"Go ahead," she offers, pushing the basket in my direction. I thank her and immediately take the eggs and set some water to boil.

As I do so, Bethea taps the other item she has brought, set delicately on the table between her and Uncle Penn. It's a letter folded twice, which she opens to peruse, though it's clear she already knows its contents.

"My aunt lives in Dionysius," Bethea says. "She's in good health but getting on in her years. She is finding it more and more difficult to get by on her own."

Uncle Penn remains quiet. He seems to know something that I do not.

"I've taken the liberty of writing to see if she might desire some assistance, and I've just heard back from her."

My heart sinks a little. Bethea is going to be moving. She's been invaluable to us, imparting apples and eggs and other little necessities. And now we are losing her, too. I try not to let my disappointment show. I don't want Uncle Penn to think I can't manage to take care of us both. But the truth is, I'm not sure that I can.

I crack the eggs as I ask, "When will you be leaving?"

Bethea startles. "I'm not," she replies, and I nearly sigh out loud in relief. "I've asked on your behalf."

Now it's my turn to startle. "I thought you said she lives in Dionysius."

"She does."

"But that's much too far to travel for work."

Bethea remains quiet, letting the offer sink in. She doesn't intend for me to stay here. She wants me to move in with her aunt in Dionysius. But no, I couldn't do that. I could never leave Uncle Penn. He and Aunt Trudy raised me since I was orphaned at three years of age. They took me in. Cared for me. Loved me. How could I abandon him now when he needs me the most? No, there must be another way.

"I've discussed the matter with my husband, and he's in agreement," Bethea continued. "We've told her that you're his daughter from a previous marriage. Educated six years and knowledgeable about running a household."

My eyes widen. I haven't got *any* education, and I know nothing about running a household.

Bethea merely goes on, saying, "Penn can come and stay with us. We'll take good care of him. My husband is gone working so much. He knows I'll be grateful for the company." She gives Uncle Penn a gracious smile.

Uncle Penn's eyes remain glued to the table, though. To the letter. I can tell he's already reconciled himself to this unexpected chance. He knows it's our best option. Our *only* option. But I haven't had the time to come to terms with it.

I've been to Dionysius only once in my entire life. It's a large city with many more people than Perseus. The hustle and bustle is overwhelming. I couldn't possibly leave the only town I've ever known. I couldn't possibly leave Uncle Penn. When would I ever see him again?

But it's clear the decision has already been made. There's no way Uncle Penn will let me stay. Not with this kind of opportunity. It's a lie to elevate my position in a better city. In a better home. In a safe job. A *good* job. In the city, I could even meet someone. Marry. Be assured a secure future. The prospect is everything I could ever hope for. Everything he would ever want for me.

Except that it's a prospect that doesn't include Uncle Penn. My heart splinters.

The eggs are done. I slip three of them onto a plate, which I hand to Uncle Penn. Suddenly, I'm no longer hungry, but I sit down with my own eggs anyway, poking at them with a fork. It would be rude not to eat after Bethea was kind enough to bring them for us. What she has done to procure me a job is a gift as well, but it's a difficult one to accept.

"When is she expecting me?" I ask.

"We leave in a week. I'll teach you all I know about running a home, and then I'll take you to Dionysius myself."

"But why …" I can't find the words, but Bethea seems to understand what I'm asking.

"Because you're a good person, Cory. You deserve this chance. Take it."

I always knew Bethea was fond of me. Maybe I've been the child she could care for since her own passed away. I suppose she knows a thing or two about how hard it can be to get a leg up in life. After all, she came from some money and married down. When her first husband died, she had already lowered herself to such a degree that the choices of marriage partners previously available were no longer options for her. She remarried as best as she could but not quite on par with where she could be now if only she'd married well the first time around. I only know these things because people talk about people like Bethea. They gossip about people who take risks and then flounder. They judge them for decisions they swear they never would have made in the same position. But what do they really know? I suppose it helps them to feel better about their own misfortunes.

"We'll start first thing tomorrow," Bethea says. "Come by and help me put together a room for Penn. I'll show you how to properly dress the bed and tend to a lady in the evenings. Aunt Farryn, that is, though you'll refer to her as Lady Havard."

Lady Havard.

She sounds like a noblewoman far too prim and proper for company the likes of mine. Then again, it's not really *my* company she believes she's getting. She thinks she's getting a young woman with education and skill in domestic service. I don't know how Bethea thought this was a good idea. This Lady Farryn Havard will see through me in an instant. She'll know I'm a fraud. And Bethea will pay the price for lying.

Bethea politely slips out, leaving Uncle Penn and me to discuss the arrangement, and the weight of the load I'm being asked to carry descends upon me.

"Uncle, I can't."

"You can," he assures me, "and you will."

Despite the faith Uncle Penn has in me, I have none in myself. My breathing quickens. He lets the wave of panic wash over me. He knows how terrified I am. If he's scared too, he doesn't show it. As the surge of fear finally turns into tears, he pulls me to him in a tight embrace.

"You're the light of my life, Cory. But your light shines too bright for a place like Perseus."

AT THE FIRST HINT OF DAWN, I MARCH OVER TO BETHEA'S home as requested. It's quite a bit larger than ours, which makes the sense of loneliness she must feel all the more palpable. There are so many rooms here and only two heartbeats to occupy them.

I hardly remember Tobin, who was four when he passed away. I was eight then. I can picture his stubby legs tramping through the tall grass behind the house, but it's the only memory of him I generate. Well, except for the funeral when his ghostly white body was lowered into the ground. It was the first time I had ever seen a dead body. The *only* time in fact. I shut my eyes at Aunt Trudy's funeral so as not to see her as an empty vessel. I hope I never have to see another.

Bethea meets me at the back door and ushers me inside. "Thank goodness you're here early," she says. "We have so much to go over." She seems more panicked than I was last night.

Maybe the gravity of the situation is finally sinking in. Maybe she sees now what a bad idea this is.

"I hope you're ready to learn."

"I am," I say firmly, if only to inspire confidence in her and maybe myself, too. If she isn't sure I can do this, how can I ever be? It seems to work, as Bethea gestures with a nod for me to follow her.

She shows me the room that will be Uncle Penn's, where a much finer cushioned chair than the one we have is placed in the far corner. It looks as though it has been untouched for years. I'm sure he will be more comfortable sleeping there than the bed where she has laid out sheets, pillows, and blankets for me to practice with.

Bethea talks about the many different kinds of sheets and pillows and the patterned wool blanket that fits around everything. We go step by step through the process of putting it all together, which is a far more complicated setup for sleeping than I've ever seen. She adds that Lady Havard's bed will have posts at each corner and curtains connecting them on three sides. I'm to draw them closed for her at night.

"And you'll have a solid bed like this in the servant's quarters," Bethea says. It hadn't even occurred to me to consider my accommodations. A bed like this one every night? That sounds wonderful! "Now, in the evenings, Aunt Farryn will expect you to lay out her nightgown and nightcap. She'll take a cup of tea to help her to sleep. You'll have to prepare it and leave it on a tray on the bed, and don't forget to bring her sugar with a teaspoon. That's the smaller of the spoon sizes, you understand?" I can't imagine why anyone would need spoons of different sizes, but I nod my understanding anyway, and she goes on. "It's also a good idea to take the kettle in case she wants a second cup. You do know how to make tea, don't you?"

I nod. It's one of the only things I can make.

"Good. Now she's still able to change into her nightgown on her own, but don't hesitate to assist if she asks. There's little room for modesty between a lady and her maid. You'll need to brush out her hair. One hundred strokes. She may want you to braid her hair or pin it in curls before bed. Do you know how to do that?"

I have braided hair a couple of times before, but I am no expert. Mine is barely long enough to practice on and I prefer to let it hang loose to shroud the scar on my face. Bethea demonstrates the steps for each, and I practice braiding and curling her hair. So far, it all seems to be going well. That is, until she asks, "Can you read?"

"No," I admit, feeling my cheeks flush. I shouldn't feel ashamed for not knowing how to read considering I never had any schooling. Still, I'm aware that it's a sign of the lower class to which I belong. "Aunt Trudy taught me letters and sounds and how to spell my name, but that's about all."

"That's a very good start," Bethea says. "Well, no time like the present. Aunt Farryn enjoys a good book, and her eyes tire easily. Since she's under the impression that you're educated, she may ask you to read to her."

"What am I supposed to do if she does that?"

"You'll read, of course. It isn't that difficult. I'm sure you'll pick it up in no time."

Dread washes over me. I have less than a week to learn to read? It doesn't seem possible.

My second day of training starts with more reading lessons, whereby I stumble through the words, trying them out sound by sound. I get most of them wrong.

"You're doing great," Bethea encourages me, but I know this isn't true.

After what feels like hours, we finally move on to other tasks. We can skip sewing, ironing, and laundry, as those are chores I'm quite familiar with. I also know enough about gardening to keep Lady Havard's flowers alive, but Bethea shows me how to replant them in new pots when they need fresh soil. She selects a potted plant of her own and tilts it to the side. Holding firmly to the stems, she gently tugs and taps until the roots break free and all the loose soil has fallen away.

"The roots can become tangled up in there, so you have to be gentle with them. If you pull too much or go too fast, they will break off and the plant will have a much harder time growing in a new pot. Everyone fawns over the beauty of the blossom up top where light is absorbed, but it's the roots below you need to protect. They provide the nutrients."

Bethea has me go through a variety of household chores. I've done most of these tasks before, such as dusting, stacking firewood, and burning logs in the fireplace. She has me go through the motions anyway just to get my feet wet. Other tasks, like beating a rug or plumping pillows, are new because we don't own these niceties, but they are fairly self-explanatory and simple.

Bethea is surprised by my vigor, but I'm used to working long hours outdoors. This is really nothing compared to that. True, my leg is beginning to throb, as it sometimes does after too many hours on my feet, but I ignore it. It's really more of an annoyance than anything else.

Even after these tasks, my work for the day is hardly done. Bethea takes me to the kitchen and explains that I'll need to be able to take inventory of things like silverware, plates, and teacups. I've learned to count pretty high and Aunt Trudy taught me some basic math skills, so I feel fairly comfortable that I won't have a problem keeping track of Lady Havard's kitchen items. Bethea tells me I'll need to notify Lady Havard when things break or go missing, as such items are wont to do.

Then Bethea turns to cooking, the one chore I've been dreading all along. She's seen me make eggs. She knows I can cook a chicken if I need to – but it never turns out particularly well. Ever since Aunt Trudy's death, whenever we've had chicken, it's usually because Bethea cooked it herself and brought some over to share with us.

She starts with spices and herbs and teaches me which ones go well together or might be preferred with certain foods, then she quizzes me. It's a lot of information, but I listen well and fare adequately. She addresses my wrong answers and says she'll quiz me again tomorrow. The long day ends with a return to reading, but I'm so tired by now, I've forgotten the morning's lessons. She sends me home with the book to practice, but I'm asleep as soon as I fall upon my hay sack.

When I try to read again the next morning, the words come out a bit more smoothly, but I still merely stumble through at a snail's pace. I have to sound them out one by one using my finger as a guide. When that's over, Bethea hands me a quill, an ink bottle, and a sheet of paper.

"Aunt Farryn sometimes sends correspondence. You can see by her letters that her handwriting is shaky. She will eventually want you to write them for her."

That familiar sinking feeling returns. It seems like every day brings a new, daunting task. Reading, cooking, and now writing. I will never pull this off.

"Don't worry. I have an idea to buy you time on this one," Bethea assures me. "But you need to practice just the same." She has me form the letters just as they are in the book until my hand understands how to move.

Just like yesterday, we spend the second half of the day in the kitchen, where we talk about vegetables. I know their names. I've helped grow some of them before. But I don't know how to cook them. She teaches me slicing and peeling and tells me which parts to keep and which parts to throw out. This much seems easy enough, though cutting them is slowgoing. I nick my finger more than once, and she demonstrates the best way to hold the blade. She tests me on how long to cook the various vegetables and I get most of them wrong because by now I'm thoroughly exhausted. She lets me go home early for some extra rest.

The remainder of the week passes in much the same way. As I've caught on quickly to the smaller tasks, we focus on reading, writing, and cooking. Reading, writing, cooking. Over and over and over.

On the last evening when I return home, I curl into a ball at Uncle Penn's feet and lay my head in his lap. I cry myself to sleep with his arm draped over me.

When I wake up in the morning, I'm certain Uncle Penn never went to sleep. He savored our last hours as I could not. He won't be making the trip to Dionysius with Bethea and me. It's too long and too bumpy a ride each way. Plus, what would Lady Havard say if we showed up with Uncle Penn in tow? I'm supposed to be Bethea's stepdaughter after all, not this frail man's niece.

I snuggle up to him until I hear Bethea outside with her horse and cart. "It's time," Uncle Penn announces. I start to cry again, and he pulls me upright. Then he draws me into an embrace so tight I can barely breathe. "I love you," he asserts with urgency. "I love you and this is only goodbye for now. Not forever."

I hope and pray he's right. To the gods, I pray the half-piece Uncle Penn gave at the temple will garner celestial goodwill to bring us together again soon.

BY THE TIME BETHEA AND I ARRIVE IN DIONYSIUS, THE FEAR in my chest hasn't abated one bit. It's been a foreign ride to a foreign city where a foreign life awaits me. And I don't want it. Bethea quizzed me on the way to pass the time and help keep my mind occupied, and while I was fairly successful in my responses, I'm still a bundle of nerves.

I'm astonished when I see Lady Havard's neighborhood and home. The exterior is smooth and bright with black shutters on the windows. Several stairs lead up to the front door, edged on both sides by ornate railing. Either the architecture has changed since my last visit to Dionysius years ago, or this wasn't the part of city I visited back then. I'm betting it's the latter, but I don't remember well enough.

We take our bags from the cart – the ones Bethea packed for me and herself – and carry them to the door. I tug at the traveling clothes she had given me for the journey. They were hers once upon a time, and she made some quick adjustments so they would fit me, but the skirt still hangs a little too long.

Bethea knocks on the door and a woman quickly answers. She has a strict face, wears a clean apron, and looks far too young to be Lady Havard. Even Bethea looks surprised.

"Can I help you?" the woman asks, evaluating us.

"I'm Farryn Havard's niece," Bethea says. "She's expecting us."

The housekeeper steps aside and lets us enter, never proffering a smile.

"I wasn't aware Farryn already had help," Bethea says. "She didn't mention anyone in her letters."

"I'm here only temporarily. I'm employed by Lady Wryn. She sent me to work here until Lady Havard's … help arrives." She notes the last part with a look of contempt directed at me and stares at my scar, reddened by the hours it took to travel here under the hot sun. I'm afraid this woman probably does everything perfectly to attend to Lady Havard, and I'm going to be a sour disappointment in her stead.

Seeing my face fall, Bethea gives me a nod of encouragement. I return a weak smile, then turn my attention to our surroundings. This is a beautiful home where everything is polished to a shine. The furniture is plush and inviting in rich colors like burgundy and deep blues and greens. There isn't a thing out of place and it's absolutely spotless. *This* is where I'll be living? Or working rather. Not even the Martins' home was this elegant.

"I'll show you around," the woman says and quickly describes the layout of the house, naming the various rooms and pointing in their general direction rather than guiding us through the home.

She then beckons with her finger, turning on her heel, and we follow her into the kitchen. It's smaller than I would have expected given the size of the sitting room we just passed through. Down the hallway behind the kitchen, the woman opens a door. "These will be your quarters."

She points out the washroom and tells me that I am to bathe on a daily basis. "Lady Havard has such disdain for uncleanliness." She wipes at her nose as if to indicate that we stink. We did just spend over three hours traveling in the summer heat, but I'm not sure she would consider that reason enough to explain our haggardly appearance.

Bethea and I enter my new bedroom.

"And how long will you be staying with us?" the woman asks Bethea.

"A few nights," Bethea responds, dropping the bag she's been carrying on my bed. I follow suit with my own bag. I suspect the housekeeper ought to have taken Bethea's from her, but it's clear she doesn't think us worth the effort.

Bethea wipes her hands together to clear the dirt and grime from them. "Might there be a place to stable the horse and store the cart?" she asks.

"I'll summon Thomas," the housekeeper curtly replies, as though we ought to know who Thomas is.

She starts to leave when Bethea stops her, asking, "And just where might Aunt Farryn be?"

"With Lady Wryn, of course. They're taking a carriage ride around town and doing a little shopping. If there isn't anything else you need, I must get started on dinner."

She doesn't wait to be excused before departing, and down the hall we soon hear cabinets opening and closing and pans clanking.

"You'll get the hang of things in no time," Bethea assures me. She immediately starts digging through my bag. She puts away my shoes and the few changes of clothes I have in the armoire. She pulls out a few books, stacks them on the nightstand, and directs me to practice my reading every evening before bed. Then she pulls out several sheets of paper, a quill pen, and a small ink bottle. "Practice writing by sending me letters. I'll return them with corrections as needed."

I'm relieved Bethea won't feel that far away after all. We will still be connected by letters.

She extracts one last item and stuffs the empty bag into the bottom of the armoire where extra blankets and pillows are stored. She's holding a piece of wood with a couple of straps around it.

"This is a brace. If ever Lady Havard asks you to pen a letter and you don't think you're prepared, simply slip this on your arm and tell her you've aggravated an old injury. I've already informed her of your childhood accident, so she won't ask questions, I'm sure."

I like this idea. "What about reading?" I ask.

Before she has a chance to answer, we're summoned by the housekeeper to meet my new employer. Bethea gives me a silent reminder to smile, watch my posture, and curtsy when introduced.

There are two women in the sitting room when we enter. I assume the older lady stationed on the blue-cushioned chair is Lady Farryn Havard, while the relatively younger one must be Lady Wryn.

"Bethea," Lady Wryn says, her nose upturned.

"Hello, sister," Bethea replies, and my eyes widen slightly.

Lady Wryn is the picture of nobility. Wrapped in an expensive shawl, she holds her head high, revealing elegant earrings that tug on her lobes.

"I'm only here to deliver Aunt Farryn home safely. I suppose that's your horse in front? She looks awfully unkempt. She could use a fresh bath, too."

"You're quite right," Bethea says. "Of course, I'd like to see you after pulling a cart with two women twenty miles in this heat. Those feathers you call hair would be sticking out in every direction. I seriously doubt you'd look or smell much better than my healthy mare."

"Oh, ladies," Lady Havard intercedes, "it's just like old times."

Lady Wryn huffs. "And just like old times, I'll take my leave now that present company has become … polluted."

Lady Havard thanks her niece for the afternoon, and Lady Wryn departs. On her way out, she notifies the housekeeper that someone will come to retrieve her by day's end. That is, now that help has *finally* had the decency to arrive.

"Bethea, dear, it is so good to see you," Lady Havard says, turning a kind smile to my escort.

"And you, Aunt Farryn," Bethea replies, drawing her aunt in for a hug.

"And this must be young Coralyn I've heard so much about."

At hearing my name, I dip into a shallow curtsy.

"We call her Cory," Bethea clarifies, smiling. She beckons me with an outstretched arm and when I approach, she places her hands gently on my shoulders as though presenting an expensive gift.

"Well, I'm so pleased to meet you. I'm sure we'll get along swimmingly." Lady Havard seems kind. I don't know what I was so worried about. Surely this woman will be patient as I acclimate.

"I must tell you, Cory has been having a small problem with her eyesight in recent weeks," Bethea says.

I'm not sure why she says this. My vision is perfectly fine.

"She's been experiencing some blurriness up close, which unfortunately has been interfering with her reading."

Oh, I see.

"I'm so sorry to hear that." Lady Havard sounds genuinely concerned.

"If it's not too much trouble, I thought I might see about finding eyeglasses for her tomorrow."

"By all means, take all day if you need. We have plenty of time to get settled."

Lady Havard rings a bell on the side table and the housekeeper appears carrying a tray stacked with everything needed to present tea. I watch her carefully, observe where she places the tray, remembering everything atop it. I note whether she serves the tea or allows Lady Havard to collect it herself. I pay close attention as she asks if anything else will be needed, then as she vanishes at Lady Havard's wave. She practically makes herself invisible. That, I can manage.

Once the housekeeper has left the room, Lady Havard leans forward conspiratorially. "She doesn't have the most cordial manner, does she?" she whispers. "Frankly, I'd have preferred this week to myself, but Harriet insisted."

Bethea prepares a cup of tea for herself and her aunt. "Of course she did. Harriet's sour you're taking on a maid that *I* found for you. Frankly, I don't know how you've got on so well without more help over the years."

"Oh, your sister has been very helpful. She has in fact provided a great deal of assistance for a long time. She's always made sure I'm taken care of. I've merely preferred a simpler approach to life."

"Well, I for one think it's fitting that that cantankerous housekeeper she sent you works in the Wryn household."

Lady Havard chortles at the joke made at her other niece's expense. She quickly composes herself and sighs, "I just don't know why the two of you never could find a way to get along."

Bethea shrugs. "Harriet likes to win. And she never stops celebrating her victories. I made my choices, and she took them as wins for herself. I'm no longer a sister she has to best but a commoner she can snub that snubby nose at."

Lady Havard giggles again. "She does have quite a snubby nose. Perfect for turning up. Thank goodness it's not a trait from *my* side of the family."

There's a tapping on the front door that interrupts the conversation. Bethea starts to get up to answer but remembers herself. Here, there is a housekeeper to do such things. I also remember myself and move to answer the door, but the housekeeper beats me to it.

"I was under the impression you had been trained for this post," she sneers at me in a low voice. "Answering the door should be second nature, should it not?"

She eyes me with disdain at my hesitation to respond to the knocking. Of course I would be found out by a woman who knows exactly what she's doing. Thankfully, she will be gone by tonight.

"Apologies, but there was no answer out back," the guest says in a poor man's accent. He holds his cap in his hands. This must be Thomas. He's young, maybe early twenties, with dirt streaked across his face that he tries to wipe away with a sleeve. "It will be a half-piece per night for the horse and another half-piece per night for the cart."

Bethea jumps up. "Is it the stable boy?" She greets him at the door, pays him, and thanks him for his help. He takes the pieces and politely bows his head.

Through the window, I can see him retreat, horse reins in hand. "Where's the stable?" I ask the housekeeper. But she has already disappeared again. *Right*, I think. *I'm invisible.* And I'm left without an answer to my question.

The next day, Lady Havard loans us her carriage to drive through the city in search of eyeglasses. Bethea informs the craftsman she's in need of glasses with lenses that do not alter vision. He looks at her askance but doesn't refuse the business. We are told to return in three days' time to pick them up.

Bethea then takes me to the town center where people are lined up on either side, clearly awaiting something. The pathway cut between them leads directly to the castle.

"What's going on?" I ask.

"The princess must be returning from her country tour," Bethea answers. "They make a show of it every time. They bring out all the flags," she adds, pointing them out, "to encourage attendance so she knows she's adored by her people. Her carriage will take her through here and then right on home." She then points to the castle, which stands taller than everything around it. It's barricaded by a tall wall, broken only by the ornate gate in the center through which the beauty of the castle can be admired by all.

"How do you know all this?"

"I grew up here, remember? The queen used to be the one to travel around until a couple of years ago when Princess Giselle came of age and took over in the queen's stead. Would you like to stay and watch her arrive?" she asks.

I consider it for a moment, but when the horns blare, the decision is made for me.

Everyone crowding around begins craning their necks to get a look at the approaching carriage. It's enclosed but moves slowly so that the princess can lean out each side in turns, waving to everyone she passes. The crowd *oohs* and *ahhs*, blowing kisses to their princess and tossing flowers in her path.

The carriage is surrounded at each corner by guards on horseback. The horses pick up their feet in near perfect unison to a practiced height. I've never seen horses so well trained as these. I study the guards to see if I can find the one who so generously helped me back in Perseus, but they all look the same from my vantage point.

Once the princess has passed us by, the crowd begins to disperse. The gates of the castle draw apart at her approach, and the carriage becomes smaller and smaller the farther it travels. Some still watch as the princess's entourage disappears into the safe confines of her castle, a world apart from their own.

Bethea places a hand on my back by way of ushering me away. "Now if I remember correctly, there's a shop nearby that sells a skin balm Aunt Farryn insists is unparalleled in its healing properties. I expect she'll send you off to purchase some for her at times. Let's hunt it down, shall we?"

We travel up and down the streets in search of the shop in question, passing taverns, fruit stands, locksmiths, farriers, cobblers, fashionable boutiques, and a plethora of other trades. I try to commit as much of it to memory as I can.

"Ah, here it is!" Bethea announces, and she pushes her way into the shop. It doesn't take her long to track down the item, and she purchases a single bottle. She opens it to breathe in the scent and then holds it up for me to do the same. We both delight in the aroma of the lavender infused oil. "Now how about some refreshments?"

I nod and follow her back outside, down the block, and into a tavern filled with all sorts of people. I see men and women in finery, those of the working class, and even children scurrying in between legs.

"This is Ned's Tavern," Bethea tells me. "Best brew in town."

We find a spot in the corner and Bethea waves down a barmaid to order a pair of drinks. I've never been in a tavern except for the time I went looking for work in Perseus not so long ago. I tend to think of them as riotous establishments, and Ned's is doing nothing to challenge that notion. It's crowded and loud and bodies shove into other bodies.

"I'd say it's not usually like this," Bethea says, "But that's not entirely true. Ned's is the place to come if you want some excitement in your life, though I expect it's a little louder than usual today in celebration of the princess's return."

The barmaid brings over two steins and places them on our table, which is sticky and shaky. I've never had "brew" as Bethea calls it. I slowly take a sip while Bethea watches me. It's bitter at first but once I get the first swallow down, the second is much smoother. It's different from anything I've ever tried. I take another gulp and as I lower my mug, I spy a familiar face not ten feet away. I recognize him almost immediately, and he's studying me in return. I shyly bring a hand to my face, trying to mask the scar I'm sure he's staring at. He approaches and I instinctively shrink back.

"Where have I seen you?" he asks.

I feel silly now to think he was gawking at my scar when he only wanted to know who I am.

"Umm, you stabled our horses at Lady Havard's manor yesterday."

Recognition dawns and his look of confusion turns to smiling satisfaction. "Aye, that's it. Thomas Freye's the name. And you are?"

"Coralyn Perle. Cory for short."

"Mighty nice to meet you, Miss Perle," he says.

I like the singsong rhythm of his accent.

"Would you like to join us?" Bethea asks. "Cory's new in town, and it's only right she knows at least one person other than Lady Havard."

"Oh," Thomas says. He seems a touch shy himself and takes a hesitant step forward before glancing back at his party, lost somewhere in the crowd. "Um, where are you from then?"

I tell him I'm from Perseus. As he's never left Dionysius, he isn't familiar with the town but knows it isn't far.

We have a brief chat before Thomas is pulled away by a friend.

"Wait a minute," Bethea calls, and Thomas yanks his arm free. "If it isn't too much to ask, why don't you show Cory around town some time?"

I hope I'm not blushing too deeply.

Thomas takes a step closer.

"Sundays are her day off," Bethea adds.

"If it pleases you, I could come 'round late morning."

I gratefully accept.

"And should you ever need anything, I can be found on the east end of Crowley Lane, if I'm not in the stables. Whoever you ask there can point you to where I live." He nods politely, tipping his cap, before he's finally yanked into the raucous crowd.

When we've finished our drinks, we head back to my new home, where I'm tasked with making dinner. Bethea keeps watch, telling Lady Havard it's the first time I've had a position where I'm responsible for everything and that she wants to be sure her stepdaughter can manage. In truth, she's really giving me tips so that I don't mess anything up.

Mercifully, dinner goes off without a hitch. I assist Lady Havard to bed, as Bethea stands by chatting with her aunt, again keeping tabs on my every move and all the while providing subtle reminders.

Finally, I settle in to my second night in the Havard manor and snuggle into my new bed. I look over a page or two of a book before falling peacefully to sleep, following the lead of the slumbering sun.

Princess Giselle

IT'S BEEN MORE THAN TWO WEEKS SINCE I LAST SLEPT IN MY own bed. While the estates and manors where I stayed on my trip were all very nice, there's something about finally coming home again that's immeasurably gratifying.

As soon as I reach my bedchambers, I throw myself onto the plush mattress and curl up for a long nap. It's been a long, exhausting trip, and I deserve some time to relax and catch up on sleep. By the time I awake, my lady's maid, Veronica, is peeking into my room wanting to dress me for dinner.

"I don't want to go this evening. I just want one night off. My parents will understand," I tell her. Although I had kind hosts everywhere I went, it always felt more like I was there to entertain them.

Veronica says she'll bring a plate up for me instead to partake of at my leisure.

"That will do fine, but I'd first like a hot bath with a glass of champagne."

When the tub has been filled, Veronica pins up my hair and helps me out of the day clothes I have yet to shed since returning home. I slip into the hot water and shivers run up my body. It's delightful, and I sink all the way in.

Veronica brings in a petite silver tray carrying a single chalice bubbling nearly to the brim. She carefully places the tray on the round pedestal by the tub. Beside it, she sets down a bell should I need to summon her.

"Anything else I can get for you, Your Highness?" Veronica asks, and I tell her no.

"Oh, wait!" I call before she exits. "Fetch me my pink nightgown, the silk one."

Veronica nods.

"And summon him at 9:00 if you don't mind."

"Summon who, Your Highness?"

I scowl. "Anselm, of course."

Admittedly, Anselm is not the first member of the Royal Guard I've invited into my bedroom, but I've been seeing him – and only him – for months now. There were only two or three others before him anyway. No wait, there were … maybe there were four or … well, who's counting? Perhaps Veronica had thought I'd moved on to someone else by now. But she would be wrong. I don't plan to move on from Anselm any time soon. He captures my attention in a way none of the others have.

Veronica stutters through a response that sounds half like an apology and half like an excuse that she only wanted to be sure. Finally, she curtsies and exits.

Alone at last, I taste the first sip of champagne I've had in two weeks and shake off the irritation of the moment just passed. The cool, bubbly liquid in contrast to the hot water is a splendid combination. I can feel every muscle in my body relaxing. My mind relaxes too. I've heard so many complaints and concerns and problems voiced to me in the past couple of weeks that I can hardly stand to hear about one more thing that isn't simply perfect. And to think, I have to do it again in six months. No doubt the time will fly by. I take another sip and quickly down the drink.

I soak for a long time. Twice Veronica pours in more hot water. Finally, I drag myself out, select a fresh towel piled at the foot of the tub, and step onto the mat. I pat myself dry and examine my figure in the full-length mirror. I turn to both sides, run a hand over my flat stomach, check every curve, and smile in satisfaction. It's easy to see unwanted changes when you leave your daily regimen and travel for two weeks, but I've neither lost nor gained anything I did not want to.

I slip into the nightgown and saunter into my bedroom. True to her word, Veronica has set out a dinner tray along with a fresh bottle of champagne. I pick at a few of the fresh fruits and vegetables.

I check the time and see it's nearly 9:00. I tousle my hair so that it falls just the way I want it to. I pinch my cheeks, add the tiniest bit of color to my lips, and then return to my bed. I'm propped up on my side with my nightgown drawn up so that the full length of my smooth legs is on display. I don't need a mirror now to know I how enticing I look.

Right on time, there's a soft knock, and I call out, not too loud, "Come in." It's loud enough for him to hear, and Anselm pushes open the door. He doesn't make it two steps inside before he catches sight of me and his jaw drops. I give him a seductive smile and beckon him with a finger.

"I didn't think you'd want to see me tonight," he says, inching toward me.

"Whyever not?"

"I thought you'd be exhausted. I thought you'd want some time to yourself for a change." He reaches me and sits down on the bed, unfastening his boots and yanking them off.

"Nonsense. There's no one I'd rather spend my evening with. Seeing you everyday for two weeks but unable to take you to bed, it's been maddening."

Anselm runs a finger down my leg, twisting his body as he does. He spots the champagne and gets up to retrieve it. He uncorks the bottle, carefully fills a chalice that he hands to me, pours another for himself, and returns to his spot on the bed. I sit up to drink my champagne. He clinks my chalice, and I take a big gulp. He follows suit and quickly refills our empty cups. A wave of tipsiness washes over me.

I study Anselm's eyes, a deeper brown than syrup but just as dulcet. His skin is tan, several shades darker than mine, and the muscles of his arms can be felt through the thick guard's uniform he wears. I can tell it's a fresh outfit and he's washed off since our return to the castle. Not that I would have minded if he hadn't, but I'm far more tempted by him this way.

I impulsively snag a fistful of his shirt and pull him to me. Both our glasses of champagne spill as mine drops to the floor and his splashes onto the bed.

I fall back, drawing him on top of me. His lips quickly find mine and his hands roam hungrily up and down my body. He pulls back only to tear off his red sash. The gold buttons on the front of his uniform take some doing, but we make quick work of it. I start on his belt, then move to the button of his pants as he struggles out of his top, having neglected the buttons at his cuffs. By the time he's tossed the top away, I've given his undone pants a good tug. He slips my nightgown up and over my head before finishing the job I started and crawling out of his pants. The entire disrobing process is completed in haste, and his lips promptly descend upon mine again. As we've been unable to see each other like this since we've been traveling, our anticipation of this moment has been building.

He gives deep and urgent kisses and my bare legs wrap naturally around his hips, drawing him closer. He's warm, and I crave the heat radiating off of him. Our breaths are hurried and my chest heaves, which draws his attention, first with his hand and then with his mouth. Just as I reach the point that I can no longer wait, he positions himself, thrusts, and releases a groan. The motion elicits a moan of my own and I arch beneath him.

Anselm is a thorough lover. Every thrust elicits another ripple of pleasure, magnified by the way his hands massage me, at times with a soft caress and at times with a firm grasp.

I can tell he's about to climax as his thrusts become more urgent. He can tell I'm close to the same peak as my nails dig into his back. We move fluidly together and before long, in perfect harmony, the familiar pulsing sensation sends shivers through us both.

He buries his head in my neck as he catches his breath. My fingers rove through his nearly black hair as I do the same. When both our heartbeats have returned to a relaxed pace, he presses a gentle kiss on my neck and slides off of me. He leaves an arm draped around my stomach, and I let him admire my body from this new angle.

Whenever we finish making love, there seems to be a momentary sadness when the truth of what this is – what we are – or aren't – screams through the silence.

I know Anselm does not love me. He's only here because I've requested his presence. I also realize that he does not want to turn me down either because he is enamored by my body or because he feels he cannot do so by virtue of my position. Maybe both are true. I get what I want because of who I am. And while I want Anselm, I'm not sure I love him either. I think he knows that too.

Neither of us dares give voice to these realities. It would destroy what we do have, though it's much harder to find words to verbalize exactly what that is.

When the silence has gone on long enough, we collectively decide without speaking that the obligatory moment of despondency will be shelved until the next time I summon him. Only once it has passed do we allow ourselves to pretend it never existed in the first place, and Anselm gets up to collect our chalices. He pours us both another glass of champagne, but I hardly touch mine.

IN THE MORNING, VERONICA DRESSES ME IN A BEAUTIFUL red gown with gold trimmings. I'm required to report to the king and queen and their advisory council about the things I've heard during my tour through the country. I figure it will look good in front of my parents to wear our nation's colors. What doesn't look so good is my late arrival.

My parents have already been introduced by name as His and Her Majesties Silvanus and Ophelia Rothrys. They wait alongside the council until I enter and find my seat. Their grim faces clearly indicate they are not happy that I slept in too late.

When everyone is settled, the questions begin. What did the people say? What's the general feeling of the nation? What issues were brought up the most? Are there any issues particular to certain regions or towns that need to be addressed?

I field their questions as best I can, and I think I do fairly well. They seem satisfied at least and most of the things I tell them are what they already expected.

"Perseus is a poor town," I note. "It seems worse off than the last time I was there. I even saw some ruffian who dared rob a young woman right in front of me. Right there in the town square. She was assisted by Ans—, er, by a guard. I saw another guard run to track down the thief."

"And was the poor girl's money returned?" my father asks.

"I can't say for certain. I know they tried, but my understanding is that the girl disappeared before her money could be returned to her."

My mother leans forward. "We ought to redouble our efforts to encourage investment in businesses there. The soil isn't particularly good for farming, though they get by with some. They could do a good trade in woodworking and fashioning home goods, I imagine."

My father nods. "The town's location is fortuitous if not for the soil then for the thoroughfares. It's impossible to travel east without going right through Perseus." He turns to me and asks, "What do you think should be done?"

I've never been asked policy questions before. I wrack my brain. "It could help to lower their taxes. If they're able to keep more of what they have, they might be able to reinvest in local businesses themselves."

My father considers this, then says, "And what about the rest of the country? Do we lower their taxes too?"

I shift uncomfortably in my seat. I see how my suggestion might not work after all. Other towns and provinces would protest that their own taxes have not been reduced. We surely cannot cut taxes throughout all of Apollonia. We rely on those funds to subsidize the Royal Guard, which isn't paid well enough as it is, fix roads that are in need of constant repair, and run a variety of social programs like hospitals and orphanages. It isn't cheap running a country and the money has to come from somewhere.

I'm not sure how to respond to the push back. I'm not a politician, though this is surely the start of the grooming process. The day will come when I'm the one heading this nation. These tours are meant to familiarize me with the country so I can speak intelligently about the various provinces and their ways of life. I've always considered the day I take the crown to be a long way off, so I've never bothered to give much consideration to these journeys.

The meeting continues and my father asks me to contribute here and there but without asking me questions of much import. I suppose he wants to teach me a lesson that I'd better start taking my position more seriously. There's no better way to do that than to expose my ignorance, though it's evident he doesn't want to rub it in too hard. I impart simple replies that are met with nods by those around the table. It's supposed to instill confidence in me. I'm not blind. I know exactly the kind of ploy they're enacting. I feel like a child being led through basic training tutorials. It's undoubtedly the start of a series of hoops I'll have to jump through, hoops that are meant to prepare me for the position I will inherit. The transparency of the current tact is just a little patronizing.

As the meeting adjourns and the council members filter out, my parents approach me rather than take their leave. "Giselle, might we have a moment?" It's my father that asks and I feel a sense of dread that I'm about to be chastised in private.

"Some developments arose while you were traveling, and you need to be apprised of them."

My parents have never had difficulty discussing any matter, so when they glance nervously at each other, I stiffen in anticipation.

"Correspondence has arrived from Callinor," my father says, pausing a moment before continuing, as though unsure of his next words.

Although I had expected him to once again highlight my incompetence, nothing he has said thus far comes as a surprise. Correspondence from a friendly nation is nothing to be concerned about.

"The royal family is now in transit for a visit to our nation. They are expected to arrive tomorrow and stay for a week, maybe two, depending on how things unfold. Your mother and I will host Their Majesties Gastogne. It will be your duty to host their son, His Highness Devayn."

I'm starting to understand. This isn't just any visit to renew a long-standing alliance with our neighbor to the north. This is an arrangement for me to meet the Royal Prince whom my parents would like me to marry. If it hasn't been set up already, this might be a trial run to see how things go. As I'm my parents' only child and will one day take the throne here in Apollonia, it's imperative that I wed a prince who isn't firstborn. One that is not next in line to inherit a nation of his own. Devayn is the Gastognes' third son, which means it is unlikely that he will sit on the throne in Callinor. He's also just one year my senior. The match is sensical from my parents' perspective, and probably from the Gastognes' perspective as well. Moreover, it would reinforce our alliance for many years to come.

"I see," I reply. In an even tone, I add, "Then I'll be sure to be a gracious hostess."

My parents each breathe a sigh of relief. I know what they expect of me. I love my parents. I would do anything they asked of me. But they surely know how dismaying this is. Their own marriage was arranged after all. I try to remain optimistic considering it worked out well for them. All hope isn't lost. Yet.

I take my leave and wander back in the direction of my chambers. I'm halfway there when I turn and walk toward the gardens instead.

I know Anselm is patrolling the exterior wall of the castle. I cross the floral expanse, scurry up the stairs of the corner tower, and exit along the eastern wall. The first guard I meet isn't Anselm, though he directs me where to go. When I find him, I pull Anselm into the nearest tower for privacy and sit on the stairs. He can see I'm distressed and takes a seat beside me.

"What is it?" he asks. He glances back at the wall, nervous at the prospect of being caught having left his post, though he knows I can bail him out of any trouble. He is tending to the princess after all.

I tell him about the conversation I just had with my parents. His face betrays nothing, and I cannot tell if he's upset by the news or not. Part of me hopes he is, as the realization that a betrothal is on the horizon has stirred feelings in me for Anselm, which I either never felt before or simply never acknowledged. I never thought I loved him but now I'm not so sure. It was much easier to ignore such complicating factors as feelings when the affair was inconsequential.

My face falls but I refuse to let myself cry. Anselm places a hand on my back and draws me in for a comforting hug, but he doesn't say a thing. I wish he would give me the tiniest hint of what he is feeling, what he is thinking, but I get nothing.

"Come by tonight?" I ask with pleading eyes.

He nods before saying, almost in a whisper, "I have to get back to my post."

I let him walk away from me, but he doesn't leave before forlornly squeezing my hand, like he doesn't want to let go. When he finally slips away, I try to hold onto the warmth of his hand passed on to me. But it quickly dissipates.

IT ISN'T MUCH PAST NOON WHEN WE RECEIVE WORD THAT the Gastogne family is only a mile away and we take our places outside to await their arrival. I wear an opulent gown, one that conveys wealth and influence.

When their carriage pulls up, Her Majesty Gastogne is helped out first. She waits for her husband before the pair of them approach, offering us smiles and kind greetings. Devayn follows behind them, standing tall with a hand behind his back, the other hanging stiffly at his side. He obediently bows his head to each of us in turn but doesn't offer his hand, so I keep mine clasped before me.

My parents reenter the castle first, followed by Their Majesties Gastogne, followed next by Devayn, and I trail behind. Devayn was hardly affable in his greeting. He was a bit too reserved, even rude by letting me bring up the rear on my own. I suppose he is as apprehensive about his stay here as I am. I will let this one slide.

We exchange only a few words with the Gastognes – none from Devayn – before they are escorted to their chambers by the domestics. They will have some time to rest and settle in. When they've gone, my mother squeezes my shoulder and offers me an appreciative smile. I can see she is grateful for the way I've handled the initial meeting. I wonder if she also saw how Devayn handled it, standoffish as he was.

As my parents take their leave, I'm left to my own devices. I can't keep pulling Anselm from his post to keep me company, so I consider my options. I can return to my bedroom and sulk until my presence is required at dinner. Or, I could do something more productive with my time – *but what*?

I have a thought and send Veronica in search of our Callinor ambassador. Meanwhile, I return to my antechamber to await him.

"Ambassador Kinsey," I greet him when he arrives.

"Please, Your Highness, call me Jareth," he replies, bowing courteously.

"Jareth," I amend, gesturing to the table where I'm already seated, offering him a chair of his own. He accepts, and as he settles in, I continue, saying, "You know the Gastogne family well, do you not?"

"I do."

"As I'm sure you are aware, I'm to host His Highness Devayn for the week, and I can't say I know anything about him. I was wondering if you could provide some insight, so I might know how best to receive him."

Jareth inclines his head, accepting the assignment. "His Highness is something of a master at archery. I'm sure he would love any opportunity to display his gifts. He has quite a fondness for horseback riding. More than once he's managed to slip by his guards to take an excursion through the countryside on his own, which gives his parents quite a scare as you can imagine. Let's see … he's got something of a sweet tooth and often indulges in an extra helping of dessert." Jareth laughs as he adds, "It's a gift of youth to be able to do so." He looks off, thinking, until he's struck by another feature, and he states, "Oh, and he has an interest in the sciences. He studies subjects like geology and mineralogy. He's really a very bright young man. Reserved by nature, but he always meets the obligations of his position, even those of a social variety."

A picture of Devayn's character is starting to form in my mind. "And does he have many courtiers?" I ask.

"As many as any prince might," Jareth provides. "But he doesn't pay much heed to most of them."

I understand. I've had my fair share of courtiers, but I've only indulged them insofar as my own desire for flattery would extend. As they knew I would never be intended for any of them, any liaison never went very far. But Devayn … as the third son, had he shown interest in a young woman of the court, he may very well have been given his parents' blessing for their marriage.

"Maybe he's just shy," I offer by way of possible explanation.

"One would think, Your Highness."

By the tone in his voice, though, I'm not sure if he agrees or not. I thank Jareth for his time and information, and he kindly offers his services should I ever desire them in the future. For now, I have an idea of what to do next.

I change for dinner that evening. There will be a ceremonial feast of sorts to welcome our guests. The wine will flow, the food will be bountiful, and the music will play ceaselessly in the background. Dozens of noble families have been invited to attend the affair. Everyone knows it's a show of our nation's wealth and culture. Everyone is also aware that nations are never as wealthy as they appear, but this much goes unspoken. Still, the charade will continue each night we host our royal guests.

My family and the Gastognes are seated at the end of our U-shaped dining table. My parents occupy the middle seats and Their Majesties Gastogne sit on either side of them. I am placed beside His Majesty Gastogne on one end, while Devayn is placed by Her Majesty Gastogne on the other. The legs of the U stretch out before Devayn and me with various nobles placed along the sides accordingly.

Mindless chatter begins almost immediately and drags on through the course of the meal. His Majesty Gastogne is kind and turns his attention to me often, including me in the conversations that unfold. He expresses delight at having made my acquaintance since he last saw me when I was but three years of age, much too long ago for me to recall. He thanks me in advance for any attentions I should bestow upon his son during their stay.

"Perhaps His Highness Devayn would enjoy a ride through the countryside tomorrow," I say. Devayn is too far away for me to ask him directly. "The mountains of Clymene are beautiful this time of year. The flowers are in full bloom and stretch practically all the way to the peaks."

"That's a lovely idea," His Majesty Gastogne replies. He leans forward and looks down the table at his son, who is slurping his soup. His voice booms louder than mine ever could as he asks, "Devayn, did you hear that? Her Highness Giselle has invited you for a ride on horseback tomorrow. What do you say?"

"If it pleases Her Highness," Devayn replies to his father, not acknowledging me, though I'm also peering down the table at him. His voice is softer than his father's but audible to all nonetheless.

His Majesty Gastogne looks pleased. As for me, I've always hated the phrase *"if it pleases."* It does not please me. His acceptance of my offer is certainly no favor to me. I smile politely just the same.

The following morning, I don my riding outfit and make my way to the courtyard where our horses for the journey have been prepared and await us. When I arrive, Devayn is nowhere to be seen. I stand by my horse, Calliope, biding my time awaiting my guest's arrival. Veronica stands beside me, dutifully in attendance. I've instructed her to accompany us only if Devayn brings his valet.

The minutes tick by. I'm huffing on the inside but maintain a composed exterior. Or at least as much as I can manage.

Devayn finally emerges, saying, "My apologies, Your Highness. I got lost. A young maid found me wandering and kindly showed me the way."

I'm not sure whether or not I believe him.

He still refrains from taking my hand in greeting, but he does have the decency to offer a slight bow. He is unaccompanied by his valet, so Veronica understands she will stay here at the castle.

"Yes," I say, "the castle grounds can be difficult to navigate if you are unfamiliar with them, but I'm sure you'll figure it out in no time." It's a warning not to keep me waiting again.

He merely nods once, taking my meaning. To avoid any awkward silence, I introduce him to his ride for the day. "This is Clio. We've had her a long time and she's one of our older mares, but she's well-mannered and strong. I think you'll find her amenable to your every command and perfectly capable of our tour today."

Devayn puts his hand to Clio's nose and lets her sniff him. He runs his other hand down her neck several times and pats her. It's already far more consideration in a greeting than he's afforded me, not that I would appreciate it if he stuck his hand in my face to smell. I'm careful not to roll my eyes in full view of everyone present at his extended greeting ritual with the horse. So I patiently wait until he indicates that he's ready to leave by sticking a boot in a stirrup and pulling himself atop his mare. I'm helped onto Calliope, and we depart in the direction of the Clymene Mountains.

Four guards accompany us, and Anselm is among them. I don't know how he got stuck with this post except that he often serves as my escort on various excursions. Perhaps it was merely assumed he would also attend to us today. Or perhaps he volunteered …

Devayn and I make little conversation until we reach the foothills, though I do point out a few sites here and there, which he acknowledges by turning his head in the direction I point. Finally, the radiant yellows and reds of the flowers sprinkled throughout the region come into view. It's a picturesque sight for anyone familiar with the area or not. One never grows tired of gazing upon the brilliant blossoms that flourish here.

I can see Devayn is taking in the view, appreciating the scenery, and I commend myself for this good idea.

He trots Clio up the path, and I follow behind, remembering the day not so long ago that Anselm and I snuck away to visit these mountains. I glance back at Anselm and try to decipher whether or not he's remembering that evening himself. He meets my eye, but he's just so frustratingly unreadable. I don't allow my eyes linger on Anselm too long and give Calliope a quick kick in the side. She hurries up beside the prince. Devayn, after all, is my guest. Not Anselm.

As my intractable companion remains annoyingly quiet, I try to invite him into conversation. "The holy books say these mountains were carved by the gods and seeded by Chloris herself. The flora returns every year and only disappears briefly in winter. They can survive fairly harsh weather conditions, and it can get quite cold up near the peaks where you can see they grow anyway."

Devayn still does not respond, but he appears to be taking in the information I provide. He's a damned tough nut to crack, but I'm willing to bet I'm ten times the headstrong royal he is. Even if it takes every damned day of two damned weeks, I *will* win this silent battle he's waging against me. He *will* befriend me if I have anything to say about it. And I do. I have everything to say about it.

"There's actually about a half-dozen different varieties of flowers blooming here," I continue. "That doesn't include the shrubbery and greenery, but those mostly occupy the base of the mountains, as you can see." I keep supplying information about the landscape. But the more we ride, the more I see Anselm everywhere.

Over there is the tree we climbed after standing on our horses' backs to get up into it. We hadn't tied up the horses and they had wandered off in search of grass to nibble. Anselm had to drop eight feet to the ground to retrieve my mare for me to lower myself onto. The going up was much easier than the coming down.

There's the patch of grass where he laid me down and we made love. I gazed upon the bright moon as he moved above me, his breath on my ear, and then he warmed me with his body in the cool night air. He even plucked a flower and tucked it behind my ear.

There's the path that leads to the pond where we swam for an hour in nothing but our own skin. Then we lay on the grass to dry before dressing again.

I shake the memories away and continue talking. "If you like these mountains, there's another chain to the southeast of the city that's equally resplendent – the Zethes. They're about a day's ride from here but well worth the effort." I know everything about this region where I grew up. I could go on forever if I had to.

Finally, Devayn breaks in. "I must say, Your Highness, you are remarkably adept in the art of elocution."

I'm taken aback, both by the fact that he has finally spoken and at his words. I can't decipher his tone. *Is he telling me I talk too much?* Why that little …! "I think if you'd bother to notice, you'd find that I'm remarkably adept in a great number of things, *Your Highness*." Now it's his turn to try and decipher *my* tone. "Perhaps we ought to be getting back. We don't want to be late for dinner," I huff, and I turn Calliope around and head back in the direction of the castle. As I trot by Anselm, I say at a volume that only he can hear, "You'll come tonight, won't you?"

I gallop off before he can respond. Before he can hesitate at the invitation now that Devayn is in town. I won't be rejected by men twice in a single day.

Dinner takes far too long to pass. It's evident that Devayn dreads this meal as much as I do, as his responses to the questions posed by our parents about our day are as banal as mine. Yes, we had a fine time. Yes, the mountains are beautiful. Yes, it was lovely weather for such an outing.

Finally, the chatter breaks into exchanges held between neighboring dinner partners. I'm grateful Devayn and I are seated so far apart. I am in dire need of a break from trying to pull any communication whatsoever out of him. It's exhausting. *He's* exhausting.

I peek down the table, though, and see him speaking with my father just two seats away from him. Their discussion seems good-humored and effortless. I'm inwardly incensed by his obstinance, which he displayed with me all day, when he's clearly quite capable of carrying on a conversation like a normal human being.

When I'm finally allowed to quit present company, I practically run to my chambers for a bath before Anselm arrives. I'm so frustrated I could scream. Who does he think he is? I put so much time and energy into today, the least that snobby brat could do is give me a little more than *"You are remarkably adept in the art of elocution."*

I plunge my head underwater in the tub and soak my hair in the soapy water. I hold myself there until I run out of breath and emerge drawing in a large gulp of air. A part of me wants to cry. I've never been treated with such disregard, and it makes me furious. I don't deserve this. I've done nothing wrong. I've done nothing but conduct myself as the perfect hostess. I'm a *princess* for crying out loud. And still he treats me like I'm not even there. Like I'm nothing. Like I'm invisible.

I try to clear my mind and let the warm water soothe and relax me. But it isn't enough. I dry off still angry. Still embittered by his graceless, detached manner.

Anselm enters my bedroom before I've had the chance to change into my nightgown. No matter. Wrapped in my towel, I march directly over to him. I give him a shove and knock him backward onto my bed, certain that the intensity on my face signals exactly how this encounter will go.

I let my towel fall, giving him a quick moment to draw his eyes up and down my body before I climb on top of him. I kiss him greedily as his hands run across my body with equal earnest desire. He helps me with his pants, and neither of us bothers with any other articles of his clothing.

I know the effect I have on Anselm. It takes no time at all for him to be ready. There's a vehement need within me and judging by the look in his eyes, there's an animalistic need in him. Climaxing doesn't take long for either of us.

I suck in deep breaths as I fall forward to lie down on his chest. He places a hand on my back, dragging a finger up and down in a shiver-inducing way, as he also waits for his heartbeat to decelerate to a casual pace again.

The familiar sadness comes, this time amplified by the indignation accrued over the course of the day at Devayn's obstinate manner. I can't recall the last time my emotions were so unbearably strong. I don't want to cry, but I cannot help the teardrop that wells. I catch it before it slides across the bridge of my nose and falls onto Anselm's shirt.

He's alerted by my hand's sudden movement to my eye and tries to push me back to read my face. But I hold firm and keep my head planted next to his heart and the steady thrum that echoes in my ear.

Oh, screw it! I think. As if the desperate way I made love to him isn't evidence enough, my refusal to show my face when I wipe away a tear surely is. I let out a whimper, hating myself for the way my emotions are getting the better of me. I am not a woman who cries. I am a woman who wins. So why can't I beat back these feelings that are overtaking me?

My chest convulses as I work through my tears, though there aren't many, thank goodness. Anselm keeps his arm around me, holding me until I'm calm. He doesn't say a word. He knows me well enough to know that I don't want pity or consoling. That this display is embarrassing. I love him for the way he neither leaves nor tries to fix me.

It doesn't take long until I regain control of myself again, though it takes much longer to pull myself off of him. When I finally do, he remains steadfast and quiet.

Anselm is gone by the time I wake up in the morning. I have no idea when I fell asleep or how long he stayed. I'm still embarrassed by what transpired last night and a part of me is glad I don't have to face him right now. Another part of me is terrified by what he must be thinking. He saw how Devayn treated me all day. He must know why I ordered him to my bedroom. He understands that my tears were not over him. Is he bothered by this or is he unaffected? Do I even really want to know the answer? I think either response might somehow cause me more grief.

I wrap my bedsheets more tightly around myself. I'm still naked, which makes me feel exposed and vulnerable, reinforcing the pitiful way I felt last night. I wish I were clothed, but I don't want to get out of bed to dress either. If I get out of bed, I have to face the day. If I face the day, I have to face Devayn. And Anselm. And the caustic emotions they each instill in me.

How did I get myself into this mess?

Anselm

I DON'T KNOW WHAT THE HELL GISELLE IS THINKING.

It must be some time after one before I finally slip out of her bed, fasten my pants, and make my way to my own quarters. I share a room with three other members of the Royal Guard and one lets out a whistle when I enter.

"Shut up," I snarl in the dark and climb into my rack.

He knows exactly where I've been. They all do. The same place I go every night that I'm not right here. I'd be lying if I said I wasn't more than happy to oblige the princess in her sexual exploits. It doesn't take much more than a glance at her flawless, naked body, and I'm raring to go.

I don't know how many times I've found myself in her bed over the last few months, not that I'm complaining. But I knew it would come to this. It was only a matter of time before the princess was going to be matched with some prince and this little fling she started with me would go up in flames. It's going to burn us both, I just know it.

I'm not the first guard she's seduced, but I had hoped she would have moved on from me by the time the inevitable betrothal came. That way, some other unsuspecting dolt could be the one to figure out the delicate balance of pushing her away without pushing too hard. How to snuff the flame of the impending fallout without snuffing the flame of her passion. And my gods, that woman's passion runs wild.

No such luck, though. I'm the unlucky bastard who risks being ensnared if she lets this blaze blow up into an inferno.

I don't sleep all night. Thank the gods, I have the day off. It's much easier to avoid the princess when I don't have to be on castle grounds. When I'm on patrol, I never know when she'll track me down and tear me from my post, whether she's impassioned by her desires of the flesh or her unfettered emotions. Either way, she uses me to rein them in. I've come to expect that in the evenings, I'll be summoned whenever something happens that unsettles her. She channels her fervor into baser instincts in the hopes that the throes of sexual ecstasy will temper their intensity. But it never works. And she never learns.

I recognize Giselle hasn't considered how this may impact me. She thinks about her own heart, her own future, her own life. There's nothing wrong with thinking about her own best interests. But the way she has been catered to all her life has taught her to think first of herself and second of others. She's not particularly good at moving on to that second part though.

When I finally convince myself to get up, I elect first to visit the temple. If I'm going to find a way out of this, I'll need all the grace the gods will allow.

The temple I attend isn't the only one in Dionysius, but it is the largest and the closest. It has a grand fountain in the center of the room ringed by a cushioned kneeler. I toss two pieces into the water and take up an empty spot, dropping to my knees and bowing my head. It isn't too crowded at the moment, so I don't have to worry about staying too long and blocking the spot from other parishioners coming to pay their respects. Good. This is a big mess I'm in, so I think I'll be a while.

When I've finished my prayers and tapped my forehead in thanks to the gods for listening, I next head to Ned's Tavern. They've got a fine brew and an even better morning meal. This early, they aren't too busy either.

"Morning, Ned," I greet the proprietor upon entering.

"Anselm, how's the morning?"

"Fair," I reply and place my order. I take a seat, tossing him several coins to pay in advance.

"And the princess?"

All of the Royal Guard frequent Ned's, so he's intimately familiar with the rumor mill. Gods know I've been a prime topic of conversation given my relationship with Giselle. I only need to give him an exasperated look for him to know how disordered things have become.

"Aye, I've heard the Gastogne prince has come to town. Rumor has it he's there for her hand."

"His *parents* are there for her hand is more like it. The kid's a spoiled brat. Doesn't seem interested. I had to spend all day yesterday with him and Giselle. Took a ride out to the Clymenes."

Ned groans. He doesn't envy me those wasted hours. "So I guess she'll be moving on from you then, what with her intended around."

I take a sip of the brew he set in front of me and give him a hard look over the rim by way of responding.

"No? Surely you jest!"

"You can guess where I was last night," I say, wiping the foam from my mouth with the back of my hand.

"Well, you're one lucky bastard to share that woman's bed."

"I *was*."

Ned gives me a look to say he takes my meaning.

I no longer consider myself lucky. Lucky was the *last* guy she seduced.

"So what are you going to do?"

"Haven't the faintest, Ned. Haven't the faintest."

Ned starts scrubbing down the counter. A barmaid brings my meal and I dig in. I think our conversation has ended when Ned speaks again from several feet away, still cleaning, "Hey, I saw your cousin in here this week. A few times actually."

"Oh? How is Thomas these days? I ought to go see him. It's been much too long."

"Bastard gets taller all the time. Must have a couple inches on you now."

"No," I say, dragging out the sound. "I had at least an inch on him last I saw him. He's older than me by four years. How is it he keeps growing?"

Ned shrugs. "Blessed by the gods."

"I wouldn't say that," I mutter, almost more to myself. Thomas is poor. He comes from even more meager means than I do, and that's saying quite a lot. He's a stable boy in the city, I know. He did his four years in the Royal Guard and got out the year I went in. That was two years ago.

Several more patrons enter the tavern and Ned turns his attention to them. I finish my meal and decide to pay Thomas a visit. I haven't got anything else I must do and I sure don't want to go back to the castle.

Thomas lives on Crowley Lane in a room he shares with another former member of the Royal Guard. I can never remember his name, though I've met him a handful of times. I knock and hope that Thomas answers, as it's long past the time when I could appropriately ask for a reminder of what his roommate is called. When I see the familiar face that does not belong to Thomas, I think to myself, *I'm one unlucky bastard*. Today won't be my day either it seems.

"Hey, Anselm," he greets me, and I feel a twinge of guilt that he remembers my name.

"Hey," I say cheerfully, "Thomas home?"

"Sorry to say he isn't."

"He's working Sundays now?"

"No, but he had plans with a young lady's maid."

My eyes widen at that. If Thomas is seeing a lady's maid, it would reflect an improvement in his station.

"Not sure it's quite like that," the roommate adds. "But he's been tightlipped about her so who knows?"

"Well, tell him I've been 'round and I'll stop by again next week."

The man whose name I don't know closes the door, and I take my leave. I've one more destination to pay a visit. The one place I prefer to spend most of my days off.

Faizal Sarif is one of the best blade smiths in all of Dionysius. Matter of fact, in all of Apollonia. I met him the week before I was drafted into the Royal Guard. He is an old acquaintance of my mother's, and she sent a letter with me when I came to the city alone. He was the only person she knew here. That is, other than Thomas, though he's my relation on my father's side. My mother wanted me to have another friendly connection in case I needed anything. I still recall when I handed Faizal the letter. He read it, and then he gave me a wide smile and threw open his arms, saying, "A son of Yasmeen's is a son of mine. You are always welcome here."

Faizal has been gracious enough to teach me the art of sword making in the little spare time I have. When I arrive in his shop, he ushers me in, wearing the same broad smile every time I come by. He collects the sword I've been working on a little bit each week and supervises as I beat, shape, and carve the steel. He gives encouragement, makes small suggestions, and reminds me of little tips and tricks to mold the sword. He teaches me about weight and balance and holds my sword up to inspect the lines. He helps me design the hilt and chisel it into shape. We work all day, though Faizal is far more skilled and efficient than I am. In no time, he can craft an elaborate sword only nobility could afford.

I take the tongs and hold the pieces in the forge as often as necessary in order to make adjustments. When I'm satisfied, I dunk them in the quench tank to harden the steel. Once that's done, the metal is tempered until it can be gently sharpened and polished.

"Any word from your mother?" Faizal asks while we work.

"She wrote last month. She tells me not to worry about her, but a couple of weeks ago, I also got a letter from the temple priest who checks on her daily. He tells me her health is failing. I get the idea it's going fast."

I don't think I've ever seen Faizal's face fall, so when it does, I'm surprised by how devastated he appears.

"You must go to see her," he asserts. His voice is replete with solemnity.

"I can't. It's a full-day's ride one way. I only get Sundays off. We aren't allowed the privilege of taking extra days unless we have reenlisted after our first four years. There are never any exceptions even in matters of life and death. We're property of the crown."

"Isn't there anything you can do? Talk to the princess. You're friendly with her, right? She could make an allowance."

"Now's not the right time for that. The princess is a wreck these days. I doubt she would let me leave her side."

"You would deny your mother a final chance to see her only living son? You have two years left in the Royal Guard. It doesn't sound like she will make it that long."

These are things I've already considered. I didn't hear from the priest until the day before we left with the princess on her biannual country tour. The journey didn't pass close enough to my mother for me to take a quick detour to see her. The entire trip, I wondered if I would find new correspondence when I returned to the castle but there was nothing awaiting me. I took that as a good sign.

I take it upon myself to return my sword and hilt to the cabinet where Faizal stores them until my next visit. I look outside and see the sun beginning its slow descent. I've been here all day and it's time to return to the castle.

"I'm trying to figure it out, Faizal. I don't want to miss a last chance to see my mother either."

Faizal nods his understanding and places a hand on my arm. He has to look up to meet my eyes. "Have you visited the temple?" he asks. "The gods may have the answer. I'll pay a visit myself and see if they'll tell me."

I thank him for his kindness. In fact, I did include my mother in my prayers when I went to the temple earlier in the day. But I haven't received word from the gods yet. Assuming they see fit to tell me anything at all.

I head back to the castle hoping Giselle won't summon me tonight. I'm exhausted, mentally and physically, and could really use a good night's rest.

As I walk up to my quarters, I find Veronica waiting outside. I'm already shaking my head and she looks at me with sorrow.

"She's a mess," Veronica says, meaning Giselle. "She'd like to see you."

"I don't suppose you could tell her I'm not feeling well."

"Then she'll only want to come check on you herself."

I know it's true. There's no escaping Giselle tonight, so I turn and walk toward Giselle's chambers. I want to get this over with.

I knock on Giselle's door and hear her invitation for me to enter. Her face is red. It is obvious she's been crying.

"Rough day?" I ask, taking a seat on the bed where she's curled up.

She nods and reaches for me. There's no telling what Devayn put her through today but she clearly wants me to distract her from the day's worries in typical wanton fashion. She sits up, puts a hand on my face, and kisses my cheek. I don't respond. I'm too tired to take the lead and part of me is hoping she'll give up if I don't.

"Kiss me," she whispers.

I turn my face a few degrees toward her and halfheartedly place my lips on hers. She easily reads my reluctance to engage with her tonight.

"You don't want me?" she asks.

I groan inwardly. Of course she would make this about her. But as I'm not eager to discuss either the issue with my mother or the problem of this affair while Devayn is under the same roof, I elect to answer her question by way of kissing her harder.

She pulls me down on top of her. She doesn't want this dalliance to be impetuous and unbridled tonight. She doesn't have a fury she needs siphoned off. She wants me to make slow and passionate love to her. She has an emptiness in her heart she needs resupplied with attention and affection. And I'm the only way she knows how to get it. No matter how impermanent it is.

Once I get going, I can give her just what she needs and my exhaustion will quickly be replaced by my own carnal need. Then I will be able to collapse and sleep through the night. I have no doubt that when we're through, she will be more than happy to keep me here until morning.

Cory

BETHEA HAS BEEN GONE FOR SEVERAL DAYS NOW, SO I'VE HAD to stand on my own two feet here in Dionysius. I'm grateful Lady Havard has been so kind in Bethea's absence. She hasn't reprimanded me too harshly for my mistakes, but I know she expects they will not occur again once addressed.

Lady Wryn came by this morning to take Lady Havard to temple. Lady Havard had already been apprised of my plans this afternoon to be escorted around the city by Thomas, which she thought was a marvelous idea. She gave me license to stay out as long as I like.

I dress in a change of clothes Bethea brought for me. I notice the glasses she purchased for me sitting atop my dresser. As they don't alter my vision, I can easily wear them when reading to keep up the ruse. Bethea suggested that if Lady Havard asks me to read, I ought to poke out a lens and hide it. That way, I can feign vision problems again.

I pick up a book to practice my reading while I wait for Thomas. I appreciate Bethea for coordinating this outing, as well as Thomas for agreeing to it on his day off. It's nice to have a friend in such an unfamiliar and busy place.

From my quarters, I can easily hear any knocking at the back door. Even though Lady Havard isn't home, propriety dictates that someone of his social status is not considered a front door guest. I only get through a paragraph before I hear three soft taps.

I meet Thomas on the back steps. I'm standing three steps higher than him and his eyes are level with mine. In only a few days' time, I'd managed to forget how tall he is. His slender build only accentuates his height.

Thomas takes my hand to help me down the stairs, then offers me his arm, which I accept. "I thought we might start at Erato Gardens," he says.

"That sounds lovely."

His etiquette makes me feel like a lady. I've never been treated with such refined civility before, and I like the way it makes me feel. Slipping into the persona of someone who isn't invisible is a pleasant affair, no matter how short-lived it might be.

We make surprisingly easy conversation on our walk, getting to know one another. He tells me he grew up in Dionysius on the fringes of the city where his family worked a small piece of land. He had moved to a more central location after his tenure with the Royal Guard where there were more opportunities to make a living. He's never traveled anywhere else.

"How did you come to work the stables?" I ask.

"Good fortune," he says, smiling. "After leaving the Guard, I didn't have many prospects for employment except to return home and work the land, but I didn't want to do that straight away. It will always be waiting for me once my parents pass away. I wanted to make my own way even if I didn't make much. I happened by the stables one day when the stable master was in the middle of sending away the young man who had my job before me. It seems the lad could never show up to work on time and often slept in the stalls right there on the hay. I offered my services on the spot and have worked there ever since. Two years now."

"Did you like being in the Royal Guard?" I remember the kindness the guard in Perseus had shown me after I was robbed, as well as the

20-piece coin he gave me. I have good feelings associated with the Royal Guard because of him.

"Oh, it was all right. When I went in, I intended to stay if only for the sake of job security. But I had little interest in the position once I got there. Plus, you get a little extra remittance when you get out, some fare to last a week, enough for anyone from far away to get back home and still have a share left over. But that little bit was an enticing reason to leave the Guard and find a new line of work. A friend and I used our remittance to rent a place together."

"It's lucky you were able to find employment so quickly," I say and tell him of the difficulty I had finding a new job after being let go by the Martins.

"Yes …" Thomas says with uncertainty, "though I was hardly familiar with horses."

I say that I find that difficult to believe. Everyone has some degree of knowledge about horses. They're the best means of transportation after all.

He explains that growing up his family had been too poor to own a horse on top of the steer they had. When he did travel by horse, he sat in the cart behind. In the Royal Guard, he always served in positions on foot. "The guards on horseback are favored, higher ranked. I was never among them. They had me doing menial tasks, so it took me some time to learn how things worked in the stables. But I finally did."

There is solace in knowing someone else had walked into a job they knew nothing about and fared well. I suppose he had done it twice now including the Royal Guard. But I don't confide in Thomas about my utter lack of knowledge regarding domestic service. It seems like it would be a betrayal somehow to Bethea, who has gone out on a limb for me.

We arrive at Erato Gardens and I'm amazed by the size. We walk a mazelike path bordered by shrubbery. There are outcroppings for benches or flowerbeds and Thomas leads me to his favorite spots.

I tell him Perseus doesn't have too many flowers, as the soil is inadequate for growing much. Sure, we learned various methods to improve our chances of a good harvest, but we frequently lost half our crops or more. As tending to the crops was often part of my job, it was easy to feel disheartened when they failed to sprout. I learned early on that the work I did was insufficient, so it's no surprise I feel so insecure about my current employment.

We walk in silence for a while, enjoying the scenery. I'm enamored by the colors everywhere. Perseus is clouded by brown and an ugly shade of dark green. The only colors we really see there are in the sky at sunrise and sunset and while the colors are beautiful, they only occur twice a day and then quickly fade.

"I don't suppose you're hungry?" Thomas finally asks once we've completed a leisurely lap. I had been so captivated by our surroundings that I hadn't noticed the rumbling sensation in my stomach.

"There's a little place up the way I know. Could I take you?"

I flush a little. I don't want him to spend any money on me considering he probably doesn't have much, but it would be rude to turn him down. I accept the offer and Thomas leads the way.

We come upon a row of eateries, taverns, inns, and pastry shops. It looks to be an area frequented by citizens of the lower class. I couldn't picture someone like Lady Havard ever coming here. I see a few people who are evidently homeless. Occasionally, a proprietor shoos them away from the front of their establishments. Grimy children play chase in the street, running between the legs of men and women who shoot them dirty looks. A few people greet Thomas. He acknowledges some of them by name and all of them by a tip of his cap. Thomas must come here a lot.

"This is Nyx Notch, so called because it's a dead-end down the way," Thomas says, indicating the entire street. He opens the door of the last shop on the left, which bears a sign that reads "PIA'S." It's small and a bit dusty inside and only a couple of people are dining here.

A woman bustles in from the back and beams upon seeing us. She approaches and throws her arms around Thomas, saying, "I wondered when I might see you again." Then seeing me, she adds, "And who might this be?" She gives Thomas a look as if to imply a romantic interest between us, which causes the both of us to blush.

"Pia, might I introduce you to Miss Coralyn Perle? She's new in town from Perseus."

"Cory," I amend.

"It's mighty fine to meet you, Coralyn 'Cory' Perle. I'm Pia." She has the same accent as Thomas, indicative of an underprivileged background. The poor of Perseus don't sound the same as the poor here but it's easy to spot people like us. Our threadbare habiliments are a dead giveaway anywhere.

"It's nice to meet you too," I say.

"Pia and I grew up as neighbors," Thomas explains. "And now look at her. She owns her own business."

"Oh," Pia says, as if to imply her success is nothing.

"Everyone loves her food. You're about to find out why."

"I'm flattered you've chosen to patronize my establishment," Pia says. "Let me whip up some croquettes for you. Potato or fish?" She looks between us for an answer before turning and calling back at us, "Never mind! You'll have both!"

Thomas pulls out a chair for me before sitting himself. There's a moment of awkward silence as words fail us both and we each glance down timidly. Then he brightens, as he says, "Tell me about what life is like in Perseus."

I tell him about my aunt and uncle who raised me after I lost my parents in an accident that also left me injured. I mention the limp that often evolves by the end of the day, and I shyly indicate the scar on my face. He looks at the mark with compassion, in such a way that I don't feel as abashed about it as I typically do. I tell him how I miss Uncle Penn, whom I had to leave to find employment to support us both. But other than that, there isn't much else to tell. My life has been simple, which he understands. His upbringing was similarly filled with work from an early age, the same activity day in and day out. There isn't much room in the lives of the impoverished for much else.

"And yet you must have had some education, seeing as how you've been trained in domestic service," he comments.

"Well, not exactly," I reply, unsure how to get around the answer. "I've been taught some things, it's true." I don't specify that my training consisted of Bethea giving me a few quick lessons in the week before I came here. "But I'm rather unprepared for some other aspects of my job. My reading and writing skills are basic at best and my cooking is frankly unpalatable." I giggle, adding, "Lady Havard has been kind not to spit it out right in front of me!"

Thomas laughs more heartily than me, saying, "It can't be that bad."

Pia soon emerges with a plate of croquettes. She waits until we've each taken one to try. They're a bit too hot and I feel steam fill my mouth. Pia smiles in eager anticipation of our reactions. Thomas swallows his with sublime satisfaction. After a moment, the savory taste of potato with melted cheese takes over my senses. It's cooked to perfection with a crisp breading that makes the bite more delicious than anything I've ever tasted. Not even Aunt Trudy ever cooked so well. "That's amazing," I say, finally swallowing. "I'm jealous."

Pia is delighted at how I've enjoyed her food.

"Cory was just telling me she can't cook," Thomas explains, snatching up another croquette.

Pia looks aghast and declares, "Every woman should know how to cook!"

"Especially me," I add, "as I'm a lady's maid and housekeeper now, the only one in the home, so it all falls to me."

Pia lurches, grabbing the back of Thomas's chair by way of composing herself. She's never heard of such a thing. A housekeeper that can't cook. "How do you manage?" she asks.

"Poorly," I tell her.

"Well, we can't have that. You need to learn to cook, if not for your lady then for your husband. You aren't married yet, are you?" Pia asks. She looks at my hand to see if she can spy a ring. I blush while Thomas pretends he isn't listening.

"Of course not. I'm only sixteen," I reply.

"Well, what's that got to do with anything? Sixteen is plenty old enough. I was eighteen when I got married. Had four kids since. Four kids in four years. Just you wait, Cory Perle. I bet you anything you're married by summer next, a pretty girl like you. In no time you'll have a full brood to cook for."

The dread at the thought must be plastered all over my face because Pia laughs. I even notice Thomas trying to suppress a smile.

"You'll come here every Sunday for a lesson in cooking, do you hear? I won't hear you say no."

"Really?" I exclaim. I'm so happy by the offer I don't know what else to say.

"You'll be sure to bring her, won't you, Thomas?" An unspoken message passes between them by the way Pia looks at him.

"Happy to," he replies. Message received.

Thomas sticks an elbow out to again offer me his arm when we're ready to leave, but we don't go before I've thanked Pia profusely for offering to teach me how to cook. The croquettes were also on the house, so I'm glad Thomas didn't have to dip into his own earnings for me.

On our walk back to Lady Havard's, we take the long way. The very long way. Thomas and I have suddenly found a lot to talk about so when we arrive at the back door, I'm surprised to find that dusk is already setting in. Normally, I would relish the hour, but after such an enjoyable day as this, I'm not ready for it to come on.

Thomas removes his cap with one hand. He gives me the other to help me up the stairs but doesn't let it go when I've climbed them, only three steps. I turn to face him, to tell him what a wonderful time I had and to thank him sincerely. But words don't come when I see the way he looks at me or when he bends slightly to kiss my hand. His lips are smooth on my skin. It's a sensation I've never experienced before, nor have I even considered how someone's lips might feel. Sure, I've had Uncle Penn or Aunt Trudy plant a kiss on my cheek, but this is different. They are family. And Thomas is … I'm not sure what Thomas is exactly. But surprisingly, I enjoy the feel of his lips on my hand, equal parts gentle and firm.

"Thank you for the pleasure of your company today, Miss Perle."

I nearly stumble over the words as I say, "I had a marvelous time. The pleasure's all mine."

He waits until I've gone inside and shut the door. I surreptitiously watch him through the window and see that he lingers a moment longer before replacing his cap and traipsing off.

Princess Giselle

I CANNOT BELIEVE THAT DAMNED DEVAYN IS KEEPING ME waiting *again*. This is three days in a row now. At least this time we aren't leaving the grounds, so I don't have to suffer my embarrassment in front of an entire entourage, Anselm included. Since we aren't traveling anywhere, I'm sure my lover is somewhere walking the perimeter atop the wall at this very moment.

I consider what it was like to wake up beside him this morning. He doesn't usually stay the night after we've made love, but he had seemed especially tired and fell asleep quickly. In truth, it was a bit awkward upon waking. He didn't say anything. He simply kissed my cheek, dressed, and left with only a nod in farewell. I'm afraid he's starting to tire of me, which breaks my heart. It's one thing to invite a man to bed who wants to lie with me, as I always thought he did. It's another entirely if he visits purely out of obligation and has no real desire to be there. As I think about it, our lovemaking did lack a certain passion last night. What changed in the 24 hours since the last time we were together when it was so furious and intense?

Devayn finally makes his appearance and I shift from concern regarding Anselm to dismay regarding His Highness. He's alone as he approaches, tugging at the cuffs of his jacket. "Your Highness," he greets me stiffly.

I turn a shoulder to him. "I must say, I am surprised you haven't obtained a more thorough sense for castle grounds after wandering them for three days. Is your perpetual tardiness because you're simple or because you're rude?" I think my blunt retort catches him as off guard as it catches me. I immediately wish I could pull the words back into my mouth. My mother is going to be disappointed when she hears about this, as she inevitably will. There is no way a boor like Devayn won't tattle the first chance he gets. I told my parents I would be a gracious hostess, but it's an impossible task. Devayn brings out the worst in me.

He doesn't reply to my surly question. He merely says, "I understand you have archery targets set up for us today. By all means, lead the way."

I sneer at the sarcastic tone in his voice. Then I turn on my heel and march down the path without bothering to check that he is behind me. I don't care if he follows me or not. In fact, I would prefer it if he didn't.

At the field, there are already several targets assembled. I find my bow cradled in a stand beside another bow set out for Devayn. Quivers filled with arrows are set at the appropriate distance before each target, four quivers for each of us. I tug on the gloves tucked into my belt, lift my bow, notch an arrow from the first quiver, and aim at the center of the six concentric rings. I let the arrow fly. It hits the third ring of the target, which is disappointing for my first shot. I repeat this series of steps for each of the remaining five arrows in my first quiver. When I've emptied it, I tally my score in my head and move onto the next target.

Six more arrows go flying from my bow, one at a time, sticking into the board, and I tally my score again. I finish up the round on the third set and then the fourth and final set. All the while Devayn is standing aside wordlessly, watching my little drama unfold. Once I've emptied my last quiver, I drop my bow carelessly to the ground.

"My score is 176," I announce as I walk off. He's welcome to stay out here and shoot all he wants. I'm not going to waste my time on him anymore.

I don't see Devayn again until dinner. He enters casually – and on time – as though nothing devolved this morning at all. The habitual pre-meal prayers are muttered, and the first course is served. I sit glumly beside His Majesty Gastogne, hoping he isn't so kind as to invite me into much conversation this evening. I hope he doesn't ask about my day. I've spent hours trying to think of what I might say to explain my outlandish behavior, even though Devayn deserved it.

The entreaty to enter into conversation doesn't come from His Majesty Gastogne, though. It comes from my mother. She peers down first at Devayn and then at me and asks about our time playing archery.

"It was delightful," I hear Devayn respond.

For you, maybe, I think, *and only because we didn't spend more than ten minutes together.*

"Her Highness Giselle is really quite a proficient archer."

I have to work hard not to roll my eyes at his words.

"She warned me of her many talents, but I had no idea just how far that extended. Of course, she came up short against my score of 192."

This is obviously a message to say he stayed and played the entire four rounds on his own. And that he bested me.

"192?" His Majesty Gastogne scoffs. "Sounds like you haven't been getting in enough practice, son." To the rest of the table he brags, "Devayn is often able to hit the target no fewer than five times in six."

"Is that right?" my mother says, sounding impressed. She peers around His Majesty Gastogne to look at me. She's pleased at what she's hearing about archery today, but the truth of how it all unfolded is obscured by Devayn's craftily worded responses. Instead of looking back at her, I'm watching Devayn, who meets my eye with a sly smile.

What is he playing at?

Dessert is finally served and it's a pie I don't care for. I don't like molasses particularly, but I see Devayn is devouring his own serving. I remember what Jareth said about his taste for sweets, so I beckon a servant to my side.

"Is it all right, Your Highness?" he asks, evaluating my untouched slice.

"It looks fine. I was wondering if you might pass mine along to His Highness Devayn with a message. Tell him his own skill for elocution demonstrated this evening is remarkable and kindly ask if he would mind refraining from displaying such talents in the future."

The servant hesitates, realizing I've asked him to tell Devayn I wish him to bite his tongue, but as I do not withdraw my request, he bows, takes my plate, and I watch him carry it to the prince. The message is delivered and Devayn looks down the table at me with a glint in his eye. He takes my meaning and I turn away, chin raised.

It isn't long before my father leaves the table indicating we are all free to follow suit. I scoot back my chair and head directly for the exit. I can't wait for my bath and I hope Veronica has already thought to heat some water to draw it.

In the next room, Devayn hurries over to me. "Your Highness," he says.

I reluctantly stop because we have an audience. Plenty of nobles slowly filter from the dining room and are passing by.

"Could you be bothered to join for me a walk outside?" he invites, offering me an elbow.

I have no choice but to take his arm. Our parents could be watching.

Devayn leads the way to the exit that takes us to the gardens. It's quite clear he has learned his way around the castle, which only serves to anger me. All his tardiness has been intentional.

The night air outside is cool, but it does little to quench the heat of my rising temper. Once I'm sure we're out of visual range from any spectators, I drop his arm and pull away with exaggerated flourish. I want him to know just how repugnant it is to have to take his arm.

He tries to hide a smile, and it enrages me all the more. *What is he so damned happy about?*

"I thought we handled the evening marvelously," he says.

I scowl at him. "Is that all you wanted to tell me?" I'm annoyed and turn to walk back inside.

"No," he says, grabbing my arm to stop me, "I wanted to apologize to you."

I'm stunned. He wanted to *what?* I'm at a loss for words and even though he's the one who pulled me out here, I can tell he's struggling to get out his next words.

"I misjudged you. I didn't want to come here to meet you and I was fuming the entire trip down. I held it against you and that was unfair."

"But why ..." It's all I can manage to get out, but the implication is clear.

He draws in a deep breath, readying himself for confession. He finally sighs, "Because I left someone in Callinor. I blamed you for taking me away from her."

"But Jareth said ..." He had said Devayn didn't show any interest in the *courtiers*. So maybe his love interest isn't a courtier at all. I think of Anselm and I can relate.

Devayn laughs, "You asked the ambassador about me. I wondered how you knew so much about me and the things I enjoy when I know so little about you."

"Oh, but it seems you know so much. You know I'm a no-good brat only out to steal myself a prince. You know I'm not worth a modicum of respect. You know I'm only good for talking your ear off. You know ..."

He puts up a hand to stop me from continuing and interrupts, saying, "I was wrong. I was wrong and you were right to accuse me this morning of being rude. I *was* being rude. I shouldn't have treated you so terribly and I'm sorry. Is there any chance we can start over?"

"To what end? You already have someone. You can return to Callinor and be with her. My parents will find someone else for me."

"I can't actually," Devayn remarks, looking at the ground.

"Why not?"

He doesn't meet my eye. He merely shuffles a foot on the ground, digging a small hole with the toe of his shoe. "Because she's already married."

I'm certain the shock is written all over my face when he finally lifts his gaze to look at me. I knew my own love affair was illicit but my gods. He's sleeping with a *married woman*?

"I don't know what to say," I respond.

"You don't have to say anything. That's really why I was upset, I guess. I knew that coming here meant it was over between us for good. I just wasn't ready for that. It wasn't your fault, but I took it out on you and I'm sorry."

"I understand," I say, now looking at the ground myself. My voice catches and it's a dead giveaway.

"Oh no," he says, "you have someone else too."

I peer up at him conspiratorially. "I'll tell you if you tell me."

Devayn smiles, offers me his arm, and we walk deeper into the garden. "She's a domestic in the castle. A maid. She comes in to tidy up my chambers, make my bed. That is, after we rumple up the sheets together."

I laugh, "He's a member of the Royal Guard. Probably prowling the perimeter as we speak."

Devayn's eyes widen and he looks around, trying to spy any guards, but we're shrouded by the trees of the gardens. We keep walking and talking, revealing secrets and other tidbits it's clear the other will understand. It turns out the life of a prince in Callinor is rather similar to the life of a princess in Apollonia.

When I return to my chambers, it's way past midnight. For once, even though I'd like nothing more than to be drawn into his warm embrace, I don't summon Anselm.

Anselm

I'VE BEEN DIRECTED TO ESCORT THE PRINCE AND PRINCESS once more. Dawn is barely cracking, and I was informed only an hour ago of this trip after I patrolled until midnight. It seems the royal pair made their plans very last minute.

On my way out, I'm handed a letter by the servant who makes the mail rounds. I shouldn't be surprised he knows to which guard to hand the letter addressed 'Anselm Odrin.' As the princess's plaything, just about everyone knows who I am.

I'm dismayed to see the letter is from the temple priest rather than my mother. I can tell by the handwriting. I slip it into the lining of my sash and hurry out. I don't want to be late and I'm cutting it close. I'll read it later.

Giselle and Devayn have elected to visit the ancient ruins in Sarpedon. This week is a holy week when many people make pilgrimages to the ruins. I don't believe Giselle ever has, so it's something of a surprise that she suddenly wants to go now. She has the entire week after all.

No matter. I'd actually like to see the ruins myself, as I've only seen them briefly in passing when I first made the trek from my hometown of Memnon to Dionysius to join the Royal Guard.

We have to leave early because the roads leading to Sarpedon will be crowded and it will take quite a bit longer than normal to travel there. Not to mention, the roads get worse every year. Others making the pilgrimage will surely move out of our way, but it will be slowgoing anyway. We have extra guards, including some from the Callinor contingent who traveled here with the royal family. We're happy to have them considering the trip is unplanned and the path has not been scouted in advance.

Giselle and Devayn travel by enclosed carriage. When they're safely inside, I direct my horse into position behind them and the entire entourage departs, moving in unison.

On our way, travelers call to the royal pair who wave at almost everyone we pass. They keep it up for most of the trip to Sarpedon, which is over four hours away. I'm actually impressed they give so much consideration to the nation's citizens. A part of me can't help but wonder if Giselle merely enjoys the attention and Devayn wants to ingratiate himself to the populace. I silently chastise myself for my cynicism. I know Giselle. She may be self-centered, but she isn't a bad person.

Halfway to Sarpedon, we stop to rest and water the horses. I keep an eye out but take advantage of the break to open the letter I'm carrying. In it, the priest says my mother's health continues to decline and he isn't sure she will survive to the end of the month. *Three weeks until then*, I think. *How can I possibly find a way home in three weeks?*

I fold up the letter and stuff it back into my sash. There must be a way, I tell myself, but I also know that I'm property of Apollonia for two more years. I go where I'm told, patrol where I'm told, and otherwise remain close to the castle and the royal family. A three-day trip, minimum, will hardly be permitted. There's an aching in my chest knowing I'm already going in the direction of home as we head toward the ancient ruins, but I'll have to turn around and head back to the castle before I even get halfway to Memnon. To where my mother inches closer to death.

I'm too restless to sit so I pace along the portion of the street where I stand watch. Despite the crowds of people and the many who stop to sneak a glance at the prince and princess, everyone is well-mannered and respectful. The royal family is well received wherever they go. I observed as much on the country tour we so recently took. Despite her faults, Princess Giselle is certainly beloved and with good reason. She knows that as her parents' only heir, the entire nation will be her responsibility one day. She is always gracious and attentive when listening to the many grievances voiced to her. She could easily shrug them off, as they are not yet her obligation to address, but she doesn't. She's quite good at heeding the nation's sentiments.

When our break is concluded, I see Giselle looking at me. The prince says something to her and she nods, keeping her eyes trained on me, and I can only imagine what she must be thinking. Probably planning our next tryst. Another guard ushers them back into the carriage and waves the crowd on their way. I climb onto my horse and we continue down the path to Sarpedon.

The second half of the trip takes longer as more and more travelers join the throng, coming from different directions. The other guards and I stiffen as the crowd swells; there are more people to keep our eyes on.

By the time we reach Sarpedon, we see swarms of people. The other guards are as nervous as I am, and I privately denounce the royals' wish for such a spontaneous trip. With only a single day to plan, we could have come up with a security detail we could be comfortable with. As it is, we have to make it up as we go along. We are well trained but lack the necessary preparation for this trip, so we remain alert and mindful. It isn't that easy with my mother forever in the back of my mind. I gaze down the road past the ruins, the road that leads home, and then censure myself for the moment's distraction.

Giselle and Devayn elect to walk the ruins, so a handful of guards stay behind with the carriage and horses as I and a few others take up our positions around the royals on foot.

Devayn offers his arm to Giselle who smiles broadly and accepts it. His other arm is held behind his back. I don't know why but I feel a twinge of jealousy. Maybe because I'm aware of how Devayn has treated Giselle and she's right to be upset about it. She has been a good hostess to him. And now they're putting on a show. Even if I don't have feelings for Giselle, I don't appreciate that this royal pain taking her arm is making her out to be a fraud in front of the people of her own nation, as she has to smile and giggle as though she enjoys his company. Their relationship is not a good one, but I must admit they sure are play acting well. It must enrage Giselle that she has to pretend to like someone she despises. If there's one thing she hates, it's stifling her strong emotions. I'm fully expecting to be called to her bedroom tonight so she can unleash her pent-up ire.

It's hard to really take in the ruins as I keep watch. It's particularly warm and I notice Giselle wipe her brow more than once. We approach the central fountain where prayers are offered, and the royals kneel there. Water isn't running any longer of course but a pool of brown water sits in the basin and priests still come to collect the offerings. Giselle and Devayn each carry a 50-piece and drop them into the murky water. Then they tap their foreheads, rise, and continue on their way.

Before long, the two sets of guards switch details and I get something of a break by the carriage. I still scan the crowd though and when I do, I see a face that's somehow familiar. The girl meets my eye and approaches me directly. Even right in front of me, I can't place her.

"Hello," she says, a bit shyly. "I didn't think I'd ever encounter you again."

I must look perplexed, as I'm still unable to recall how I know her.

Her eyes drop for a moment before she fills in the gaps, saying, "You helped me in Perseus. You gave me a 20-piece and a ride home."

I'm taken aback. This is the same poor girl from Perseus who was robbed in the town square? She looks so different. She's wearing traveling clothes for the journey and I can see she is with a pair of women, one perhaps in her forties and the other more elderly. They're clearly both women of means and I wonder how this girl came to be in their company. And to have traveled all the way to Sarpedon at that. It's a long way from Perseus.

She can see that I'm trying to put the pieces together, so she explains her newfound employment in Dionysius. "I brought these for the temple fountain, but I'd like you to have them instead. I owe you eleven pieces after all," she says and holds out three pieces, but I don't take them.

"You don't owe me anything. It wasn't exactly my own money that I gave you."

"Oh?" she asks, evidently concerned that I'd stolen the money for her.

I lean in closer and lower my voice, "I took it from the princess's traveling coffer. I knew she would never notice and if she had, she wouldn't have minded. She would have given it to you herself if I'd spoken to her about you."

"She sounds very kind," the girl says, pocketing her coins.

"She is," I tell her, realizing more fully for myself that despite her imperfections, she is compassionate. She does care.

"As are you," the girl says. "What's your name?"

"Anselm Odrin."

"I'm Coralyn Perle. You can call me Cory." She smiles and offers her hand for me to shake. "If you won't take these pieces, please let me repay you somehow. You have no idea what that 20-piece meant to me. And to my uncle."

I'm trying to think of something, but I'm still distracted by how different she looks. In Perseus, she was dirty like she'd been working outside all day. Her hair was stringy, her clothes were torn, her face was serious, and she was thin as a stick. Now she looks put together. She has nicer clothes, and her hair is washed and pinned, though she still uses her tresses to hide behind. Even her posture is more upright than I remember.

"I'm going to try to see my cousin next Sunday," I say. "I'm not sure but I think he might be courting a young lady. Perhaps the four of us could have an outing then? A picnic maybe in the Erato Gardens?"

"That sounds delightful. I'm no cook but I can put together a few sandwiches for us."

She tells me where I can find her in Dionysius and then rejoins the pair of women. I watch as they walk off toward the temple to pay their respects. I'm still surprised by how much the girl has changed. I never would have pinpointed the familiarity upon seeing her had she not approached me and told me. The transformation is remarkable. Her features were easy to miss before, muddied as they were and made more indistinct by the frown she wore, replaced now by a pretty smile. All cleaned up, it's plain to see that she's really quite an attractive girl.

There's a bustling that I see out of the corner of my eye. I turn to find the royal pair approaching the carriage together. I guess they've decided they are finished touring the ruins, so I start preparing the horses. They cordially speak with people who approach them, and I can mostly hear wishes of good fortune to them in their courtship.

It dawns on me that this is why Giselle wanted to take a trip to such a public place. Devayn couldn't possibly ignore her in front of so many others. His nation of Callinor is a close ally and the border is only a half-day's journey from here, just past my own hometown of Memnon. If he treated her poorly, word would travel quickly back to Callinor and his own reputation there would be harmed for how he treated Apollonia's only heir and his intended. Truth be told, I'm rather proud of Giselle's clever scheming.

At last, we're ready for the return trip and take our leave at a leisurely pace. It's been a long, hot day and we don't want to overwork the horses, so we move slow and steady.

Giselle and Devayn are able to ride in peace as the number of people to wave at dwindles. I wonder if she's celebrating her victory today. Devayn was the picture of genteel propriety and it must madden her to see he's quite capable of such politesse while stubbornly refusing to display any to date. Until she forced his hand, that is. *Good for you, Giselle*, I think. I'll tell her I'm proud of her when I undoubtedly see her tonight.

Sure enough, that evening I receive a summons to meet Giselle in her room. I wonder how long she can keep this up with me. I wonder when the prince will learn of the affair and the whole thing will explode in our faces. I'll be ousted from the Royal Guard, my future prospects for employment obliterated. I have to tell her this can't go on.

In her room, Giselle wears a light blue nightgown. I can't help but find myself turned on no matter how many problems I have that need sorting out. The champagne bottle is already open. She must have started without me or maybe she took an opened bottle from dinner. She doesn't rush at me or openly seduce me like normal, which takes me by surprise. With the exhausting day we've had, I expected her to fall upon me immediately, to release her pent-up emotions in a flurry of lovemaking. But she doesn't.

I go ahead and pour us both a glass of champagne. When I sit beside her on the bed, she drinks, surveys me, but still she doesn't say a thing, so I start. "I want you to know I think you handled today marvelously."

Her face transforms. I think the sincerity of my comment means a lot to her and she smiles, even blushes a little. "I thought you'd be upset with me," she says. "I knew you'd be tired and would be assigned to the journey anyway. But it's because you're such a valued member of the Guard. You always look out for me."

I don't tell her it's my job. She knows it is. But protecting someone is a lot more intentional when you know the individual as well as I know Giselle. When you care for them.

I down my glass and place a hand on her knee. Now's as good a time as any to get this evening started. She takes my hand in hers and seems to hesitate before pulling me down to her. Giselle moves slowly, giving me deep kisses, more intimate than any she's ever given before. Everything she does is visceral. This time, I don't feel like I'm an outlet for her passion. This time, I feel like I'm the object of it.

Undressing is slow. Methodical. It has the effect of augmenting my lust for her, craving the moment when she finally pulls my hips to meet hers and she releases a pleasurable groan, reveling in the experience of taking me in for that first thrust.

This isn't lovemaking for lovemaking's sake. This is lovemaking for the sake of us. Of Giselle and me. It's for the sake of sanctifying this foolhardy affair we've carried on for months now.

Out of the blue, an odd feeling courses through me. I get the sense that the end of us is near. Very near. So I wonder why it is that I pull her closer when the end is precisely what I've been hoping for.

When we're done, I hold her, and we share the silence, somehow knowing that breaking it would be some form of desecration. It feels like something sacred just took place between us. It's an experience like we've never had before.

We lie together for a long time, neither one of us moving, and I'm pretty sure Giselle eventually drifts off to sleep. I don't how long it takes but I drift off myself and when I awake, it's morning and Giselle is gone.

Princess Giselle

WHEN I SLIP OUT OF ANSELM'S ARMS AND RIFLE THROUGH HIS clothes for the letter, I don't know what I'll find. I saw him reading it. I saw the look of consternation on his face as he took in the message. I also know it isn't the first correspondence he's received. I can't help but wonder what could possibly be going on that he isn't telling me and that's causing him such grief.

I make my way to the antechamber, where I light a candle, unfold the letter, and quickly read in the dim light. It's from a temple priest in Memnon. He's sending word to Anselm about his mother's state of health, which is very poor and declining rapidly. Instinctively, I touch a hand to my heart where sadness wells.

This is serious. I can't imagine the anguish I would feel if I knew my mother were dying and I could not get to her. I fold up the letter and hide it. I may need to hold onto it for a while. I only hope Anselm doesn't notice it's missing.

When dawn breaks, I rise before Anselm, careful not to wake him. I want him to be able to sleep in, if not to restore his energy then to allow him a longer reprieve from reality, a world where his mother is dying.

I dress in something simple without Veronica's help and slip out of my bedroom. I have a small bite to eat and then head to the gardens and find my favorite stone bench. It sits under the shade of a large oak tree. Hours pass that I sit here, thinking, formulating a plan.

I don't know what time it is when my mother finally stumbles upon me. She's accompanied by Her Majesty Gastogne and His Highness Devayn. "Here she is," my mother announces. They had evidently been looking for me. I'm not surprised my mother knew where to locate me. She's found me here before when I've wanted to do some thinking. "Giselle, dear, your guest would like a word with you."

I move to one side of the bench, offering the other side for Devayn to sit. He does and once our mothers have taken in the sight of us sitting side by side, they cheerily move on and leave us alone.

"I didn't mean to disturb you if wanted time to yourself," Devayn says, but I wave off his concern. I've been out here on my own long enough. "I wanted to say I thoroughly enjoyed your company yesterday. I'm happy you talked me into it. It was nice to have a break from our parents' incessant watching and waiting too."

I laugh. He makes a good point. More than once I've found myself wanting to blend in with wall décor to avoid detection around my parents. For once, I don't particularly like the abundance of attention I've been getting. Then again, I've never had anything as personal as this courtship be such a public event either.

Devayn goes on, saying, "It made me realize what my obligations are as well. Not that you're an obligation. I don't mean that."

"I know what you mean. You're a prince of Callinor. I'm a princess of Apollonia. I understand."

Devayn places a hand on my back and says, "The girl back in Callinor, she was never really mine and I was never going to have a future with her. In the days that I've been here, you've shown me a whole new world. Your world. I resented being here at first, but I don't anymore. It's beautiful here. And I'm thankful you've opened my eyes to it."

They are very kind words, and I'm grateful to hear them after the things I've been sorting out today. The tension I carry in my back and shoulders loosens, and he senses the change.

"What's the matter?" he asks, realizing I haven't been hiding out to avoid anyone but to contemplate some things that are vexing me. "Is it your guard?"

He means Anselm of course. He has a maid and I have a guard. And just like Devayn is starting to let his maid go, I have to follow his lead and do the same with Anselm. I knew it last night when we made love for what I was sure would be the last time. It was a passionate goodbye, a beautiful goodbye, and for some reason, it breaks my heart.

I won't cry, I tell myself. No, *demand* of myself. Life is a series of hellos and goodbyes, an ever-changing whirlwind of events from the first breath until the last. And who in their right mind would want it any other way? No, saying goodbye to Anselm isn't anything to cry about.

"Yes, it's the guard," I finally say, "but it's a great many other things too." It's Anselm. It's his mother. It's Devayn. It's Apollonia. It's my future as the nation's queen. It's my primitive understanding of politics. It's all the expectations. It's all that's at risk if I fail.

It isn't just Anselm I'm saying goodbye to either. I'm saying goodbye to what life was like mere days ago. I can feel it slipping away and the future is staring me in the face. A future where the weight of the world is on my shoulders. It's no wonder my parents want a courtship to blossom. They know what it's like, and they don't want me to shoulder the burden alone.

It occurs to me then that Devayn can help. "Devayn, when are you going back to Callinor?"

He furrows his brow, clearly mistaking my meaning.

"I'm sorry, I don't mean it like that. It's just that ... I think you might be able to help me with something. If you're willing. If your *parents* are willing."

I divulge everything to Devayn about Anselm and his mother. Devayn tells me a date hasn't been set to return to Callinor just yet. "It depends on how things go with us, I think. Another reason I was so dismissive to start. I thought if it didn't go well, I could get back to Callinor faster."

I understand the added apology in his words, implicit by his tone.

"Do your parents know about Anselm?"

I never really thought about it before. It's a pretty open secret, I know that much, but I have to think that if they knew, Anselm would be long gone. Especially now that the Gastogne family is in town. They would never let me risk embarrassing Devayn and his parents by continuing to invite a guard into my bed. I tell Devayn as much, adding, "If they find out, Anselm risks losing his position in the Royal Guard and any real opportunity for future employment."

I finally realize how selfish I've been. I never considered the risk Anselm took to indulge me in my little games. No wonder he's been so distant since Devayn's arrival. His entire life is on the line if the affair is truly exposed, and I've been too caught up in my own miseries to give it any thought.

"It would be the same with Maris," Devayn tells me, meaning his maid. "Except that since she's married, she'd be looking at imprisonment on top of social castigation."

"Then we can't tell them anything," I conclude.

"Yet," he qualifies.

Yet, I ponder.

I realize what has to happen now. Considering guards can never take leave in their first four years, I can't get Anselm to Memnon without my parents' blessing. And they will never agree without learning what he means to me. If they know the extent of my relationship with him, they'll dismiss him from the Guard. While that might get him to Memnon, he would go in disgrace, left to face a life of shame and poverty. In order to keep Anselm from losing his post, my parents must see things the way I do. And they're going to want something in exchange.

It's perfectly evident what my parents want more than anything. A betrothal between me and Devayn. If I can give them that much – something that will be a commitment for the rest of my life – then surely they can let Anselm keep his position here – something that will salvage the rest of his life. His future never would have been placed at risk in the first place if not for me. He shouldn't have to pay forever for my mistakes.

But even if my parents do forgive me my sins and choose not to punish Anselm but grant him leave, it still wouldn't get him to Memnon.

"Which is why you want to know when we're going back to Callinor," Devayn finishes fleshing out my idea. "You want us to provide him transportation."

"Would that be all right?"

"With me, yes. With my parents … they wouldn't relish spending a day in a carriage with a guard from another nation, even one that is our closest ally."

"What if you went back engaged?"

Devayn gives me a mock look of surprise. "My goodness, Your Highness. Are you asking me to marry you?"

I'd fairly well accepted that Devayn and I were never going to get out of an engagement to begin with. The entire affair had been decided before the Gastognes ever left Callinor. At least he and I are in agreement that we can use this relationship to help Anselm. Devayn's maid, too, for that matter. Though, as we talk, Devayn increasingly suspects his parents are aware of his liaison and brought him to Callinor in order to break it up. That bodes even better for us to realize our plan if I'm wearing a ring by the time they make their return trip. In such a case, they might be under the impression their son's illicit romance has ended. Still, we're going to have to sell it that we've fallen for each other if they're going to be truly convinced. If we have a prayer of sparing Maris imprisonment.

We spend the rest of the afternoon conspiring and discovering we work remarkably well together. I learn that Devayn has an unparalleled sense of humor and by the time we make it to dinner, my stomach is hurting from so much laughter.

We're a bit late to dinner, as we were out too long in the gardens. Devayn and I arrive together and enter the dining hall with my arm on his. The room is already full and everyone is seated, waiting on us. He whispers something to me that makes me giggle a little too loudly in the otherwise quiet room.

Finally reaching our end of the table, Devayn pulls out my chair and I sit, apologizing to the room for our tardiness. Noting the amity between us, I'm certain our parents do not really mind. Convention would dictate that they are supposed to express vexation by the delay we've caused everyone, but all four of them are clearly trying to hide their delight at the sight of us together.

While Devayn and I planned the whole thing for the sake of appearances, I couldn't help but enjoy walking in on his arm, laughing with him, and then spying him repeatedly at the end of the table. If I'm being honest with myself, I'm not sure where the contrivance ends and the budding feelings begin.

The next day, Devayn and I elect to have a rematch in archery. We take turns launching our arrows. Devayn even helps me adjust my grip in increments, improving my aim. I get the feeling he might have modified his score down when he said he shot a 192 at dinner the other night. He hits one target after another. I think he must not have wanted to embarrass me. But I'm confident my score was perfectly respectable considering how quickly I took my shots.

"In Callinor, guards are required to be trained in archery. Sword-fighting and hand-to-hand combat, too. Everything a militiaman would need to know." Devayn steadies his arm, exhales, and launches another arrow.

"Our guards get that training, too," I counter, stepping up with my arrow already notched.

"Yes, but Callinor is along your northern border while the sea is to your south and west. Apollonia is most at risk from the east, whereas Callinor has numerous nations along our northern and eastern borders. It's imperative that we have a well-trained standing militia at all times, whereas Apollonia can get by with much less. Our guards are expected to be ready to answer the call to arms at any time to act in support."

I lift my bow, and Devayn nudges my elbow a fraction of an inch, following my arrow line. I release and watch the arrow soar into the target. It's far from the first target I've hit, but I can certainly tell how his adjustments are helping. I smile in satisfaction.

"Very good," he applauds me. As he notches his next arrow, he continues to talk about Callinor. "We require that all guards have a certain level of training before they can enlist and if they don't meet the standards, their requisite years of service are postponed for a year."

"Postponed?" I've never heard of such a thing. The notion seems ludicrous. "Wouldn't some men fail on purpose to indefinitely put off joining?" I ask.

"For some, yes, because they might have family obligations or other such concerns, but it doesn't get them out of militia duty if we go to war. Any appeal of a temporary exemption is typically overshadowed by the appeal of the severance they receive after they've fulfilled their term. It's generous, so there's incentive for them to go ahead and start." Devayn takes aim again, concentrates, and when he's ready, he exhales, releases, and the arrow goes flying. I can't tell if it's in the target or just outside. He curses under his breath, clearly dissatisfied.

"If they have to meet basic standards before enlisting, how are you able to ensure they receive sufficient training?" I ask, preparing my next arrow.

"We send targets to each province along with an abundance of arrows and bows. They aren't expensive to fashion, so it doesn't cost us much. Young men are expected to practice. There's social pressure, too. Men are rather fond of showing off, you know," Devayn says, smiling. "Plus, we instituted annual competitions where the winner of each province is awarded a small sum."

"Incentive," I reiterate, and he nods.

It takes us an hour and a half to get through our four dozen arrows. Devayn wins, of course, but my score improved by twelve points. We decide to play one more game, which takes us even longer for all the breaks we have to take as our arms tire.

"I'm impressed," he tells me when we're finished. "I was impressed the other day when you flew through all your arrows and still hit the target as many times as you did. With a bit of concentration, you've improved dramatically. You'd be a masterful archer in Callinor's militia."

"Well, you can tell your countrymen that the princess of a neighboring nation could rival them any day. How's that for incentive?"

Devayn laughs, a sound I'm growing quite fond of hearing. We leave our bows and waltz back to the castle arm in arm.

As morning arrives and I leave behind the world of the dreamers, I find that Devayn is the only thing on my mind. We decided we need to make our blossoming relationship more visible to our parents, so we arrange to have some local musicians, poets, and performers come to the castle. We even hire a master of ceremonies to introduce the acts.

My parents think it's a wonderful idea to share our cultural artistry with the Callinor royal family, though their culture is much the same as ours. We set up in the great hall, just my family, the Gastogne family, and a handful of noble families. It takes all day for our servants to arrange the area, but I thoroughly enjoy selecting the décor, designing the layout, and directing its execution. Devayn stays close, offering suggestions that will impress his parents.

When he's near, I notice him finding excuses to place a hand on my back, at my hip, at my elbow. He even boldly takes my hand when we sit down for a break. He turns my hand over, examines my palm, and draws a finger down the creases.

"You know, we could invite a palm reader," I suggest, "a fortune teller."

"Not a bad idea. It would be interesting to know what our futures hold."

Yes, it would be interesting. "Then I'll see that it's arranged."

Their Majesties Gastogne arrive in style for our gathering. My parents look equally lustrous. But my breath is truly taken away when I spy Devayn. He wears dark blue and gold. I'm already seated when he arrives and upon approaching, he takes my hand, kisses it, and doesn't let go as he takes the seat beside me. He keeps my hand in his, and I can't tell if this is a show for our parents or not. In my heart, I suspect not.

It isn't long before everyone finds their place and the entertainers filter in. There's a lutist, a flautist, a trio playing various horns, and then my favorite, a harpist, sits to play.

The music is beautiful. The songs range from upbeat to plaintive, and I'm captivated by the range of emotions they so readily evoke. I feel Devayn's fingers weave through mine, and I'm convinced his heart is turning the same way mine is. I give him a squeeze in return, an acknowledgment that I know he's beside me even if my eyes are trained ahead.

The last to play is a quartet comprised of two violins, a viola, and a cello. The music starts and it's a cheery melody. I'm surprised when Devayn stands, my hand still in his. He bends slightly and says, almost in a whisper, "Your Highness, would you care to dance?"

There's certainly space enough for dancing, and I accept his offer. As it turns out, Devayn is a rather proficient dance partner. He leads and twirls me effortlessly.

We're enjoying ourselves immensely, and the evidence is written all over our faces. So much so that it inspires Their Majesties Gastogne to follow suit. Not to be outdone, my own parents join us in dance. Soon enough, every nobleman is spinning his wife on the dance floor and having a marvelous time of it.

Alas, the music ends. While everyone sees fit to applaud the musicians, Devayn and I hardly notice anything but each other. His gaze is intense, and his grip at my waist holds firm. For a moment, I suspect he might try to kiss me. When the music has ceased long enough and it's clear we are the last remaining couple in a dancing pose, he finally steps back and walks me to our seats. If our parents are watching us, I don't notice that either.

The next to arrive are the performers. There are jugglers, magicians, contortionists, snake charmers, and a whole host of others. Our guests are amazed by their skills and *ooh* and *ahh* at correctly guessed cards, feats of acrobats, and other tricks that boggle the mind. We clap at every show, laugh at every joke, and I'm delighted to see how enjoyable the evening is turning out for everyone.

The poets read their works, tell excerpts from epics, play act scenes with aplomb. All the while, the crowd is enchanted.

And then the final guest is introduced. "To close the night," our master of ceremonies says, "we wish to impart good fortune to each of you. Please welcome Madam Miriam."

A woman enters who isn't anything I'd expect a fortune teller to look like. For one thing, she must be in her twenties. Her hair is cut short at her neck. She wears a cloth vest, but her arms are almost entirely bare. She does wear a long skirt that drags along the floor, and I wonder if she's barefoot. My parents would be aghast and dismayed if a guest in the castle didn't deign to wear shoes.

The woman evaluates each of us in turn. She approaches a man and asks to take his hand. The man obliges, and she studies it curiously. She turns her attention to the hand of the woman beside him and then she smiles.

"Another child," she says, and the couple widens their eyes. They've already raised three children to adulthood. But Madam Miriam goes on, "Within a year, he will make his appearance." I can't tell from here if the woman is pleased or merely surprised.

The palm reader moves on to another pair, another fortune. She tells about jobs, money, family, health, and most recipients seem satisfied by their news. I suspect Madam Miriam doesn't say anything ominous on purpose.

Finally, she approaches my parents. She runs a finger up and down the lines of their face-up palms, scrutinizing them, comparing them. She speaks without looking at them, saying, "A prosperous kingdom shall be your legacy, but obstacles arise nonetheless. In personal matters, a lesson will be learned but only if the heart is open and willing. A closed heart will breed contempt." My parents nod in thanks for the fortune, and she moves on to Devayn's parents.

She evaluates Their Majesties Gastognes' hands. "Hmm ... you've been wise and discerning in your leadership. This is a quality you may need to rely upon, for there is a confession on the horizon, one that will impact many lives. Whether in good ways or bad is in your hands." She curls Her Highness Gastogne's fingers, as though wrapping up the message within them and returning her hand. The couple eye one another with curiosity, contemplating the message.

Devayn and I are last to have our palms read. We present our face-up hands, and she peers into them. It doesn't take her long to see something, and she says, "A new season is upon you both. Your roots are already intertwined. Find a way to nurture and grow them together or they will fray and wither away. Tangled roots are not easily separated."

Madam Miriam starts to step away when she peeks once more at my hand and pulls it back to her for inspection. She sighs and drops her voice such that I'm not sure anyone else but me and Devayn can hear. "Tread carefully," she says to me, "as your roots have already been entangled with another. You will need to be gentle to break free. Failure to do so could mean the death of one or both."

I know precisely who she's talking about, and the message fills me with dread. I have to go about this with my parents exactly the right way or Anselm will pay with his future. And that will destroy me in turn.

Madam Miriam finally takes her leave, and the master of ceremonies provides closing remarks, wishing us a good rest of the evening. A round of applause goes up for him and the performers he introduced.

Devayn and I are discussing our fortunes when his parents approach and we rise to greet them. Her Majesty says, "We had such a wonderful evening. Thank you both for putting it on. Brilliant idea, really. Giselle, we must have you and your parents to Callinor some time for a similar occasion. We would simply love to host you."

"Thank you, Your Majesties. I would be delighted to accept such an invitation any time."

"I hope you don't mind if we retire early," she adds. She seems tired, and the pair of them exit, bidding my parents good night on their way out.

Then my own parents approach us. "Giselle, Devayn," my father says, "well done. Though I'm surprised your palm reader saw fit to encourage us to have open hearts. Perhaps we are mistaken in thinking we already do."

"You aren't mistaken," I say.

"I didn't think so," my father replies, smiling. He kisses my cheek, and my parents also retire.

The noble families filter out one by one and servants arrive to restore the hall to its original design. I'm almost sad to see it taken down. To know the evening has truly ended.

"Might I walk you to your room, Your Highness?" Devayn asks, and his etiquette makes me blush. I take his arm and walk closely to him at a deliberately slow pace.

At the door to my chambers, he gazes at me the way he did on the dance floor. "I hope you won't think it an act if I kiss you, princess."

I give a slight shake of my head and then his lips are upon mine, gentle from start to finish. It makes my head spin, awash with desire. Typically, I would grab him by the shirt and pull him into my room. But something tells me this isn't a typical kiss. Or a typical man. Something is different with Devayn. And I can't help but wonder at how our separate lives have suddenly started to grow together.

I realize it's been three days since I made love to Anselm. Three days since I even last saw him. I don't believe I've ever gone so long without seeing him since we first started enjoying each other's company months ago. Even during our two-week country tour when we couldn't share a bed, I still saw him every day.

It's also been three days since I took his letter, the one that's tucked away in my desk drawer now.

I HAVE VERONICA DRESS ME IN SOMETHING THAT LOOKS regal. I make sure my shoulders are back and my chin is up as I evaluate how I look in the mirror. I try to shake the unease away from my face but still I see a small crease between my brows. I've never been good at masking my emotions.

"Thank you, Veronica," I say when she's finished.

"You look lovely, Your Highness. Is there anything else I can do for you?"

"No," I tell her and try to give her a smile in gratitude. I haven't always been as courteous to Veronica as I ought to be, but she's never once failed to be so to me. I draw in a deep breath and think, *Here goes nothing.*

I find Devayn waiting outside my bedroom. Right on time. We walk through the castle to my parents' antechamber where they take their breakfast. My father's valet announces our presence, and we are invited in.

My parents aren't expecting us, so they await our announcement with interest.

"Going somewhere?" my mother asks.

"We hadn't planned to," I reply.

"Well, you certainly look nice to be sticking around here," she says.

Yes. That's by design.

"Mother, father. His Highness Devayn and I would like to discuss something with you if it isn't too much trouble."

My father invites us to sit, gesturing to the available chairs, but we decline and remain standing instead. That's how he knows this is serious.

"Are you familiar with the guard Anselm Odrin?" I ask.

They both shake their heads, which confirms that they have no idea I've been sleeping with him. I was hoping that they had already heard. That they'd overlooked it as an inconsequential romance they knew would run its course. No such luck.

"Well, I'd like to ask a favor on his behalf."

"Oh? And what's that?" My father asks, taking a bite of bread.

"His mother is dying. She'll be gone very soon. I'd like to send him home to be with her." I evaluate their faces. Compassionate but resolute.

"If he's at least in his second term, he's free to take the time," my father says.

"He isn't."

He's about to return to his breakfast when my response makes him lean back in his chair again, sighing, "Giselle, we can't grant such a favor. What you do for one, you'll have to do for all. You know that. How is it you're even aware of his personal circumstances? Did he come to you about it? Because that would be highly inappropriate."

"Oh, no!" I quickly reply. "He doesn't even know I'm discussing the matter with you."

"Then how do you even know …" my mother asks, the incomplete question clear.

How do I know so much about a guard's personal life?

"Well, I … came to learn of it indirectly, not straight from him. But he's meant quite a lot to me, which is why I'm coming to you."

Both of my parents furrow their brows. "They all mean a lot," my mother says, "for the risks they take for us. What makes this one guard mean so much more?"

"Because … he's been a member of my personal watch for some time and … I've become … intimately familiar with him," I say, gauging their reaction to my word selection. My mother reacts but my father doesn't. She's worried about my meaning, while he hasn't yet picked up what I mean by 'intimately.'

"I hope you haven't made poor choices, dear," my mother says, clasping her hands in her lap, "for his sake." Now my father understands.

"If I have, the fault would lie with me and me alone. Anything that transpired was at my entreaty. As he answers to me as I see fit, he would have had no choice but to comply, wouldn't you agree?"

"I'm not sure I agree with that," my father says. I can see he's angry. And embarrassed to be having a conversation on the topic of my private life. In front of Devayn at that. I open my mouth to reply but nothing comes out.

Devayn sees me falter and jumps in, saying, "Giselle and I have discussed the matter, and truth be told, I've disclosed an illicit affair of my own in Callinor. I assure you there is nothing you could fault Giselle for that you could not also find fault for in me."

"Be that as it may," my mother replies, "Giselle is our child, not you."

"And it was a child who made poor, self-interested choices but a matured young woman owning up to her mistakes standing before you now," I say.

"We cannot grant your request regardless of whether it's made by a woman or a child," my father chides, clearly irritated now.

I glance at Devayn and he nods to me in support. "I had hoped I could speak of his circumstances without revealing the extent of our relationship. But seeing as how it is out in the open and you're disinclined to provide any leniency, I'd like to strike a bargain on his behalf."

"You want the boy granted leave *and* you don't want him dismissed for his misdeeds," my mother astutely surmises.

Devayn takes the smallest step forward and says, "In truth, Your Majesties, I'm quite anxious for him to maintain his employment here as well."

My father is astonished. "*You?* You come to court our daughter, she admits to being with another man, a guard no less, under this very roof, and *you* want his behavior excused?"

"Your benevolence in the matter would serve as an example to my parents when we next visit them and I make a similar confession. I hope I haven't damaged my character in your view by my own admission of guilt."

"Well, out with it then. What's your offer?" my father asks me, all but ignoring Devayn's remark.

I ready myself. This is the bargaining part of the conversation. "It's important you know that Anselm has meant *everything* to me." The declaration is genuine. I may not have fallen head over heels in love with

Anselm, but he has been steadfast in his devotion to me. As a guard. As company in my lowest hours. As an outlet for my wildest emotions. As anything I needed him to be. Madam Miriam was correct to suggest we have become very much enmeshed. And now I have the difficult task of undoing something I never ought to have been caught up with in the first place. "If I put myself in his place and it were your lives in the balance, I would be brokenhearted to be a day's ride away without any hope of being able to make the journey. If you would allow him to visit his mother and to keep his position in the Guard – and Devayn will be making a similar request of his parents on behalf of his paramour – then he and I would agree to be married in order to ensure the peaceful alliance of our nations for many years to come."

My father, who has hardly been able to meet my eye, finally lifts his gaze but only to give me a look to say that isn't good enough. "Giselle, a match with a prince of Callinor is asking very little of you. You are the sole heir to this throne. You know as well as I do that whether the time is now or ten years from now or once your mother and I are dead and gone, you will marry practically and do what is best for this nation. Frankly, it would be even better for Apollonia if we asked you to marry a prince of Tympane."

Tympane is the nation to our east, the nation with which Apollonia has a much looser alliance. I suppose he's right that asking me to wed Devayn is hardly asking much of a princess destined to marry for political advantage.

I hesitate, realizing I have no other advantage to barter with. And yet, it makes me wonder why my parents haven't tried to arrange a marriage with a prince of Tympane. His Highness Cyrus is an eligible option after all. And then it dawns on me, as I recall what Devayn told me about Callinor's militia.

"Would that be better?" I ask. "Because if an alliance with Callinor doesn't remain strong, how do we protect our border from them?" Devayn is listening closely. "Callinor has a standing militia that exponentially exceeds ours in numbers, training, and weaponry. It's necessary for them because they have so many other nations to protect themselves from. But we do not. If we keep Callinor in an alliance, we need only to maintain a militia sufficient to defend against Tympane, a nation smaller than ours by more than half and significantly poorer and less developed. It's far more important to maintain an alliance with Callinor, which is why you need this arrangement to work out."

My mother looks impressed. I'm not sure even she had considered the ramifications if it clearly was not going to work out between Devayn and me. But I know my father has. These were his motives to begin with and he kept them from me.

He rubs his knuckles, weighing my argument. "It still isn't enough," he finally says. "It doesn't change the fact that you will marry for the good of the nation."

I shake my head. "I don't have to marry at all."

"Oh no? And who will the throne go to then? You have to have an heir."

"Fine. Then maybe I'll marry Anselm." It's a childish thing to say so impulsively, but it gets my point across.

"*A guard?* You'll do no such thing!"

"It's only *assumed* I'll marry because it's what's assumed of every young woman, me in particular. There is no law that requires me to marry a man of royal or noble breeding. There is no law that requires me to marry at all."

"Well perhaps there should be!"

"Dear," my mother says at her husband's raised voice, "the battle or the war."

While I know this conversation is the battle, I do not know what war she refers to. My marriage? An alliance with Callinor? My plea to save Anselm?

There's an awkward moment of silence as my father and I both quell the heat of our rising tempers.

"Would it make any difference if Giselle and I were engaged before my family's departure?" Devayn inquires. That much at least gets my father's attention. "We could make the announcement on our last night."

My father taps a finger on the table, contemplating. Announcing an engagement would mean there's no going back. It's virtually tantamount to marriage itself. At long last, he says, "Speak to Their Majesties Gastogne. When you've finished, tell them we are anxious to confer with them. We'll summon you back once we've reached a decision on the matter." He huffs, correcting himself, "*Matters.*"

Devayn gives a quick bow to my parents before exiting behind me.

When we are alone again, the emotions I held back in front of my parents threaten to overtake me. I pace the room, unable yet to search out Devayn's parents in their own antechamber. That conversation went nothing like I expected. Like I had hoped. I've exposed Anselm and I have no guarantee he will be safe. *What have I done?*

Devayn pulls me around the corner for privacy should my parents quit their chambers unexpectedly. He wraps his arms tightly around me as I try to catch my breath. He whispers comforting words, letting me know I'm not alone in this. And when I've finally composed myself, we head off in the direction of Their Majesties Gastognes' quarters.

I can do this, I tell myself, not at all believing it.

Devayn and I bide our time for hours after we've conferred with his parents. He suggests we go eat but I can't stomach the thought of food. He suggests a walk and I consent considering I can't keep still with my frayed nerves. I'll be delivering news of some kind to Anselm tonight, and I can't bear the thought of it being ruinously bad.

Devayn shares in my apprehension for his maid's sake, but he's far better at taking it in stride. Finally, Devayn's valet tracks us down, telling us our parents want an audience with us to impart their decision. It's only thirty minutes until dinnertime. If it's good news, I can eat. If it's not, I don't know how I'll make it through the meal without bursting into tears. For a woman who prides herself on not crying, I sure have been doing a lot of it lately.

We meet them in the great hall and none of them betrays their verdict by their stern faces. Devayn takes my hand rather than my arm when we stand before them, a contingent of two confronting an army of four.

My father initiates the conference with a grim voice, saying, "Disappointment does not even begin to describe how we feel about the position you've put us in. You have both behaved carelessly, childishly, and gave no regard for how your actions might impact others. On top of that, you come running to us to fix it, asking to be absolved of any real repercussions. They are hardly the behaviors expected of future monarchs. For that, we are gravely dismayed, though perhaps we bear some responsibility in failing to bring you up appropriately.

"Having said that …" My eyes brighten at the change of tone. "We have reached a consensus. Your palm reader warned Their Majesties Gastogne about an impending confession and that their response would carry great significance. We, too, were advised to keep an open heart. Against my better judgment, we have agreed to meet your terms."

I exhale an audible sigh of relief.

"But there are conditions."

Whatever they are, I'm sure I can meet them.

"Should the guard Anselm be removed from service, the reason why may well become public. We cannot have the reputation of the only princess of this nation so tarnished. Therefore, he will complete his term, but he will not be eligible for reenlistment, nor will he ever again be assigned to your detail for the remainder of his term. He will be demoted, unable to advance further."

My father looks to His Majesty Gastogne who picks up from there. "The maid Maris will be offered a new post in the home of a noble family. She will not be allowed to visit castle grounds in the future but neither will she be locked up for her misconduct. Her husband will also be apprised of the liaison so that he may make his own decision about how to proceed with their marital affairs. Whether or not he makes it public is not up to us, though we can provide him some incentive for his discretion."

His Majesty Gastogne defers once again to my father, who says, "The two of you shall announce your engagement on the evening of Wednesday next when we have a farewell ceremony for the Gastogne family. We will renew our faithful alliance at that time, marked by the joining of our families by your impending nuptials. You will not fail in convincing both of our nations of your love for one another, whether authentic or not. A date will be set for you to wed in no more than one year's time. You will also be expected to bear children within five years hence so that we may be assured of our lineage here in Apollonia. Are we agreed?"

"And what of Anselm's mother?" I ask.

"Oh, yes," my father says, "the guard may be granted leave. As it is unclear how long his mother has left, he may take up to thirty days to tend to her, say his goodbyes, and manage affairs of any estate he is left. His missed days will be added to the end of his term."

"And," His Majesty Gastogne adds, "we shall provide him passage to Memnon when we return to Callinor, departing Thursday morning next."

"He will have to find his own way back, walking if he must," my father says. "We will not allow him to borrow a horse of the Royal Guard for personal purposes. Bending the rules so dramatically for one guard will be looked upon unfavorably as it is. Gifting him such a fine steed for so long a journey, a steed that is property of the crown, would be asking too much."

I nod my understanding.

"Giselle," my father continues, "when you see the boy and impart the news, I want it to be the last time you correspond with him so long as he is a member of the Royal Guard and finds residence here. I'll let you figure out how, but do or say whatever is necessary to keep him from coming around. I've no idea what kind of feelings he may have developed for you, but from this moment forward, he deals with it on his own."

I nod again, slowly this time. I think I feel Devayn squeeze my hand, but I can't be sure.

"And finally, Giselle, you are hereby required to attend meetings with our advisory council on a daily basis. You will be given more responsibilities, which I expect you to fulfill with prodigious results and without complaint. Where your mother and I have failed to train you in your personal life, we will not make the same mistake in your political life."

"And Devayn," His Majesty Gastogne adds, "you will relocate permanently to Dionysius in six months' time. You will also be tasked with apprising yourself of the nation's laws and the monarchy's authorities in order to best assist your wife when she inherits the crown. You will be imparted duties at the discretion of Their Majesties Rothrys. You will reflect well upon our family and our nation in your fastidious performance. You were born a son of Callinor. You will now be a son of Apollonia."

"Is anything we have said unclear?" my father asks.

Devayn and I shake our heads no.

"Good. Then are we agreed?"

"We are," Devayn and I say in unison.

"Then we'll see you shortly for dinner."

Devayn and I hurriedly exit hand in hand.

As I await Anselm in my room after dinner, I am aware that it's the last time I will see him. Of course my parents will do everything they can to ensure he is kept away from me, which takes little more than telling his superior to reassign him to new posts. But it's up to me to ensure he has no desire to be in my proximity.

The silence in my bedroom is deafening and my hands shake holding the letter I'm about to return to him. I'm so angry at myself for what I've gotten him into. None of this was his fault and he'll be punished nonetheless, barred from reenlistment, barred from the most prestigious posts. He earned those placements and now they will be taken from him. Because of me. Because of my selfish ways.

When Anselm enters, it's all I can do to meet his eye. But my parents have reminded me of my position and my authority, and I have to start practicing the role.

I haven't given any consideration as to how to start this conversation, so I pull out the letter by way of confessing my sin. He spots it and knows instantly what it is and that I stole it from him. He knows I've read it and summoned him to discuss its private contents.

"I wish to return this to you. I just … why didn't you tell me?" I ask and immediately chastise myself. It's a childish plea, and I already feel I've botched how to go about this.

The anger radiates off of him at my question. I understand because I harbor the same anger at myself.

Before I can try to amend my opening, he says, "*Why?*"

I falter, trying to eke out something rectifiable, but the words are lost, caught in my throat.

"Because it's none of your damn business," he sneers.

I deserve the acrimony in his voice and he's right. It is none of my business, but I made it my business anyway. Still, it stings hearing him acknowledge that he kept me at a distance. I had deluded myself into thinking we were closer than that.

"I just … I thought you trusted me," I whisper. I wish I could take it back as soon as it's out. It sounds like an accusation, but I don't mean it that way.

"You don't know a thing about me, Giselle. My family. Where I'm from. Nothing. You never bothered to find out anything about me because it was never important to you. *I* was never important to you for any reason other than what I could do *for you*."

He's absolutely right, but I never realized it until now and I didn't expect to hear him speak those words. Not with such recrimination in his voice. My face betrays me once again as my mouth hangs slightly agape. "But I could've …"

"No, you couldn't," he says before I can even finish the sentence. "You have the Callinor prince to entertain. You've hardly been able to help yourself with all the emotions he's stirred up in you. And with him here, you think the Guard would *let* me leave even with your blessing? They need more guards right now, not fewer."

I hold the letter out for him to take. It is his after all.

"Keep it," he says, "a souvenir of our last night together."

My already aching heart fissures like broken glass. He turns to go before I've even told him what I need to impart.

"Wait."

"Are you ordering me?"

I don't have a choice in what I say next. If it's no, he'll leave. So I hold my head up and say, "Yes." I inch toward him carefully and when he turns away, I stop in my tracks. I work to keep my voice steady to deliver the message. "The Gastogne family is traveling back to Callinor on Thursday next. I've arranged for you to travel with them as far as Memnon. You're to manage your affairs and then return to duty in the Royal Guard within a time frame not to exceed thirty days. Your missed days will be added to the end of your four-year term."

He can't bear to look at me. I'm desperate for one last look before he's gone for good. "Thank you, Your Highness," he says, and the formality of his address is a punch to the gut.

I've been more intimate with this man than anyone else and now he's disgusted to be in my very presence. He doesn't want to know me at all.

"I'm indebted to you," he adds. "Will there be anything else?"

All I can manage is a quick shake of my head. He practically runs from the room in his desire to be away from me. The door is left ajar, but I don't care. I fall to pieces crying anyway, imagining a sapling ripped from the ground.

Anselm

I HAD BEEN WONDERING WHY I HADN'T HEARD FROM GISELLE in the three days since we last made love. And now I know. I had walked away from our last night together thinking we had shared something sacred. But what a manipulated fool she's made of me. She saw me read that letter on the trip to Sarpedon and tuck it into my sash. In a single act, she stripped my letter and my trust in her. And she has the temerity to accuse me of lacking faith in her. I now have good reason to. Since that night, while I've been trying to figure out a way to get home to see my mother, she's been betraying my confidences.

I didn't disclose anything to Giselle because I didn't want to burden her with my problems, which I didn't really think she could solve anyway. I doubted she could grant me a privilege she wasn't also able to offer to every other member of the Royal Guard. I knew the predicament such a thing could cause her in the future – her and her parents. And while I would give anything to see my mother again, I never wanted special treatment. Especially not from Giselle.

It's bad enough that the other guards jeer and taunt whenever she summons me. I've always known it was out of jealousy. But now I'll be a pariah here. As the only first-term guard to be given such charitable consideration, that jealousy will transform into contempt. And I won't even blame them for it. I'd probably feel the same if our positions were reversed, wondering why I couldn't visit my dying relative when the princess's lover could. The other guards will never believe that I didn't ask Giselle for help, and I don't have the heart to out her betrayal in my own defense.

But neither will I turn down her offer simply because I'm angry at her methods. I'm not so blind as to miss the enormous gift she's given me. And my mother.

So I'll hold my tongue, take the ostracism, and wait it out until my term ends with the Royal Guard. This is no longer the place for me.

Cory

TWO DAYS AFTER TRAVELING TO SARPEDON, LADY HAVARD and I bid farewell to Lady Wryn, who returned us safely home. After seeing the ruins, we took a detour to visit an old acquaintance of Lady Havard's, where we stayed the first night. She doesn't like to travel for very long, as it causes her body aches, so Lady Wryn agreed to house us for a second night in an inn. And now, we are back in the comfort of Lady Havard's manor.

Upon entering, Lady Havard declares she is exhausted and elects to lie down for a nap. I take the time to complete my chores. After doing some light housekeeping inside, I collect a watering can and a pair of gloves. I need to water Lady Havard's plants and flowers, as they've been neglected for a couple of days in our absence. I plan to inspect the soil as well in case any need repotting.

I exit to the back garden and find Thomas at the base of the steps. He seems almost more surprised to see me than I am to see him … outside the servant's door at Lady Havard's home … where *I* live.

He grips his cap with both hands and stops mid-stride. *Was he pacing?*

"Cory," he says, "um, you must be wondering what I'm doing here." There's a tentative tone to his voice. Paired with the rhythm of his accent, he sounds almost apologetic.

"I suppose I am, though I'm certainly not disappointed to find you in Lady Havard's garden. You seem well suited to them." I smile, recalling our venture to Erato Gardens. I mean it too. I'm quite pleased to see him.

"I wanted to know if maybe ... er, I thought I'd ask if ... um, perhaps before your cooking lesson ... at Pia's, that is ... on Sunday, of course ... if maybe you'd like to join me ... for an outing."

It takes me a moment to piece together his phrases, then I remember the plans I've already made for a picnic with Anselm and his cousin on Sunday. "Er, well, perhaps we could go Sunday next? I'm actually occupied this Sunday as it happens. I plan to see someone I met in Perseus. I encountered him out of the blue when we were in Sarpedon."

"Oh, I see ... yes, of course," he stammers. "I ... I'm sorry, I didn't mean ... Sunday next. Certainly. I'll just ... I'll go then. But ... I'll see you still, yes? This Sunday? To take you to Pia's, right?"

I'm somehow enchanted by the way he says so much so fast and still says nothing at all, so I hardly realize he's asked me a question when he finally does come up for air. "Oh, yes, of course! I'll still see you Sunday – say, 3:00?" I ought to be back from lunch by then with time to spare.

Thomas nods. Well actually, I can't tell if he's nodding or bowing or both. He sure is acting strange, but I find it endearing. Is he nervous to be around me? Talking to me? He didn't seem this nervous Sunday last.

Thomas finally places his cap on his head and awkwardly departs. I think he mutters something like "goodbye," but I can't be sure. I watch him as he walks away and once he's out of sight, I continue on my way with my watering can, where I find every plant healthy and green.

ON SUNDAY, I'M EXPECTING ANSELM AT THE BACK DOOR, SO I'm startled when there's a knock at the front. Lady Havard is surprised too because she isn't expecting company.

"If he's selling something, I'm not interested," she tells me.

I'm already holding the picnic basket I've filled with sandwiches and apples when I open the door and find Anselm standing on the stoop dressed in his Royal Guard uniform.

As Lady Havard retires to her study for some light reading, she passes by the door. Upon seeing a member of the Royal Guard, she says, "Goodness, is everything all right?"

"Oh, yes, Lady Havard. He's not here on official business. This is the gentleman I spoke to in Sarpedon if you recall. The one I first met in Perseus."

"Oh, yes, I remember now," she says, touching a hand to her forehead as if to playfully imply memory loss. "I just didn't realize how profoundly dashing he was as I stood so far away. But I can see quite clearly close up that he is a true vision of masculinity."

My cheeks burn at her words. I can't bring myself to turn and look at Anselm's reaction for fear of exposing the tomato shade of my face. Anyone with eyes can see Anselm is wildly attractive. After all, those hickory brown eyes are the first thing I ever noticed about him. But his handsome visage hadn't made me feel self-conscious until this very moment.

Lady Havard doesn't see fit to save me from further humiliation. Rather, she persists, saying "My, my, Cory. You've been here all of two weeks and already you've snagged yourself two suitors. I can't imagine how many men will be coming to call in two months' time."

"Um, Lady Havard, can I help you get situated in the study before I leave?" I say, pleading.

"No, no, I can manage on my own. I'm old, not infirm. You two run along and have a lovely day together. She practically shoves me out the door and shuts it behind us. I can hear her giggle to herself on the other side. At least one of us finds my embarrassment entertaining.

Anselm offers me an arm as he says, "Can I carry that for you?"

I gladly hand off the picnic basket.

"I apologize for Lady Havard's behavior," I say, though I'm not sure it's proper etiquette to apologize for a lady.

"I take no offense," he responds, and I can tell by the sound of his voice that he's smiling – not that I can see it as I haven't worked up the courage to look at him just yet. I'm still afraid my cheeks are too crimson, and I'm sure that my scar especially is aflame.

"I, umm, thought there would be others," I say, desperate to move on to a new topic of conversation, "your cousin and his lady?"

"Ah, yes. As it turns out, she was unavailable, so my cousin elected to stay home as well. It will be just the two of us this afternoon. I hope that's all right."

I tell him it isn't a problem at all, adding, "Though I hope you're hungry because I made enough sandwiches to feed the entire Royal Guard."

He laughs easily and the sound is melodious.

"She didn't mean it," I explain, "about suitors. About you being a … well, a …"

"Suitor," he finishes filling in the blank because the prospect is too embarrassing for me to consider, let alone give voice to, no matter how effortlessly Lady Havard had. "It's all right. I rather like the idea of treating a young woman to a nice outing."

"If you recall, you wouldn't let me pay back the money you gave me. I am the one that is supposed to be treating you," I reply.

"Same thing if you think about it. Letting me escort you on a picnic is a treat for me."

I blush again.

"Miss Perle, forgive me, but I confess I never would have recognized you had you not approached me. I'm astonished by how you've changed. You hardly seem like the same person."

"It's Cory, if you don't mind. And it is remarkable what a change of clothes and two weeks will do for a person. Just before I arrived here, I was quite disordered. Terrified, really. I just knew Lady Havard was going to see right through me as a poor country girl without the necessary training to serve as a lady's maid."

"Precisely how I felt when I joined the Royal Guard," he confesses. "I grew up in Memnon."

I've never been to Memnon, of course, but I know of it. It is not quite so destitute as Perseus but certainly a town of working-class citizens.

He continues, "I was one of the lucky ones that had some education. My mother had a few years of schooling and she taught me, but the idea of coming to the city was daunting. I'd never been away from home and I had to walk here on my own. The trip can be done in two long days on foot, but it took me three. You see, I had fallen asleep in a cart when a man offered me a ride. He didn't realize I was going on to Dionysius and he turned off the main road heading for Britomartis. I slept for an hour and had to make up quite a few miles to get back to the main road."

"I can't imagine going to a new place all alone. At least I had my neighbor to accompany me."

"Not your uncle?"

I'm impressed he remembered I mentioned an uncle in our exchange in Sarpedon.

"No, he isn't well. He's the reason I took this job in fact. He isn't able to work any longer. The neighbor that brought me here has been kind enough to take him in during my absence."

"Isn't well?" Anselm asks.

I think his voice sounds softer with the question, but I can't tell for sure.

"It's a problem of his lungs mostly. But his joints pain him, too."

The Erato Gardens come into view and Anselm finds a nice patch of grass for us to enjoy our picnic. He retrieves a pair of sandwiches from the basket. As we eat, he seems to be watching me with curiosity, as though trying to figure something out.

Finally, he asks, "Do you wonder what your uncle would think seeing you now? Working as a lady's maid in the city?"

"I'm really more of a housekeeper," I amend. "But no, I hadn't thought about it. I don't know if he *would* recognize me! How did your family react after they saw you dressed in your uniform?"

"It's just my mother left, and I haven't seen her since I enlisted two years ago," he answers. He adds that in their first term, members of the Royal Guard aren't allowed leave. "But as it happens, I'll be going home this Thursday."

"How are you managing that?" I ask, seeing as how he still has two years left in his first term.

He heaves a deep sigh tinged with sorrow. "That's a long story. Let's just say someone intervened on my behalf."

"That's a rather kind someone to have attained such an exception for you." I take a bite of sandwich and notice he is contemplating my words more than I would have thought. It seems an obvious statement to me.

"You're right," he finally agrees after a protracted pause. He doesn't seem eager to explain whatever it is he is pondering, so I don't prod.

"How long will you be gone?" I ask.

"I'm not sure. I'm allowed a month."

I'm stunned. That seems like an especially long time if such a trip really is the exception Anselm is making it out to be, and I have no reason to think otherwise. I'm curious about the circumstances, but I still don't ask, and he doesn't offer additional information.

When we've finished our sandwiches, Anselm pulls me to my feet, saying, "I need to pay someone a visit."

"Oh, well I …"

He cuts me off, saying, "Would you like to accompany me? It isn't far."

I agree and he leads the way until we arrive at a smithy. There are a few smithies in Perseus, but I've never ventured into one. Uncle Penn had warned me against them as it was the fumes from the smithy where he worked that aggravated his lungs after so many years spent there.

A man with skin the shade of chestnut approaches, his arms and mouth both spread wide in merry greeting. Anselm introduces me to the man whose name I learn is Faizal. He's somewhere between me and Anselm in height. Anselm has to stoop to embrace him.

"Faizal is second to none in blade smithing," Anselm informs me and then takes it upon himself to show me some of Faizal's creations. He makes everything from daggers to longswords. The hilts are so ornate that they're practically an art form. Some are imbued with gemstones of varying cuts and sizes. Anselm explains that Faizal uses a mix of metals in the hilts, which provide different tints to the various components. He crafts custom-made designs, some of which are worth a small fortune in price. It's evident Faizal has an unparalleled gift for sword making.

Anselm next shows me the sword he's been crafting. He tells me it will be nearly four feet in length once the hilt is attached, and then hands me the blade to test the weight. Surprisingly, it isn't particularly heavy at all.

"Faizal has blended a new kind of steel. Much lighter but just as sturdy. He's been teaching me the art of blade smithing in my spare time, and I'm happy to say I think this one is nearly finished," Anselm says, beaming.

"It's beautiful," I assert and examine the grooves cut into both flat sides of the sword, tracing a thin line beginning near the tip and widening ever so slightly as it extends toward the base. The edges remain sharp throughout, and I'm impressed by Anselm's craftsmanship. Faizal, too, stands aside watching, visibly proud of Anselm's work.

"How long have you been learning blade smithing?" I ask, handing the sword back to him.

"Not quite a year, I think. I made a few smaller items, daggers and such. This is the first sword of this length I've made," he divulges, and I'm astonished. This doesn't look like the work of a beginner at all.

"He has quite a knack for it, doesn't he?" Faizal cuts in. "Anselm's a quick study. He understands lines and balance and has an eye for design."

"It would appear so," I agree, though all I have to go on is what I see in front of me. I know nothing about making swords.

Anselm next shows me the hilt he's working on, as yet unattached. He describes the loops he's carved, one half representing the rising sun and the other half representing its descent. I see a pair of letters etched into the hilt where it will attach to the blade – *AO*.

"Odrin, was it?" I ask, trying to recall his surname, which he mentioned in Sarpedon.

"That's right," he confirms.

I hand the hilt back to him, affirming its beauty and its maker's skill.

"I'll show you again once it's completed. If you're interested in seeing the finished product, that is."

"Truly? I would love to see it," I gush, perhaps too eagerly, but Anselm doesn't acknowledge my enthusiasm if he even notices.

He merely replaces his sword pieces and we rejoin Faizal.

Anselm then directs his attention to Faizal, saying, "I wanted you to know I'm leaving for Memnon this coming Thursday. I don't know when I'll be back. It might be a few weeks, so if you don't see me for a while then you'll know why."

"I take it you spoke to the princess about your mother's health, then?"

The question posed by Faizal reveals much more than Anselm has disclosed, but he doesn't hesitate to respond despite my presence.

"Not exactly, but she was instrumental in working it out."

This small exchange has my mind racing. I had no idea Princess Giselle was particularly familiar with the guards. They always appear to keep a social distance in public, close enough to protect the royal family but too far to converse much. They are working after all. But within the safe confines of the castle, any manner of socializing could transpire. I merely had never considered it. Then again, Anselm did remark on the princess's kindness, saying she would have gladly given me the 20-piece back in Perseus. I thought he knew as much because he had spent time guarding her, observing her. Perhaps there's more to it than that. The princess of Apollonia is apparently the one interceding on Anselm's behalf. I can't imagine she would bend the rules for just any guard. I can only come up with one plausible explanation. Anselm and the princess must be *very* close.

After we've bid Faizal farewell and Anselm offers me his arm for the walk home, I ask, "Is your sword intended to be used to help guard the princess?"

My query seems to pique his interest. "No. It's just something I do in my spare time. I wanted to try my hand at it and see what I could come up with."

"I see. Well, you've come up with a masterpiece," I say.

"You really think it's that good?" He halts and looks at me as if he needs to be sure I'm not merely flattering him.

It must be the dark shade of his eyes that makes his gaze upon me feel so intense, almost alarmingly so, but I gather my thoughts quickly and reply, "I suppose it's easy to be critical of yourself when you're doing something you've never done before." Gods know I can relate. "But yes, I thought it was spectacular. Haven't others you've shown said the same thing?"

"I haven't shown anyone else," he confesses. "Only Faizal knows about it. Well, and my cousin is aware that I've taken up the craft. I even gave him a knife I made. In fact, he's the only person who owns a blade I've created. But that's the extent of it."

"I feel honored you would share it with me then," I say. "If you were to show it to others, I have no doubt they would be impressed. And I'm sure your cousin is aware he is in possession of a rare gift indeed."

Satisfied, he turns again, and we continue on our way back to Lady Havard's. "Anselm," I initiate, slightly nervous to broach the next topic given its personal nature, "is your mother in ill health?"

"Yes, I'm afraid. She'll be lucky to make it to month's end."

"I'm so sorry." I recall he mentioned that his mother is the only family he has left in Memnon. "I am glad you'll be able to see her again, though, and be with her when the gods claim her." I hope, too, that when the time comes, I have enough warning to make it to Perseus before Uncle Penn passes, whenever that day may come.

Anselm accepts my condolences.

"And the princess? You said she helped arrange the visit to your mother."

"She did. Giselle, er, *Princess* Giselle became apprised of the circumstances and saw fit to find me passage back home."

"That's mighty generous of *Giselle*," I say, highlighting his accidental slip.

He smiles sheepishly, "Ah, well, I may as well fess up. The whole thing has been an open secret in the castle anyway. Everyone knew she fancied me. And a man would have to be blind to miss *her* exquisite charms."

"As a woman unacquainted with the princess, the only charm I can be certain of is her unmatched beauty. Of what other charms do you speak?" I think the question makes *him* blush.

"Is it really gentlemanly to kiss and tell?"

"So you have at least kissed her," I conclude and he laughs.

"You know what I like about you? I think you possess a very honest view of the world. You see things as they are, not as you would like them to be."

"Is that so unusual?"

"My gods, you have no idea."

By the time Anselm and I reach Lady Havard's, I have only a half-hour before Thomas is supposed to arrive.

"I don't suppose it would be all right for me to call on you again when I return from Memnon, would it?" Anselm asks.

I'm flattered he delighted in my company so well. "You can certainly do so if it pleases you. I would enjoy it considerably, much as I have enjoyed today."

"Me as well," Anselm replies, lifting my hand and pressing a soft kiss against the tops of my fingers.

"May the gods bless your travels and your mother in her final days," I say before he leaves me at the door. He thanks me, hands me the picnic basket, and sets off for the castle.

Rather than enter through the front door where Anselm left me, I walk around back to the servant's door. I'm surprised to find Thomas is already waiting there for me.

"Well, hello," I say before he sees me and startles.

"Cory," he grins, clutching his cap nervously like he has a habit of doing, "I'm early. I thought you might be back, but I didn't want to disturb you just yet."

"You wouldn't be disturbing me," I tell him. I hadn't noticed when I first made his acquaintance at Ned's that he had a tendency to become so easily flustered. "Would you like to come in and wait while I get ready?"

"Oh, um, no. That's all right. I can wait out here in the garden if it's just the same to you."

"Very well. I'll only be a few minutes. I need to check on Lady Havard and put the basket away."

He nods and sits on the bench to await my return.

Inside, I inform Lady Havard that I'll be leaving once more. She asks me to fix her some tea and leave a sandwich for her. She looks me over with a sly expression, as though she knows something I do not, but she doesn't say a thing. As she seems contented to continue her reading in the study, I curtsy and leave her to it.

When I find Thomas again outside, he's wearing his cap and seems to have relaxed a bit. I must have simply caught him off guard when I walked up on him earlier.

Thomas walks me to Pia's, and I notice he pulls my arm rather close to him. He makes jokes, laughs nervously, and tells me I look beautiful – twice.

I must admit, Thomas looks rather handsome himself. His cap hides any hair that has grown out too long and keeps it out of his face. I think he looks nice whether he wears it or not. I especially like the way he has trouble meeting my eye when he smiles, though I do wish he would do it more. I like the way he smiles at me. I like feeling that he notices me. I like that in Thomas's company, I no longer feel invisible. I feel seen.

At Pia's, she teaches me how to bread and fry croquettes. Thomas stands close by. He's my taste tester for whatever I make. While I cook, following Pia's lead, he tucks my hair behind my ear when it falls in my face and I can't brush it away because my hands are coated in the egg-soaked breading. I don't even mind that it exposes my scar. Thomas reddens when Pia recounts embarrassing stories from their childhood together. I laugh at his expense, and he takes it in stride, which I think is remarkably attractive. I like knowing these little intimacies about Thomas's youth. It makes me feel like I've known him much longer than I have.

I even confess to a few of my embarrassing childhood moments. Like the time I screamed at temple when a spider dropped onto my shoulder.

And when I got separated from Aunt Trudy in the town square, and she found me being fawned over by the half-dressed ladies at Satine's. On second thought, maybe that was more embarrassing for Aunt Trudy than it was for me. I was too young to recognize the house of ill repute for what it was. Thomas laughs at hearing these tales but not too hard, I think for the sake of my dignity, but I wouldn't mind if he had. I feel comfortable enough to share these things with him after all.

When my croquettes are done, I hand one to Thomas. I understand now why Pia was so eager to watch us eat her own croquettes when we first came by last week. Every grimace or pleasurable groan provides information for how I'll need to adjust them for the next time.

Last week, Thomas groaned. This week, he emits neither a groan nor grimace, as he picks out a bit of fish he doesn't like. I notice that it's much too overcooked, and my shoulders droop in defeat.

"Don't despair," he says as he lifts my chin with his finger, "except for that bit, it was really quite good. You might have a future in cooking after all."

Pia lets me take home the half-dozen or so croquettes we have remaining, wrapping them up so they retain their heat. I don't know that I would trust myself to make them so well on my own, but I'm eager to try this week. The recipe isn't so complicated.

Thomas and I stay to help Pia clean up and put things away. She finally retires upstairs to the loft where she has a bedroom made up. "See you Sunday next," Pia calls and I happily agree to come by then.

When we leave, it's much later than I expected. I notice how different Nyx Notch looks now that the sun is nearly all the way down. Most people have vacated the area, though a few of unsavory appearance hang around. There are women with skirts drawn up to boast a bare leg and men looking them up and down. I watch a couple emerge from an alley, rearranging vestments as he hands a coin to her and they part ways.

"It's not safe here at night," Thomas warns. "I plan to visit my family Sunday next, so if you're coming back to Pia's, promise me you'll find another chaperone or arrive earlier in the day if you're unescorted. I don't want anything happening to you when I'm not around."

I promise him. I don't want to be walking these streets alone after dark anyway. He pulls my arm tighter as we pass a man missing too many teeth looking at me sideways. When we cross to the other side of the street, Thomas takes up my other arm instead, positioning himself between me and any leering characters. I remind myself that he was formerly a member of the Royal Guard and I wonder if the other men in these parts were too.

"Many of them were kicked out," Thomas explains, "or given remote assignments, such as escorting a nobleman or ambassador on a journey for official business. They're kept away from the royal family if they're even allowed to finish out their term in the Royal Guard. But you see, once you've been expelled, no one wants to hire you. It's sort of a black mark on your reputation. You're seen as dishonorable. After all, if you can't be trusted to look after the royal family and their interests, why should anyone else trust you to look after theirs?"

"I see."

It is nearly pitch black when we reach the servant's door at Lady Havard's. Thomas doesn't yet release his grip on me and says, "Since I can't make it Sunday next, I'm afraid I won't see you for two weeks. Unless Lady Havard takes an outing and needs her horses, then I'll be sure to bring them by."

"She will probably just rely on Lady Wryn," I explain.

"Well then, I will miss your company enormously," he says wistfully.

It's strange that I hardly know this man in front of me and yet I also know him better than almost anyone else. My life has been fairly solitary until this move to Dionysius, so it has taken me by surprise that someone so recently encountered could so quickly garner such import in my life. I will miss him, too. Quite a lot, I think.

He inclines and tenderly kisses my cheek. "Be safe, Cory. I'll be counting down the days until I see you next."

"As will I," I confide. And I know I will. I think I miss him already. What's more, I think that's the reason I don't release his hands when he starts to pull away. He takes it as a sign and leans in again, this time pressing his lips to mine.

I've never felt such yearning before, and I breathe him in, savoring the moment that won't come again for two weeks. Once he has finally pulled away and reluctantly bid me goodnight, Thomas still waits until I've gone inside before he departs.

I'm forlorn when I go to check on Lady Havard.

"A letter arrived for you from Perseus today," she informs me, indicating the folded note on the desk.

I pick it up, assuming Bethea has sent me corrections for my letter writing, and ask, "Shall I prepare your room for bed?"

She narrows her eyes at me.

The tone of my voice has surely given me away.

"Is everything all right, dear? You've had two separate outings with two different men today, and yet you seem withdrawn. I daresay I was never so down in my youth under the same circumstances."

"Oh, it isn't anything really. Thomas is busy for the next couple of weeks is all."

"The stable boy? Well, you should let the guard pursue you anyhow. Much better prospects."

"Thomas was a guard too. And Anselm will be out of town for perhaps for a month."

Lady Havard appears put out. "Men! They ensnare you with their charms and then walk right out of your life."

I have to laugh at her theatrics. Neither of them is walking out of my life, but I enjoy the womanly coalition she has created with me against them.

"I think it's time for bed after all," she says.

I curtsy and go to prepare her room.

Princess Giselle

DEVAYN WILL BE RETURNING TO CALLINOR TOMORROW AND taking Anselm with him. I haven't seen Anselm since delivering the news of the arrangement to get him to Memnon, so I wonder if he's still angry with me for taking and reading his letter. I imagine he must be.

The last few days with Devayn have been rather nice. We've taken several outings around the city and even took a return trip to the Clymenes. Anselm did not accompany us this time, as he is no longer a member of my personal watch. I dislike the adjustment. I could trust Anselm, though I have no doubts in the capabilities of the other guards. I just miss him.

I'm grateful Devayn has been around to fill in the spaces that would otherwise have been taken up by sorrow. He makes me laugh and teaches me things I never knew. He's as brilliant as Ambassador Jareth told me he was.

The castle is busy today in preparation for the goodbye ceremony before the Gastogne family goes home. The engagement between Devayn and I will be announced, and I have butterflies thinking about the moment.

I receive word from Devayn that he would like to take me to Lake Harmonia for the day in advance of this evening's ceremony. We have an estate there, so I've visited the lake a handful of times, but we have not gone in many years. The landscape is likely different now compared to my muted memories. I figure Devayn must have asked my parents for suggestions of where to take me for an outing, seeing as how he isn't familiar with the area. Of course, I accept Devayn's offer to accompany him.

I wear a dress of white and gold. Its thin fabric is well suited for being outdoors in the heat. When he sees me, Devayn falters before kissing my hand and telling me how beautiful I look. "Like a goddess," he whispers.

Precisely how you make me feel, I think. He helps me into the carriage, and we set off for the lake, which is no more than a half-hour away.

The scenery at Lake Harmonia is picturesque with mountains rising in the distance. A fishing boat drifts on the far side of the lake with a single fisherman, who is too occupied and distant to notice us. Devayn and I promenade along the edge of the lake where a seldom trod path has been carved.

"These last couple of weeks have been a surprise, have they not?" Devayn asks me.

"They certainly have. I had no idea how much life could change in so short a period of time."

"Change in good ways, I hope."

"There has been a great deal of good," I confirm, letting the unspoken implication hang that there have been vexing trials for both of us as well. We've both had to accept saying goodbye to people we hold dear. And yet, we've found commonality in the shared experience.

His Highness Devayn is no different than me. He is the offspring of a nation that looks to him for leadership, who has made mistakes of youth and been forced to find a path forward. That path has led him to me. And my path has led to him.

It's easy to recall his recent boorish manner, and yet the same man now walks on my arm, a gentleman who, in a matter of days, has made me laugh and conspired with me and danced with me and held me when I was scared. He has kissed me with easy passion and accepted my every fault.

Gods know I have a few! To think of the Devayn of day one and the Devayn of today, I can hardly believe the two men are one and the same.

The realization hits me like a ton of bricks. I'm not just falling for this man. I'm head over heels in love with him!

"Did you ever think you'd be here?" he asks, drawing me back to the moment.

"At the lake?"

He laughs, and I wonder if he had said something else I missed while I was caught up in my reveries. "No, at this point in your life. Announcing an engagement to someone you met not two weeks ago."

"I'd say I only met the *real* you one week ago. But yes, I knew my parents would arrange a marriage for me, though it was always my choice whether or not to accept their match. My parents' marriage was also arranged, but it worked out well for them. I knew they would want the same for me."

"Well, I didn't have the same expectations seeing as how I have two older brothers in line ahead of me for the Callinor throne. It came as quite a surprise when they summoned me and said we were leaving for Apollonia in two days' time and that I needed to be prepared for a betrothal."

"No wonder you hated me."

"I didn't hate you. I just didn't know you."

"And now that you do?" I peek up at him, trying to gauge if his reaction to my question gives anything away.

He grins, tilts his head closer to mine, and whispers, "I find my parents made a good selection for me. A very good selection."

We walk on merrily until we come upon an outcropping of rocks. Water from the lake splashes over them where moss grows in bunches. Devayn leans down to run his hand over the smooth, wet growth.

"Did you know rocks are just an assortment of crystals and minerals that get packed together in different ways? It happens by heat, sand, mud, anything really that can glue them together."

I did not know this.

"And the moss that crawls atop it has no roots whatsoever. It just likes the rocks for the moisture and shade."

I did not know this either.

He pulls a piece of the moss for me to examine, showing me the fibers that fall apart between my fingers. "Moss grows in a lot of different places but has no allegiance to its host."

"It's still pretty," I say.

"It is," he affirms, "but it's picky too. I prefer rocks to moss. Boulders even. An accumulation of fragments molded over time, not easily broken apart or dislocated. And still, they help moss thrive without complaint."

"Trees, too," I add, nodding to the tree line that billows out into a copse. I can see the moss from here, blooming in much larger clusters.

"Also a gracious host," Devayn says, "and even stronger than rocks if you consider that their roots can push through and weaken the composition of rocks."

"You're a wealth of knowledge today," I say.

He shies for a moment, realizing how he has lectured but not offensively so. It's edifying, and I'm attracted to his aptitude for science and learning.

He turns solemn and takes both of my hands in his. "It's better to be a tree than a rock. It will bloom again no matter how harsh the winter, but if a rock is broken, it cannot be molded together again for ages. Trees put down roots that dig into the ground as far as they need to for the tree to survive. And tangled roots are not easily separated, are they?"

I smile, taking his meaning.

He presses his forehead to mine. His breath is warm and inviting and I think he might kiss me, but instead, he breathes, "Giselle, you've been a surprise to me, and my feelings for you developed quickly once I allowed myself to know you. And thank the gods I did." He pulls back only for a moment to touch a hand to his forehead by way of gesturing the notion. Then he dips his forehead to mine once more and continues, "Because what I found is that you are remarkably adept in a great many things, just as you claimed. I just didn't realize at the time that includes capturing my every thought and pulling my heart to yours. I can't say how it happened, but I've fallen for you."

"And I for you," I whisper.

Then he pulls back once more and withdraws a ring from his pocket, holding it up for me to see. It gleams in the sunlight. "We may have been brought together by circumstances outside our doing and our commitment to one another may already be agreed, but Princess Giselle Rothrys, a union with you would be the highest privilege and my greatest honor. Before the announcement of our engagement tonight, I wanted to ask you myself with only the gods as witness if you would be my wife and see fit to make me your husband."

My heart soars and while the wide smile on my face is certainly answer enough, I fervently cry, *"Yes!"*

His smile matches mine, and he slides the ring on my finger. He's chosen a band of innumerable gold threads intertwined and overlapping, wrapping my finger in an endless loop.

I feel Devayn's arms wrap tightly around me as his lips meet mine. Again and again, we kiss and embrace and kiss some more until the flurry slows to intimacy.

"I will give you my heart every day of my life," I whisper.

"And I will guard and protect your heart as I would guard and protect your body," he vows, kissing me again, deep and impassioned, and I'm flooded with a sense of love and safety, knowing my soul has found a home with his.

THE ORCHESTRAL ENSEMBLE IS ALREADY PLAYING AS GUESTS arrive and make their way to the great hall. Veronica has dressed me in a gown of red and gold and I'm certain Devayn will be wearing the colors of his own nation, too, blue and gold.

Devayn and I will be introduced first to the swelling congregation of noble men and women, eager to send the Gastognes off in warm appreciation for their visit. Their Majesties Gastogne will enter next and my own parents will be last. There will be drinking and dancing throughout the night until finally the news of our engagement – and enduring alliance with Callinor – will be announced. Devayn and I will wade through the many congratulations we are sure to receive until guests decide it's time to retire for the evening.

And then only a matter of hours will remain before Devayn leaves me.

I'm pacing outside my chambers in the hallway, waiting for Devayn to escort me when a face I don't expect to see comes by instead. Anselm. My heart flips, wondering if he's here to see me. I'm stupidly still pondering this question even as he stops in front of me.

"You look beautiful," he says.

I open my mouth to speak but no words come, I'm so shocked that he has approached me. The last time I saw him, he was clearly livid. He hated me and the betrayal I enacted against him. I didn't mean to hurt him but that's precisely what I did, despite intending to help him. I can still envision how he ran from my room the second I let him go. My heart hurts to remember it.

"Giselle, I want to thank you for what you did for me. I behaved badly when you were only trying to show me kindness and I'm sorry. I'm so appreciative, more than what I could really express."

His words certainly mean a lot but what might mean even more is that he called me *Giselle*. Not *Your Highness* or *Princess*, even now that our relationship has become more formal in nature, though that was thrust upon us by necessity. If the Gastognes had never arrived, Anselm would still be sharing my bed.

"And I wanted to be the first to offer my congratulations for your engagement. I wish nothing more than for you to be happy, so I hope he's everything you deserve and more."

I'm not sure how he knows about tonight's announcement, but I suppose word gets around. "As it turns out," I say, "I think he just might be."

"Good," he says, as he leans in to kiss my cheek and hug me. Just as he starts to step away, Devayn approaches.

"Would I be correct in guessing this is Anselm?" he asks.

I move to stand beside Devayn and tell him he is in fact correct, though Anselm looks confused as to how this Prince of Callinor knows him. "I understand you've meant a lot to Giselle. And my family is pleased to offer you passage to Memnon."

"Thank you," Anselm says, shaking Devayn's extended hand, "I was just conveying my congratulations to the two of you."

"It's much appreciated," Devayn says.

Anselm gives me one last look then excuses himself. Devayn allows me a moment as I watch Anselm walk away. When he rounds the corner, I turn back to Devayn and squeeze his hands, finding my reflection in his eyes. I give him a soft kiss with upturned lips before he escorts me to the great hall where the start of our future awaits. A future I'm profoundly excited for.

The following morning, I stand outside beside my parents, ready to bid farewell to the Gastognes as they climb into their carriage to be taken back to Callinor.

"I'll see you in a matter of months," Devayn whispers, his head bowed to mine. My heart is breaking at the prospect of his imminent departure. I want so badly to go with him, but my parents have already set up a series of advisory meetings for me to attend. They've even hired a tutor to instruct me in the finer points of politics. They have ensured that the next few months have me so tied up in the business of inheriting a country that I won't have a moment to think about doing anything else – namely betraying their trust by renewing an association with Anselm. But I would never do that. Not now that Devayn is in my life.

Devayn is too polite to kiss my lips in front of our parents, so he settles for the cheek. I crave the feeling of his lips on mine and wish I could skip ahead six months by snapping my fingers. I can have nearly anything I want as a princess, but the instant passage of time is not among them.

"I promise to write," he asserts, "and I'll hope every day to receive word from you as well."

"Then I will have to write to you every day," I reply.

Finally, Devayn steps back so his parents can also bid me farewell, and they all step into the carriage. Not far behind, Anselm, too, climbs inside, though his hesitation to ride with the royal family is obvious. Under normal circumstances, it would be a breach of protocol and etiquette for a guard to dare join Their Majesties – but nothing lately has been normal.

Anselm is in the carriage before I can wish him good tidings, which is just as well because to do so would most certainly have been a violation of my parents' terms. As Anselm and I are not to correspond with one another, I can only watch as the carriage pulls out of sight, carrying two hearts that will forever hold mine.

I'm not sure how long I sit outside mourning their departure and distant returns. Eventually, Veronica comes to check on me and see if there's anything I need.

"Are you married, Veronica?" I ask.

She's taken aback by the question. I've never been personal with her even though most women are quite close to their lady's maids.

"I am," she answers, adding that her husband works in the kitchens here in the castle. I had no idea. I'm ashamed that I know so little about the woman who helps me run my life.

"Are you happy?" I ask. I'm not sure why I ask. I only know that I was exuberant one minute and alone the next.

"I am. Can I do anything for you, Your Highness? Is there anything that might cheer you?"

"Are you able to accelerate time?" I ask hopelessly.

"No, but perhaps the gods could speed up your perception of it," she suggests.

"I'll have to visit the temple tomorrow and ask."

"If you keep busy, Your Highness, the days will pass in no time. I've found it to be true when I'm eager to see my husband."

I smile at the thought. I'm glad Veronica has a happy marriage. "Do you have children?" I can't believe I don't know this.

Veronica blushes. "Not yet," she replies, patting her stomach, "but we might in a matter of months."

My eyes widen in astonishment. "Really?!" I exclaim.

"Word has it you'll be greeting your own little ones in a matter of years," she says.

Ah yes, within five years, per the terms of the agreement with our parents. The prospect is daunting and yet it fills me with joy at the same time. "Yes, well, I have to get through these months first."

Just then, a pair of guards walk through to the front of the castle, nodding a respectful greeting to me. They're carrying a mailbag and sifting through several pieces when one of them spies a name and stops in his tracks. He turns to me and hesitates, as though he has something to say but is too timid to speak up.

"What is it?" I ask when I realize he wants to approach me but doesn't quite know how.

"Your Highness," he says, "there's a letter here for Anselm Odrin, but I understand he's already gone."

"That's correct," I reply. "How long ago would you say they left, Veronica?"

"Close to four hours now."

I'm shocked. *Have I been sitting out here that long?*

"If you leave it with us, I'll make sure it gets forwarded to him," I tell the guard, who obligingly hands over the letter.

Once they've gone, I'm reluctant to give the letter to Veronica so that she can post it to Memnon behind Anselm. The letter feels like a piece of him that I want to hold onto for just a moment longer. Then it occurs to me …

"Veronica, you don't suppose this letter is from Memnon, do you?" I think I recognize the handwriting. It looks to be from the same temple priest who wrote Anselm about his mother in the earlier letter. But if he's writing again so soon … I take a quick look around to be sure there aren't any prying eyes. "Speak of this to no one," I whisper to Veronica as she watches me split the seal and open the letter.

I'm immediately crestfallen by what I read.

Dear Anselm,

I hope this letter finds you well. Unfortunately, I am terribly sorry to inform you that the gods have claimed your mother just tonight. Her passing was in peace as I offered prayers to the gods for her soul. Please let me know at your earliest convenience how you wish to proceed with arrangements for the estate. With greatest sorrow and prayers for your own well-being, I hope to hear from you soon.

"No," I say aloud, my voice replete with desperation. I look down the road as if I could will the carriage back. I know what Anselm will find when he reaches home and I would give anything to spare him the heartache. But there is nothing to be done. Except …

Anselm

HIS HIGHNESS DEVAYN GASTOGNE STEPS OUT OF THE CARriage with me when we reach Memnon. He even walks a short distance as a guard on horseback follows.

"Giselle has been restricted from corresponding with you, but I haven't," he starts. "I understand your relationship with her has become complicated, but I hope you don't harbor any animosity. If you could have seen her the day she spoke on your behalf, you would have seen how much she cares for you. How much she was willing to sacrifice for you. She didn't think of her own reputation. She only thought of yours. Our parents saw how impassioned she was to fight for what she believed was right, even if her means and earlier behaviors were questionable."

"Thank you. I think what Giselle and I have gone through has been resolved. I'm glad you can see what passion she exudes. One of my biggest fears in all of this was seeing that passion extinguished, so I hope you find a way to balance feeding the flame while also tempering it."

Devayn chuckles. "I'll do my best. May the gods be with you." He takes my hand to shake.

"And you in your travels. Thank you for providing transportation."

His Highness turns back to the carriage. I'm certain he doesn't want to keep his parents waiting any longer. They still have plenty of road to travel before they reach Callinor's capital city.

It's only two miles until I reach home. When my mother's house comes into view, the house where I grew up, I pick up my pace. She's only moments away, and I can only think that she will finally see me in my Guard's uniform. It will be one of the last images she will have of me before she passes on.

I break into a run, hardly even gasping for air when I reach the front door, which I discover is unlocked. The temple priest must be here.

The floorboards creak as I enter, which gets someone's attention. I hear footsteps approaching. Just as I suspect, the temple priest greets me.

"Anselm, you couldn't have possibly gotten my letter already," he says, bewildered.

"Already? The one from a week ago?"

"The one from yesterday," he sighs, and his voice is as full of sorrow as his face.

"What's happened?" I push past him to get to my mother's room. At the doorway, I see her prone body on the wood boards that form her bed, nestled upon her hay sack. Her eyes are closed, and her arms lie stiffly at her sides. The priest has already found a cloth to wrap her in, though she only lies upon it, not yet enveloped.

"The gods claimed her just before dusk," he says, coming up behind me.

Right about the time I was thanking Giselle for giving me leave, my mother was breathing her last and the temple priest was writing me a letter he would send immediately and that I would not receive.

For a time, I don't know what to do. I stand there staring, disbelieving. A matter of hours separated us from a final goodbye. I want to curse the gods for taking her now. After everything that took place to get me here, I can't understand why they would do this. I was prayerful, wasn't I? I went to temple, gave my offering, and still they have robbed me of one last moment to hear my mother's voice, to let her hear mine. The woman who raised me lies dead in her bed, and I was not here for her as she passed into the next realm.

I go to her and kneel beside the bed, taking her hand in mine. Then I weep for my mother just as a child would, craving the comfort only a mother's embrace can impart. Only this time, she is not here to answer my plea, to wrap her arms around me. *"I'm sorry,"* I whisper. And I hope she can somehow hear me.

I'm not the first guard to lose someone and not be able to say goodbye. She knew the rules as well as I did. She could not have known I was on my way. I was foolish not to write in advance. I was just so scared something would change at the last minute and my leave would be taken away. I didn't want to risk raising her hopes only to have them dashed.

I remember the last day I saw her, how tightly she squeezed me. She bit back tears until I said, *"I'll be back in four years"* in a playful tone I might have used if I were merely going to pick up something in town. She let loose a chuckle she could not help, tinged with sadness for the truth of my words. Then she slipped a letter into my pocket and told me to look up Faizal Sarif when I reached Dionysius. If ever I needed anything, he would help. I have never so desperately needed anyone as I do now, but Faizal is far away and could do nothing anyway.

I finally rise, give my mother one last kiss, and fold her hands across her chest. I pull the cloth around her and secure the ends in place. When I leave the room, I see that the temple priest has remained, giving me the necessary space to say goodbye.

"I don't know how to thank you for all you've done," I say.

"Yasmeen was a devout woman. She was faithful in her deference to the gods until the end. They would not have wanted me to let her breathe her last alone. I was blessed they chose me as her keeper."

"As am I," I say.

"Where shall we bury her?" he asks.

I already know the answer. I hate to admit I've already considered this. "Across the field where the sweetbriar bloom."

He nods, as though he could not have thought of a better place. "There, she will surely blossom and grow anew."

That night, I can't sleep. I don't know how with my deceased mother just a room away. At some point, I find myself sitting against the closed door to her room, as close as I can possibly put myself without entering. Somehow her bedroom has transmuted into something holy in my mind and crossing the threshold would be sacrilege. So I wait until the sun comes up and the temple priest returns.

He arrives early. The sun has barely breached the horizon and I wonder if he has been unable to sleep as well. He helps me carry her body and place it on the cart, already secured to his horse. I see he has thought to bring a pair of shovels as well.

I lead the horse across the field. The priest and I select a spot and begin to dig. It goes more quickly with both of us working, especially before the sun has reached its zenith. It's cool yet, so we are able to work faster than if we had waited for the sun to rise. I wonder if the priest considered this before coming over. I sure hadn't. Then again, he has more experience in the practicalities of death than I do.

We finally lower her body into the grave we've dug. The priest delivers rehearsed prayers, giving her body back to the earth and her spirit to the gods. Then we shovel the dirt back in. I collect stones and place them in a ring representing the lifecycle. From the gods, to earth, and back to the gods once more. The orb looks like both the sun and moon, light and dark, beginning and end.

The priest places a hand on my back, tells me to take my time and that he'll meet me back at the house when I'm ready. Ready for what, I'm not sure, but I accept his gracious offer and sit with her for a while as the sun continues to move across the sky.

I can feel the heat increasing by degrees and finally decide I've sat there long enough. No matter how long I stay, my mother is not coming back. I will never again see her beautiful face. This is where I must leave her. So I wipe down my dirt-riddled pants as I stand and make my way back alone. As the priest took the horse and cart when he left, I make no haste in my return to the house.

"She had me track this down for you," the priest says when I eventually reenter. I glance at the single sheet of paper. The deed from when my father purchased the house some twenty years ago. He also hands me a letter my mother wrote when she first became aware of her failing health and knew it would not improve. I don't read it yet. I don't want to. If it's the last thing my mother will ever say to me, I need to save the moment for when I'm ready. I've had enough in the way of saying goodbye of late.

Over the course of the next day, I wander the rooms of this empty house. Not much of my deceased family is left. My mother wasn't one to hold onto much for the sake of sentimentality. If she could use it, she would. If she could sell it, she would. So there isn't much here that I feel I need to keep either.

When I start my trek back to Dionysius on Sunday, I've already made plans to sell the house. This is not the life I want to return to after my service in the Guard.

I hate to put anything else on the priest's shoulders after all he's done for my mother and me, but I visit him at the temple anyway. I know he can handle this one last task and won't turn me down.

"Sell to anyone for no less than 80% of its value. I don't care how long it stays vacant. You can hold the money until I get out of the Guard and I will collect it then or you can send it to me. Take 10% of whatever you sell it for. That's for you in recompense for your help with a portion to be given to the temple. Thank you for everything."

The priest blesses me and sends me on my way.

I've changed into an outfit more comfortable for traveling. My hands are empty when I start walking save for a knapsack holding my Guard's uniform. When I leave Memnon, I also leave everything there to my past – and I don't dare look back.

I doze off overnight on the cool grass near a tall tree and rise before the sun to continue on my way. After hitching a ride to take me part of the way, I'm back in the city by Monday at noon.

I go directly to Thomas's rather than the castle. When I knock, I see the same face as last time but still have no name to go with it. "Thomas here?" I ask.

"Missed him again, I'm afraid," his roommate says.

"Where's he off to?"

"See family, I think."

"Do you mind if I come in to wash up? I've been on the road walking from Memnon since yesterday."

He lets me in. It's a dingy little apartment but it has two rooms and a washroom to boot. Not a bad find. I scrub myself off and change into my Guard's uniform to let my other clothes dry. "I'll be back for those later if you don't mind," I tell Thomas's friend.

It isn't her day off, but I decide to go next to Cory's. I knock on the front door and Lady Havard herself answers.

"Hello," she warmly greets me, though for some reason, she seems wary.

I know Cory's working and I haven't come for anything important, so now I feel that I shouldn't have intruded.

"I apologize for showing up unannounced," I say. "Is Cory available by any chance?"

"I'm not certain she's in a state for guests," Lady Havard advises.

"Is everything all right?"

"She came back a sight last night. Wouldn't say what happened. I've sent her to bed. Maybe she'll tell you more than I could get out of her." Lady Havard invites me in and leads me to Cory's room in the back.

She's in bed as Lady Havard said, though she isn't sleeping. She has a glazed look in her eyes, and I'm not sure she really sees me standing in the doorway.

"Cory," I say, and her gaze seems to focus a little. I enter and kneel at her bedside. I can see blue and purple spots forming on her neck. The same colors mixed with a sickly yellow tone spot her cheek. Her lip is swollen with a line of dried blood where it has been split open. Her hair is matted, dirty, and stuck in strings to her face, wet from either tears or sweat, but I can't tell which. She isn't crying now anyway. She's distant. Disconnected. I find her hand and hold it in both of mine. "My gods, Cory. What happened to you?"

She doesn't say anything and peers at me as though she's still trying to decide whether I'm friend or foe. If I'm the latter, she has clearly lost any will to fight against my approach, so I hope she sees me as a friend. Increasingly, familiarity creeps in, and I feel a slight squeeze of her hand as she acknowledges me.

"Anselm …" she breathes in a raspy voice. That's when I see that the marks along her neck look like a handprint. Someone has gripped her throat so fiercely that to leave these marks, I have no doubt she struggled to breathe. She probably couldn't even cry out for help if the sound of her voice is any indication.

"Who did this to you?" I ask and watch as tears start to well in her eyes. She shakes her head and I take it that she does not know her assailant. "Where did this happen?"

"Nyx …" she squeaks, but her voice gives out.

"Nyx Notch," I clarify, and she nods.

"When?"

"Last night," she barely ekes out.

"Cory, what were you doing in Nyx Notch at night? Did you not have an escort? It's dangerous there. You could have been killed." I realize I'm lecturing, telling her what she already knows. "I'm sorry. I just …" Gods, these last few days have been awful.

"Why …" she starts. "Memnon?"

She wants to know why I'm back so soon. She expected me to be gone for weeks as I told her I might be.

I sigh. In a quiet voice, I say, "The gods claimed my mother Wednesday last."

I watch as her face transforms into sorrow.

"But don't worry about that now. Let's get you better. If Lady Havard will have me, I'm going to stay awhile, all right?"

She nods and gives my hand another small squeeze.

Outside her bedroom, I discover that Lady Havard has been listening, anxious to see if I could get anything out of Cory.

She pulls me into the kitchen out of earshot of the bedroom. "I didn't know she was going to Nyx Notch. I never would have allowed it."

"It's no more your fault than mine," I say. "Would it be too much of an imposition …?"

"No, no." She waves off the question before I can even get it out. "There's another bedroom that never gets any use. Take it as long as you need. Though won't you get in trouble with the Guard if you don't return to the castle?"

I explain that I've been given some leave, which I haven't used, so my absence won't be missed.

"Very good," she says. "It's Anselm, right?"

I nod.

"She won't let me summon the doctor to look her over. Do you think you could convince her?"

"All I can promise is that I will try."

"That's all I can expect." Lady Havard squeezes my arm in thanks before filling a glass with water and handing it to me. "See if she'll drink. She hasn't touched anything since she's been back. I'm sure her throat must be hurting. She needs to at least drink something if she won't eat." She fills a second glass for herself and swallows it quickly, clearly distressed. "You don't think she was … I mean, maybe she got away before anyone could …"

"I don't know," I whisper. I'm certain Cory has never lain with a man before. I'm also fairly sure that if she was in Nyx Notch alone at night having returned looking as she does, a doctor would undoubtedly find blood between her legs. It's no wonder she doesn't want to be examined.

I spend all of the next day in Cory's room. She still refuses a doctor or food, but she has accepted more water. She will need to get up to wash at some point and if she has kept her clothes pressed between her legs, I might be able to see if they are spotted red.

In the meantime, I see she has a few books on her dresser, so I ask if she would like me to read one to her. She nods and doesn't seem to care which one I select.

After a while, I hear a noise from Cory. She's wheezing but assures me with a wave that she's all right.

"Do you want to take a break?" I ask. When the cough passes, she tells me she's enjoying listening to me read and that she can't read nearly so well.

"When you get your voice back, I'll teach you," I promise her. It's the first real smile I've seen from her since I arrived.

She finally lets me help her up so she can make her way to the washroom. She lets me examine the bruises on her face and neck. They're still dark but the swelling in her lip seems to have gone down a bit. I find her attractive still in spite of the somber look on her face. Maybe that she lets me see her this way makes me feel privileged. I can't help myself when I pull her into an embrace and kiss her forehead. I wish I had been there. If I'd only gotten the temple priest's letter in time, I might not have ever left for Memnon. Or had I come back just a day earlier, I might have stopped by to see her before she left for Nyx Notch. She might have asked me to accompany her. Then this might not have ever happened.

"I think I'd like a bath," she says, her voice breaking on half of the words. It comes out more strongly than yesterday but still scratchy. It takes a bit of time, but I heat some water and fill the tub for her.

"Shall I retrieve Lady Havard to assist you?" I ask.

She shakes her head no. "Just help me with my sleeve, if you don't mind." Her arm is sore and when I pull the sleeve for her to extract it, I see another bruise. The sight of it makes me murderous. Whoever did this to her, I want to hunt him down. I want to put the fear of the gods in him. Make him feel the terror Cory did. I think she can sense my growing rage because she hides the bruise again with her sleeve and ushers me out.

I return to her bedroom and sit on the edge of her bed. I'm thinking. Quelling my anger. Letting my emotions filter through outside of Cory's presence. I should have controlled myself better in front of her. I'm supposed to be tending to her. She doesn't need my ire making it worse than it already is.

I get the notion to pull back her bedsheets. They're clean. But when I push them back further, I see a balled-up cloth, evidently an undergarment, spotted in red, dark now that it's dried. There's no question Cory was raped in Nyx Notch. And then she somehow stumbled home on her own.

"Cory," I say, knocking on the door. "I'm going to go out for a little while. I'll let Lady Havard know so that she can check on you in case you need anything." I hear a squeaking acknowledgment on the other side of the door.

I enter Faizal's smithy with a fury that has not abated on the walk over. Faizal's typical smile immediately falls upon seeing me.

"Oh, no. She's gone so soon?" he asks.

He means my mother. I have not seen him since getting back, so he hasn't been made aware. "She is. Wednesday last," I say, trying to keep my voice steady. Just the sight of Faizal has calmed me some. "I need a favor, Faizal."

"Name it," he says without hesitation.

Faizal is a well-connected man. He has done a great deal of business selling weapons, in transactions both above board and under. He isn't a man to get in the middle of anything, but he understands there are some problems men don't require the law to handle.

"The girl who was here with me a week ago, something terrible has happened to her."

"Is she …"

"She's recovering."

"What is it you need?"

I don't hesitate a moment when I make my request, knowing full well Faizal would never deny me anything, though I feel a bit guilty about involving him at all.

"Two things. First, do you have any connections in Nyx Notch?"

I spend the rest of the day in the smithy, working on the second favor. Faizal provides me with the materials and I start forging, grinding the steel into just the right shape. I don't intend to make it beautiful. Just effective. After the other smithies in Faizal's shop have gone home, I remain, hammering, shaping, cutting, and sharpening the edges. Sharp enough that little force would be required for it to slice through skin and fat. The handle is the next order of business. It's simple, fit for a small hand. I carve my initials into the hilt.

The sun is coming up when Faizal comes back in and I'm just finishing, the hilt and blade attached.

"You did that in fifteen hours?" he asks, examining it. He tests the weight and balance and seems impressed. "Not the most beautiful dagger but the other smithies here have made worse with much more time." Faizal returns the dagger to me and disappears for a moment, asking me to wait. He returns with a sheath. The dagger slips into it nicely. "It's all yours," he says.

"And what of Nyx Notch?" I ask.

"I'm told there was a ruckus Sunday last and a girl was heard screaming before her voice was muffled."

My heart is pounding.

Faizal hesitates before going on, unsure if I'll erupt in his smithy at learning the details I don't want to hear but need to know. "I was given several names, but no one seems entirely sure which of them it might have been."

"And those names are?"

"Ivan Rhomar. Alden Gervase. Petros Wilkes." Faizal surveys me as I commit the names to memory. "Don't do anything stupid, Anselm. Whatever you're thinking, don't find yourself on the wrong end of a hangman's noose. I doubt even the princess would be able to save you then."

"Thanks, Faizal," I say, making no promises. I take the sheathed dagger and leave. I can feel Faizal's concerned eyes on me as I go.

Cory

HE WASN'T THERE WHEN I FINISHED MY BATH. HE WASN'T there when Lady Havard brought me something to eat in the evening. And he wasn't there when I went to bed. But he was there when I woke up the next morning. He was sleeping on the floor in my room with only a pillow for comfort. I watch him sleep for a while before finding the strength to get out of bed on my own. I don't know where he's been, but he's clearly exhausted. I take an extra blanket from my armoire and lay it across him. Then I make my way to the washroom to look myself over.

My arm isn't so sore anymore and the bruising has faded, more so on my cheek than my neck, which remains a deep purple. The swelling in my lip has gone, but it's still tender to the touch. I run my tongue over the cut. It doesn't sting with the blood caked there. I'd tear the bloodied scab off if I thought it wouldn't reopen the wound.

I try to dress myself in a fresh change of clothes. It's slowgoing but I manage well enough. Then I make my way to the kitchen. Lady Havard has been tending to me, and she shouldn't have to. I'm being paid to attend to her, not the other way around. I manage to set some water to boil, but I have to use both hands to lift the kettle because the muscle of my right arm still aches to flex.

I collect a teacup and saucer and set them on a tray with the kettle and tea leaves. Lady Havard likes to steep them herself. I try to lift the tray with all of its contents, but it's too heavy for my arm. I try again, but my arm just isn't having it.

"Can I help?" Anselm says from behind me, and I jump.

He was so quiet. I didn't know he was there. I suppose he's trained for stealth as a guard.

"I can't lift the tray," I say. I feel ashamed, though I know both Lady Havard and Anselm understand. I don't like feeling weak. Nervous is one thing. Scared even, I could manage. But weak … I don't know how to cope with that. If I'm weak, I can be overpowered again. If I'm weak, I can't do my job. If I can't do my job … Uncle Penn relies on me to be able to do what I must. If I can't, it isn't just me that will pay for my inadequacies.

"Allow me," he says, as he picks up the tray and carries it for me.

I trail behind him, and he sets the tray on the table in the sitting room, where Lady Havard is settled in, reading.

"How kind of you both," she says. I'm embarrassed all over again that I'm unable to do it myself. Lady Havard reaches a hand out to beckon me, and I approach. She pulls me down on the sofa and looks me up and down, then asks, "How are you feeling today?"

"Better," I say. "I'd like to start doing some things around here again, though you can see I can't seem to carry very much. It might take me a little longer than normal."

"It pleases me very much to see that you're out of bed and eager to get back to normal, but don't push yourself unnecessarily. It takes much longer than a couple of days to heal from what you've been through." Lady Havard pats my hand.

I flush at the reference to my assault. I feel so ashamed by what happened. I can hardly think upon it without feeling my face burn.

"Do you think some fresh air might do you some good? Anselm, why don't you take her into the garden. The sun shines nicely where the bench sits."

"Excellent idea, Lady Havard," Anselm says and turns to me. "How about it?"

"Well, yes, all right. On the condition you will let me know if there is something you might need," I say to Lady Havard. I don't want to feel useless, though I'm sure she can get by perfectly well without me for a few more days. When I first arrived to act as Lady Havard's maid, it wasn't because the elderly woman was helpless. It was only because she was starting to succumb to the vulnerabilities that inevitably come with age.

Anselm leads me to the backyard, stopping to collect a book from my bedroom. "Your voice is stronger," he says, taking a seat beside me on the bench. "Would you like to try reading a little today?"

"Maybe just for a bit," I answer, and he hands me the book, pointing to the paragraph where he last left off. I examine the words and try to recall everything Bethea taught me. I struggle through at a snail's pace. Anselm follows along, nodding as I approach a word correctly, providing small adjustments when I use the wrong sound. His tutelage is comforting, and I somehow don't feel as insecure when I fumble. His corrections are conveyed to encourage, not to criticize me.

I manage to get through a full page, my voice becoming increasingly raspy, before I feel it leaving me altogether. I've found the limits of my healing throat, so I give the book back to him.

"I'm impressed," he says. "Most people I know can't read at all. Those that can aren't much better than you and plenty aren't quite so good."

He flatters me. I can't possibly have done that well. Then again, I don't know how well most others read.

Anselm continues reading aloud for a few pages. When a chill sweeps through the air, he retrieves a blanket for me, carrying something else with him. "When I was gone yesterday, I went back to Faizal's," he explains. "I didn't think I'd finish so quickly, but I suppose I was motivated." He extracts a dagger from its sheath and holds it out for me.

"It's very nice," I say, though it isn't nearly as fine as the first blade he'd shown me. The design of this one looks like it has been made to be used, not admired. I touch the edge and find it razor sharp. I see his initials, *AO*, carved into it.

"I want you to carry it wherever you go," he instructs.

I don't know how to respond. The thought of carrying a knife unnerves me. But when I think of that night, what I wouldn't have given for this dagger! I accept it, sliding it back into the sheath. "Thank you," I say, finding my reflection in his eyes. I sink into them, and he doesn't look away. He merely gazes back at me.

He puts an arm around my shoulders, and I lean into him. His other arm wraps around me as well, and I relax further, immersing myself in the warmth of his body. I didn't know how tense my shoulders were until they soften under his embrace. He holds me without letting go, I think waiting for me to push away first. But I don't want to. This is the safest I've felt in days.

"How long will you stay?" My voice breaks in and out.

"How long do you need?"

"I don't know …" It comes out in a whisper. *Forever*, I think. I don't ever want to lose this sense of security.

"Then we'll just take it a day at a time."

I nod into his chest. A day at a time. I can do that.

I wish Anselm would sleep in my bedroom again that evening, though I know Lady Havard would not find it appropriate. He makes use of her spare bedroom instead, and I find comfort still in his proximity. When he comes to my room in the morning, I'm already up and dressed.

"Might you help me with breakfast?" I ask and he agrees. We make omelets with cheese, tomatoes, and mushrooms. We sprinkle parsley on top as garnish. Anselm finishes putting the tray together while I retreat to Lady Havard's room to help her dress.

"So when's the wedding?" she asks, adjusting her skirt at the waist in the mirror. My eyes widen, and she merely shrugs. "Let's not pretend he doesn't fancy you, my dear."

Fancy me? Had I missed some obvious signs?

"Oh, you think he's here just to be nice."

"Isn't he?" I ask. "Or maybe he just doesn't want to return to duty in the Guard so soon after he's buried his mother."

"Maybe," Lady Havard replies in a tone that suggests she's not convinced. I help with her hair and slip an ornate pin in place. When she's satisfied, I ask if she needs anything else.

"I know you've got feelings for the stable boy," she says, ignoring my question.

"Thomas," I amend. I do have feelings for Thomas. Strong ones at that, and she knows it.

"Thomas," Lady Havard repeats. "But perhaps you could open your eyes and see another option, perfectly suitable, right in front of you."

Anselm is a fine option, and I'm aware that Lady Havard prefers him because he's sure to make something of himself whether he stays in the Guard or not. He's attractive, attentive, and kind. Confident where Thomas is shy and nervous. Muscled and strong where Thomas tends to be more lean. Thomas is poor. Anselm, though he also comes from meager means, will not remain so. It shouldn't surprise me that a woman such as Lady Havard would encourage me toward the man with better prospects. But I cannot help how I feel.

Thomas is the boy I may as well have met in Perseus. He might have been an outdoor hand for the Martins, working alongside me. He might have struck up a conversation one day as I drew water from the well and helped me carry the buckets. He might have spent some time wooing me and then would have met Uncle Penn. Had Thomas been in Perseus, I might have led a quiet life with him and never known anything about Anselm except that he was good enough to help me when I was down on my luck. That might-have-been world doesn't seem so terrible to me.

The truth is, I think Anselm is too good for me. Especially now. I was already marred by my scar and damaged leg. Now I've been used in vulgar gratification. I'm no good for Anselm. He could do so much better than me and my cheapened body, my shattered pride.

Thomas, too, for that matter. But it's easier to match my simple life in comparison to his. We are fashioned from the same cloth. I'm the modest kind of girl Thomas undoubtedly figured he would end up with. Anselm is the handsome and resolute Guard personally connected to the princess. It's not a picture I fit into.

I can't fault Lady Havard for her preference for Anselm. Had I come from Dionysius, had I not suffered injury in childhood, had I been her niece rather than her lady's maid, things might have turned out differently. But that simply isn't the life I was born into.

I set aside the conversation I've just had with Lady Havard, and we all enjoy breakfast together. Then Anselm and I escape outside again, book in hand. I practice my reading with Anselm's thoughtful guidance until he takes over, reading much more seamlessly than I have. When we reach the end of the chapter, I interrupt before he can read on. My thoughts have strayed from the story.

"Tell me about Memnon," I prompt. "What's it like there?"

He gathers his thoughts before responding, then says, "A bit like Perseus. But greener. And not quite so impoverished but not necessarily much better in some parts of town either. Good soil for growing. Some boutique shops and not just the bare necessities. There's a small lake too. It wasn't a bad place to grow up."

"What about your parents?"

"I was eight when my father died. There was an explosion in the mine where he worked. Twelve lost their lives that day, my father and brother among them."

I did not know Anselm had a brother.

"He was fifteen and a month away from leaving for Dionysius to enlist. It was just me and my mother after that. She took me to temple every week, paid tribute to the gods, prayed for the souls of our lost family, prayed for me to find good fortune. She was a strong woman and I wanted for nothing because she worked hard to provide for us both. I wanted so much to make her proud. To be able to care for her in her later years. But I never got the chance."

"I have no doubt she always knew how much you have loved and appreciated her."

He gives me a weak smile, either unconvinced or merely sorry he didn't have the opportunity to prove it to her. "Promise me something," he says. "If ever you hear your uncle does not have much time, promise me you'll go to him immediately. Don't put it off until it's too late. If I had done something sooner, I might have been able to say goodbye."

It's an easy promise to make. I've already made it to myself.

BY THE TIME SATURDAY ROLLS AROUND, I'M FEELING MUCH better. My bruises have faded significantly. The cut on my lip is a thin line, barely visible. My voice is strong, and I have just about full use of my arm again. The only thing still demolished is my pride and I don't expect to get that back anytime soon. Maybe not ever.

In the morning, Anselm takes me outside, and I think we are going to read some more, but he leaves the book in my room. Instead, he has me sit on the bench beside him, and he takes hold of my hand.

"It won't be easy what I'm about to ask of you," he starts, "but I need to know about that night."

I stiffen and pull away from him. I've had nearly a week to tuck the memory of that night away. I'm not eager to revisit it.

"Cory, please ..." he beseeches.

I can't fathom why he wants to know. Why he wants me to relive this. "I can't," I say in such a whisper that it's like my voice has left me again.

"You don't have to tell me everything. Just what you can. Was it just one man? Or were there others?"

The memory of the night flashes through my mind. There's a sneering man who turns the corner and blocks my path. Then another man appears, and I have no choice but to turn around. But Nyx Notch is a dead-end the other way. There's only one way out, and they're standing between me and it. Were there just the two men then? Did I hear yet another voice? No, I don't think I did. There's an exchange between the two of them, but I can't remember what's said. *I don't want to remember this.* I shake my head and the memory ducks back into its hiding spot.

I feel Anselm squeeze my hand, bringing me back to the garden where we sit. It's better here. Safer. Lighter. I decide I want to stay here and avoid the dark corners of my mind.

"Was there more than one?" he asks again and my head nods in the affirmative as if answering of its own accord. There must be some part of me that wants him to know. Wants *someone* to know.

"Two? Three?"

I shake my head. *I can't think about this!* I pull my hand from him and start wringing both of mine together. I look away, unable to bear any scrutiny.

"Did they say anything?"

"I can't be sure," I whisper, noticing my legs can no longer remain still either. They bounce and I try to quell the shaking but to no avail. I start to rub my legs, turning several degrees away from Anselm. I can sense him beside me, wanting to embrace me, if only to place a hand on my back or my knee, but I pray he doesn't touch me. Not right now. Not now that the events of that night are flooding back.

"Do you remember seeing any features that stand out? Glasses, maybe? Jewelry? What were they wearing?"

I don't know what they were wearing. Wait, one of them had suspenders. And the other had a gold tooth. It almost gleamed in the moonlight. I think he did not want me to see him any better, so he spun me around, slammed my face against the brick wall and held my head in place by gripping my neck. I had screamed once, maybe twice, before his grip tightened and I struggled for air until I felt like I might pass out. I wish I had passed out. I wish I didn't have these memories coming back to me.

With my body pinned against the wall, I felt a stray hand lifting up my skirts. And then I felt … It sent an aching through me, especially as he increased his pace. Then he stopped and I felt a throbbing palpitation from him. It was over. He stepped away. But I remained terrified and couldn't move. The mild relief I felt that I might be able to get away now was quickly vanquished when the other one leaned nearly his full weight against me, taking hold of my arm to keep me from fighting. But I had no fight left in me anyway.

He said something, I think, made a threat of some kind. I was too frightened to hear it or to scream. Another hand grappled with my skirts. This time there were fingers that felt around first followed by a tongue across my cheek, right across my scar. I flinched. Hot, stale breath filled my nostrils. And then, it happened all over again. He kept his eyes trained on my face frozen in terror. I shut my eyes. The second man was done more quickly. I saw him fumble with his pants, reattach suspenders, and then they were gone. Tobacco smoke wafted through the street paired with cackling.

I stood in place for a long time until I noticed the moonlight and found there was no one on the streets. I finally forced myself to move. I walked back home, alone, limping on my tired feet. I didn't cry. I didn't even ache in the injured parts of my body. I was numb there and everywhere. I did not feel a thing.

It's only a couple hours after I tell Anselm what happened to me that he says he needs to return to the castle. He's says he has been gone long enough and ought to resume his duties on Monday. In the meantime, he has some business to attend to and has only tomorrow – Sunday – to address the matter. Still, he promises to try to see me in a week's time.

"I'll only go back to the castle if you're agreeable to it," he says. "I can stay another week if you'd like me to. I have the time to spare."

I want him to stay another month. Another year. I'm afraid that sense of safety from having him here will vanish when he leaves. But I can't keep him from his life because I'm scared. I tell him I'll be fine and will await his return. I don't let on just how anxiously I'll be waiting. I remind myself that Thomas has also returned by now from his visit home and will be dropping in tomorrow as per usual. I won't feel alone for long. I just have to find a way to make it through tonight.

"Don't go anywhere without that dagger," he tells me.

I nod. I wouldn't dream of it now.

Anselm takes two steps away from the front door and my fear at his departure surges. Then he stops, and I wonder if he can hear my pleas that permeate to my core. I wonder if that's why he's turned around. *Please, Anselm, don't leave me alone! Don't go!*

"Cory?" He closes the distance between us.

"Yes?"

Inches separate us now and still he leans in closer. He tips my chin up so I look directly into his liquid brown eyes. His voice softens when he says, "No matter what kind of crude uncleanliness was committed against you, you're still the purest person I know. And purity is what I see when I look at you. If nothing else, please remember that."

I think I tilt toward him, craving a final embrace so I can cocoon myself in the memory later when I'm alone. He hesitates and then seems to make a decision. His lips touch mine and he's careful not to press too hard on my healing wound. The sensation sends shivers through me. One kiss, then two. They're light, barely any pressure at all, which makes them stimulating in such a way that I want more. When he pulls away, he trains his eyes on mine. His gaze is replete with infatuation.

"I'll see you soon," he whispers before taking off.

When he's gone, I think my heart might explode. Lady Havard was right and I knew deep within me that she was. I just didn't want to admit that a man so exquisite could have such fondness for a girl so inadequate and tainted as me. I almost want to shake him so that he comes to his senses.

I shove back any longing for him to stay and tell myself I can't entertain such thoughts. I have Thomas in my life to consider. And the moment those men pinned me and violated me, they also laid waste to my dignity. They reminded me that even if I now reside in a nice house, I am still wearing servants' vestments. I am nobody. But Anselm is not. Lady Havard is also right that he has the chance to make something remarkable of his life.

And I will not let him waste it on a lowly, debased woman like me.

Anselm

I DON'T GO DIRECTLY TO THE CASTLE AFTER LEAVING CORY at Lady Havard's. Instead, I go to Thomas's to finally collect the clothes I left drying there. I change into them and leave my Guard's uniform instead. Thomas is not there. His roommate informs me that Thomas has returned from visiting his family, but he's currently at work in the stables. I don't have time to go and see him.

When I've changed, I head for Nyx Notch and enter a tavern there. The fact that it's barely 1:00 in the afternoon makes no difference to this handful of patrons. They are the type to drink all day, which suits my needs perfectly. I can ask a few questions and leave without concern that they'll recognize me when I return tomorrow night. These men are drunk. They won't remember much, if anything.

I approach the man nearest the door. I tend to look away when I talk so he doesn't get a good look at my face. I ask first about a man with a gold tooth that comes around at night.

"There was another fellow here a week ago wanted to know about indecent types," the man says. I figure that was Faizal's guy, the one who returned the three names. *Ivan Rhomar. Alden Gervase. Petros Wilkes.* The names are seared into my memory, running on an endless loop.

Ivan Rhomar. Alden Gervase. Petros Wilkes. Ivan Rhomar. Alden Gervase. Petros Wilkes.

"I'm curious about one with a gold tooth," I repeat.

"I think the Wilkes fellow's got himself a tooth like that. That gold one makes up half his teeth near about too. Funniest thing how it looks like it just dangles there." He laughs a drunken laugh.

"Any indecent types wear suspenders often?"

"A few, I'd say. Some men, it's the only way they can still wear the old pants that get too big when you fall poor." The man takes another swig from his stein, empties it, and peers inside, frowning when he sees only mug at the bottom.

"Any that are in good with the Wilkes fellow?"

"Ivan Rhomar, I'd say. He and Wilkes are nearly joined at the hip. He was in here earlier today. Or … maybe it was yesterday."

I'm not particularly interested in the man's ramblings. "Are they usually in Nyx Notch at night?"

"Sometimes I've seen 'em." Not helpful. The man belches and the stench is rancid. I'll just have to come back tomorrow night and hope they make an appearance.

I go back to Thomas's to change again before returning to the castle. I'm there too early to run into Thomas, who's still working, so I leave a message with his roommate that I'll be in touch again soon.

I spend Sunday at Faizal's. I work on my sword before asking Faizal what he did with the daggers I made in months past.

"I've got them around here somewhere," he says and goes off in search of them. He retrieves two of them, telling me they're the only ones he's found so far. I take just one and tell him he doesn't need to keep looking.

I carry the dagger to a grindstone and sharpen the edges as Faizal looks on with curiosity, apprehension even. "Why, might I ask, did you want that old dagger?"

I give him a look that tells him I don't need to voice what he already knows. I'm planning to kill Ivan Rhomar and Petros Wilkes tonight.

I can see Faizal contemplating whether or not to try to stop me. He even starts to say something a couple of times before either the words fail him or he changes his mind. He finally says, "I'll stay here through the night. As soon as it's finished, bring the knife back and we'll melt it down again. And one more thing." He retrieves a pair of gloves and hands them to me. "Wear them. We'll burn them too."

I nod, accepting the gloves and his offer to abet in my crime. I don't want to involve him, but it would be good to have someone to speak on my behalf that I was here late blade smithing with the man apprenticing me in the craft. I hope it doesn't come to that.

As darkness descends over the city, I make my way back to Nyx Notch. There are plenty more people out than I would have thought. Cory must have been here much later than now to have fallen into the clutches of two ruffians with no one around to answer her cries. I don't know what she was thinking. But I can't focus on that right now. I need to get my head clear to carry out what I have planned.

I make my way through the crowd, most of them jovial and heedless to my presence. I keep my head down anyway, my hair disheveled and hanging in my face. Thank goodness it's grown out long enough to provide some cover. I'm certainly overdue for a cut.

The farther I walk, the fewer people I encounter. At the back end of the Notch, it gets darker and the number of establishments dwindle. I'm not so worried about anyone seeing me back here, especially as the night only gets blacker.

I duck around the corner at the end of the last shop, which is closed for the night. *PIA'S*, the sign reads. The space where I hide is small, but it will serve well to shroud me and still allow me to hear the noises from the street, conversations and such. What I hear are ladies of the night entertaining men across the street in plain view of anyone walking by. Behind me is a brick wall and I wonder if it's the same one Cory's head was shoved against, the one that marred her cheek with bruising.

I don't know how long I've waited, fingering the tip of the dagger in my belt, but it's been long enough for the moon to rise to its full height and for the street's occupants to disperse. Finally, I see a pair of men who look like they live for trouble. They laugh together, pass a tobacco pipe back and forth, and I think, *trouble has found them tonight.*

I toss a rock into the darkened dead-end of the street. It catches their attention, and I hope they will decide to investigate. They laugh again, each one daring the other into the darkness until the one with the gold tooth – Wilkes – decides to take the lead. The other, the one with suspenders, follows behind and they rib each other for their shaken nerves.

I creep up behind them and grab the one in the back wearing suspenders. I place a hand over his mouth to stifle any yelling, fixing my other arm around his chest, hand to his neck. The scuffle catches Wilkes's attention, and he goes slack-jawed when I suddenly jerk and crack the man's neck. A young, trained guard up against a man so liquored up and taken by surprise is no difficult feat. But now Wilkes is on guard. He could yell or run before I can dump the other man's body into the shadows. Wilkes seems too drunk and stunned to be so astute, though.

I lower the lifeless body, now dead weight in my arms, and stare down Wilkes. I'm taller than he is, younger, stronger, and I've got my wits about me. I also have a knife and point the tip in his direction as I step toward him. The moonlight glinting off the blade draws his eye, and I wonder why he hasn't yelled out yet. Is he still in shock by the turn of events his evening has taken? I hope so. I hope he's terrified. I hope I've put the fear of the gods into him and he has some inkling of how Cory felt when he forced himself on her. Only Cory survived her ordeal. And Wilkes will not.

I attack him then, jumping on him, and we fall to the ground. He's pinned beneath me, and I place my arm across his neck. I lean all my weight there, watching him suffocate. Cory couldn't breathe, couldn't scream. Neither shall he. He tries to flail his legs to squirm out from underneath me, but I'm far too heavy and strong for him.

A part of me wants to carve him to pieces. Tear a line from sternum to naval, slash his guts, and pour out his entrails. That is the rage he has evoked in me.

My better judgment prevails. I draw the blade along the side of his neck in a thin, crisp line. He'll bleed out quickly, and I can keep from getting blood all over my clothes. Once it's done and two bodies lay in the black of the night at the end of Nyx Notch, I walk farther into the darkness and scale the wall, leaving them to be found by whoever happens upon them in the morning.

On the other side of the wall, I drop into a thicket not yet expanded into by the city. I use a leaf to clean the fresh blood off my dagger. Then I work my way through the brush until I reach streets that I can trace back to Faizal's.

Thomas

IT'S BEEN TWO WEEKS SINCE I LAST SAW CORY. I TOOK SUNDAY last to visit my mother, to ask for an heirloom I knew she'd bequeath me. Now that Sunday has finally arrived again, I'm anxious to see Cory today. I have so much to tell her. The trip home turned out better than expected.

The farmland that stretches out past my parents' house is owned by Lord Paden, a rich nobleman. Very rich. He unexpectedly paid a visit to my parents while I was there. He wanted to inquire about purchasing my family's land and was prepared to offer an enticing proposal he wished to present in person. He assured us we could remain on the property, work the land for our own profit, and stay until my parents are claimed by the gods. At that time, the property would pass to Lord Paden rather than to me.

I was plainly reluctant to give my parents my blessing on the matter, though they did not need it. Still, as the land and home were always my future inheritance, they were as tentative as me.

To address these concerns, Lord Paden offered to provide employment and housing for me and any future spouse. Any children of the union would have housing, though their employment on the property would be contingent on their own set of skills and devotion to their work. My job would be as stable master, overseeing the care of the two dozen horses he owns. As his current stable master is in frail health, Lord Paden informed me I could start immediately at a pay rate nearly three times my current earnings. My parents conferred, including me in the discussion, and accepted the proposal.

The entire week, I was anxious for Sunday to roll around so I could see Cory and impart the news. I have repeatedly imagined the way she would light up at such happy tidings. But I plan to tell her more. I plan to tell her I can promise her security, a home, better employment in the home of Lord Paden if she even wanted to work at all. My nerves tighten when it occurs to me that I have not truly expressed my feelings for Cory. Not in words anyway.

As I now pace outside the servant's door, trying to work up the courage to knock, I'm scared my feelings will be unrequited, that she will decline my proposal, no matter how appealing what I can offer may be.

I finally knock, and she opens the door. She doesn't look as I expected. She has some discoloration in her face, a timid look in her eye. But she still has a smile upon seeing me, which makes my heart soar.

"Cory," I say. I pull her to me in a hug, and she clutches me as tightly as I do her. "Has something happened?" Her manner has changed somehow too, and I draw back only far enough to see her face.

She drops her gaze at my question before finding some renewed resolve and says, "Could we discuss it later? I'd prefer to simply enjoy your return."

That makes me smile. "Perhaps we could take a walk then?"

She gladly accepts and takes my arm. I notice how close she walks to me, how tightly she grips my arm, and how gratifying it feels to have her cling to me.

We make a return trip to Erato Gardens, this time strolling to the pond at the far end. Lily pads float atop the water, some in bunches and some drifting off alone.

"Cory," I start when we find a patch of grass to sit upon, enjoying the view. "I thought about you quite a lot in the days since I last saw you."

"I've thought of you too," she says, and my smile feels like it's emanating from somewhere deep within.

"An opportunity arose for me when I was gone last week."

I can't read her face. It seems to be a mix of emotions, which she clarifies by asking, "Are you moving away?"

I clasp her hand and say, "Yes. But not far. Just outside the city past my parents' land."

Her face falls, though she tries to maintain her composure. That my impending departure is affecting her this way bodes well for what I plan to say next.

I tell her about Lord Paden, the agreement he reached with my parents, and the job I plan to start within a week. She tries to look happy for the fortuitous opportunity I've been given.

"There's more. I've been offered a place to stay on the property for the rest of my life, housing for the stable master – that would be me – and also for my wife."

Once again, I can't quite read her face until she finally says, almost in a whisper, "You're getting married?"

"I'd like to," I say, matching her soft tone and clasping her other hand, "if you'll have me."

I can read her face now. She's astounded by the proposal. I extract the heirloom I was given by my mother and hold it out to her. It's a ring with a simple band and an amber gem of humble size.

"This ring has been in my family a long time and every man who has used it to propose has told how the amber came from the sap of a tree a thousand years old. With it comes the love shared by generations of men and their wives. As long as it's been worn, love has never faded. Cory, I know we haven't known each other long, but my heart feels as though it's known you forever. If you would have me, I would promise to love you for as long as we have together. With the prospect of my employment, I can give you a home for the rest of our days and a heart and arms that will always hold you. Coralyn Perle, will you marry me?"

Her eyes smile as much as her upturned lips. I think she's about to say yes when her face crumbles again and my elation breaks apart with it.

"I can't," she says softly, holding back tears, "I can't say yes without first …"

"What is it?" I say, enveloping her in my arms, hoping she feels safe enough there to tell me anything.

"I didn't break my promise to you," she whispers so quietly I barely hear. I struggle to recall what it was she promised. "I didn't go late to Pia's. But I stayed there much too late. It was an accident."

I can picture Cory in Nyx Notch by herself at night and I know what she's going to say before any other words are spoken.

"There were two of them."

"Oh my gods," I mutter, squeezing her more tightly. A range of emotions courses through me but the one that never departs for a moment is anger. Not at Cory. At myself. At the vile men who prowl Nyx Notch. I never should have taken her there to begin with. I never should have left without telling her not to go there alone. Or without finding an escort for her. This never would have happened if I hadn't been so damned stupid. "Did you make a report?" I finally ask.

She shakes her head no against my chest.

I wonder if she even told Lady Havard. After a long silence, I say, "Cory, let me take you away from here. The city is dangerous. Let me take you to Lord Paden's land. We'll be safe there. We can make a life together there, you and me."

"You would still want me after …?"

"Aye! I want you no matter what. You've given me such joy in such a brief time. I can only imagine what joy we could share in decades to come."

She still can't bring herself to accept. Whether its doubt that she is worthy or whether she is lacking in love for me, I do not know.

"Here," I say, placing the ring in her hand, "hold onto this while you think it over. Meanwhile, I'll hold onto you."

She clutches it tightly, and I do the same to her frail, shaking body.

It's hours later when I finally take Cory home. She promises to consider my proposal and have an answer for me by next week. At the back door, I don't want to let her go. I don't want to say goodbye. She clings to me as well. I cup her face in both of my hands and kiss her. Her lips return the pressure of mine then part as mine do. I've kissed a few girls over the years but none with the ardor that passes between Cory and me. I grasp the back of her shirt and squeeze the fabric in a fist. The anger from Cory's earlier admission comes flooding through in a wave of intense fervor that she matches in the way she kisses me back and snakes a hand through my hair, knocking my cap to the ground.

The heated frenzy continues to mount and the moment sends tremors through me. I'd take her to bed this moment if we were already wed. I settle for passionate kisses she eagerly gives me which I accept with equal zeal, responding in turn with the same.

"I love you," I whisper when at last our lips draw apart.

"I'm scared," she whispers back.

"Since when has that ever stopped you?" I say, bestowing another soft kiss. I know the answer. *Since never.* I hope she knows it too.

I go to Pia's alone. I don't ever want Cory back in Nyx Notch. After I tell Pia what happened to explain that Cory won't be returning for any lessons in cooking, I stick around. I stay for hours. I help her serve customers, wash dishes, and sweep the floors, doing anything that needs to be done.

The time passes quickly and it's easy to see how Cory might have lost track of time here. There's plenty to do and Pia's company is endlessly amusing.

I'm not surprised then when I step outside and it's dark. Very dark. The moon is half of a sphere in the night sky. It's late enough that there aren't tavern stragglers this far down the Notch. So when I hear the brief sound of scraping and see movement out of the corner of my eye, I don't know what to make of it.

I approach the source of the sound as my eyes adjust to the dark. I come upon a pair of bodies, one of them deceased, neck twisted unnaturally. The sound I heard was the boot of the other scuffing the cobblestone. The movement was his bent leg finally dropping at gravity's command. I lean closer, checking his mouth and nose for any air. I lift a wrist to search for any pulse. Blood has spilled from his neck and I shudder upon accidentally wetting my hand with it, trying to see if he can be saved. But he cannot. This man is also dead.

I glance around. I don't think they've been dead long at all – minutes maybe. But there's no one around and no sound of footsteps. I take off running down the street to report two murders.

WHEN I GO TO WORK TWO DAYS LATER, I STILL CAN'T SHAKE the memory of what I stumbled upon. After what happened first with Cory and now with the pair of dead bodies, I need to confront Pia about where her eatery is located. Surely she can do better than Nyx Notch. I know she is staying in the loft just above the restaurant and has no need to venture out at night but just the same, it troubles me. She is staying there alone right now, as her husband and children have gone to visit his family in north Callinor. I don't like her being there.

I'm mucking stalls when an officer approaches me, I assume to ask more questions about what I reported the other night.

"Are you Thomas Freye?" he asks, and I affirm that I am. "You're under arrest for the murders of Petros Wilkes and Leo Marmus."

"What? The fellows in the Notch? But I'm the one that reported them murdered."

"You're also the one found with blood on his hands and was seen running away from the area soon after their deaths," the man says.

"I checked to see if they could be saved. That's why the man's blood was on my hands. And I ran to inform you lot as quick as I could."

"That isn't all. We've been made aware you were often at Pia's, close to the scene. You were seen there a couple of times with a girl on your arm, a girl who we are told was assaulted by one of the victims, one Petros Wilkes."

"Who told you that?" Cory said she hadn't made a report.

"Gent by the name of Ivan Rhomar, friend of the deceased. You happened to be at the scene, ran from there, show up covered in blood, and had motive to go after one of the victims if he had assaulted your lady. If you would kindly follow me then. No need to make a scene."

I drop the rake, professing my innocence. I'll oblige them for now. They're sure to uncover the truth and I'll be released. Back into Cory's arms. Back to the life that awaits us.

Anselm

I'M PATROLLING THE CASTLE'S PERIMETER WHEN I GET WORD that someone has come to see me. My first thought is that it's Princess Giselle before I remember she's under orders not to come near me. Then I think it must be Cory, so I'm eager to follow.

"Who is it?" I ask as I'm led through the castle.

"Fellow called Byron."

Byron! That's the name of Thomas's roommate. I wonder why he's here to see me.

When we reach the castle gates, I'm told I can speak to my guest just outside.

"Anselm, Thomas has been arrested. They're saying he murdered a couple of men in Nyx Notch Sunday evening. But he couldn't have. We both know he couldn't have."

Of course he couldn't have. Because I did. But no one knows that other than Faizal. How did Thomas get mixed up in this?

"I can get some money to get him released," I say.

"It's murder charges. They won't let him out for nothing. Anselm, I've heard their case against him. They're going to hang him."

"They will not," I say adamantly, then I think for a minute. "Look, tell Thomas you've come to me and I'm working on how to get him out. Tell him I *will* get him out."

Byron nods and hurries off to deliver my message.

Gods be damned! How could this have happened? I don't want to do it, but it's the only thing I know to do. I can't see Giselle, but I can see Veronica. I find her, tell her the story – leaving out my part in it – and ask her to pass it on to Giselle. She did the impossible and got me to Memnon. No one has to know my relation to Thomas, the second favor she'd be doing me. Surely she can get Thomas released and the charges against him dropped.

I have to return to the perimeter, anxiously awaiting word from Giselle. Finally, Veronica finds me and says, "The librarian plans to retire at midnight but says you may find what you're looking for in section twelve."

I get the message, coded for anyone listening nearby. *Meet Giselle in the library at midnight.*

"Thank you, Veronica."

I arrive early, walking through the castle like I'm making the rounds. In the library, Giselle stands at a tall stained-glass window. It shows Apollo, the god for whom our nation is named. In the image, he's a child clutching a golden sword.

There's no one else in the dark library this late, so I approach Giselle without fear of being caught.

"Anselm," she says, hugging me.

"Is there anything you can do?"

"Yes. And no."

My heart leaps and plummets in the same moment.

"I can speak on his behalf. Say he was an esteemed member of the Guard. It was one thing to get you leave when it would only affect how others in the Guard perceived the move. But this is going to be seen by the entire city if not the entire nation if I speak on his behalf. If they release him upon my word without any evidence of his innocence, there could be far-reaching consequences. The truth is, I didn't even know him when he was here, so my word about his reputation would mean little."

"They don't have to know that. It would mean a lot to have the nation's princess speak for him. They couldn't keep him if you do that, could they?"

"They can. And they probably would, just to prove that unless I order him free, he's in their hands to do with what they want. If I do order him free, what precedent would that set? Appeal to me and guilty men go free? I don't want to be seen as subverting our official protocols. The ramifications could be extensive."

"He isn't guilty, though."

"According to you."

I weigh whether or not to tell her how I know of his innocence. If I gave them reason to suspect me, if it were me in that cell, would she save me? How could she? Especially after she's already gone out on a limb for me once. The extent of our relationship wouldn't be an open secret just among the Royal Guard and Ned then. It would be everywhere, and her reputation would be ruined. Especially if I were now seen as a murderer who shared the princess's bed. The future queen's reputation would be in shambles along with her credibility. No, she could not save me either.

"What can be done?" I ask.

She considers this. I get the idea she's been considering it all day and has yet to come up with any very tenable ideas.

"Let me summon the lead officer and hold counsel with him. I'll be able to tell whether there's anything to be done based on how that conversation goes. I'll send word to you through Veronica. I'm sorry to have to ask you to bide your time a little while. It's the best I can do."

I thank her, even dare to hug her, and her embrace in return is warm.

"I'm sorry, Anselm. About your mother. I'll try to do what I can to keep you from losing your cousin too."

I don't sleep a wink that night.

Cory

I'M DUSTING THE SITTING ROOM WHEN THERE'S A KNOCK AT the front door. I go to answer it and find a young man I've never seen before. He's shabbily dressed, red-faced, and short, but he has an honest look about him.

"Is this the house of Lady Havard?" he asks.

"It is. Who might I tell her is calling?" I reply.

"Are you Cory Perle?" he asks, ignoring my question, and I confirm that I am. "My name is Byron. I'm Thomas's roommate and friend from the Guard. He asked me to send for you."

"Is everything all right?"

Lady Havard enters then, saying, "Who is it, dear? Solicitors? Tell them to go away."

"Um, no, Lady Havard. A friend of Thomas's. Byron, was it?"

He nods. Byron then proceeds to explain what's happened to Thomas. He tells me he's locked up in a cell and that he did not want me to know but as it looks as though he will not be able to come by tomorrow as per usual, he wanted me to know why. "He also says that he still awaits your answer," Byron adds, "whatever that means."

I smile, knowing exactly what it means, and finger the ring I've kept in my pocket.

Lady Havard steps forward and asks, "Is there someone filling in for Thomas retrieving horses?"

"I don't know, milady," Byron replies.

"Perhaps you could do us a great favor and check. If there is no one, could you retrieve our horse and carriage yourself? I could pay you quite handsomely for your trouble. I believe my lady's maid and I need to pay a visit to the jailhouse."

Byron agrees and when I've closed the door, I turn to Lady Havard. Before I can even ask a question, she says, "Oh, please. The guard stayed here a week and all he could manage was a quick peck or two before leaving."

I didn't even know she saw that.

"You see this Thomas boy once after two weeks and you're smiling and humming all day every day, head up in the clouds. You think it takes a genius to know what love looks like?"

"He wants me to marry him," I tell her.

She steps closer to me, wraps an arm around me like she would a daughter and says, "Then I have no doubt you'll be a very happy woman and he will be a very lucky man. Now let's go get your husband out of jail."

In the carriage with Byron at the helm, I watch the passing scenery as I ask Lady Havard, "Are you sure you find a marriage with Thomas agreeable? I've hardly known him long at all. And you wanted me to choose Anselm only days ago."

She takes a deep breath and looks outside. She sighs, "Dear, it may come as a shock to you but I'm well aware you don't have the training to be a lady's maid."

That is *not* what I was expecting to hear.

"Don't get me wrong. I think you've done marvelously. But I saw those glasses Bethea got you. Your eyesight is fine. I saw that brace you've got tucked away. Finely crafted excuses not to read or write. I saw Anselm teaching you to read outside. I even read the letter Bethea sent where she made all those corrections to your writing. I do apologize for that breach of confidence. And my dear, how did you never learn to cook?"

I blush, but she shoos away my embarrassment.

Lady Havard continues, "What Bethea did not realize in our exchanges before you arrived is that I was not really asking for a lady's maid or housekeeper, though the assistance is appreciated. My husband, Osman, died over twenty years ago. I've been on my own a long time, and being alone has its perks, no doubt. But what I was asking for from Bethea was a *friend*."

Lady Havard is telling me she has simply been a lonely widow. I always knew she didn't need much from me, but I had no idea she didn't really need anything but my presence.

"Now when I married Osman, we had been acquainted only three months and I knew I loved him that fast. When he passed away, I gave myself six months to grieve him. I told myself that after that, I'd focus on my own life. That's what he would want me to do. But now that I'm getting on in years with no idea when the end might come, my unwanted kinship with loneliness has been renewed.

"But dear, I understand a whirlwind romance better than most. Osman and I had just that for the entire thirty years we were together, start to finish. It's why Bethea and I remained good friends. She married down for love, and I understood that when none of the rest of the family did. You recall how her sister still looks down her nose at Bethea.

"When it comes to you, Cory, you've got a good head on your shoulders. You came to a new city where you knew no one out of love for an ailing uncle. You learned a variety of skills in no time. You have done what you needed to do to care for yourself and others, including me. Now it's time to follow your heart. If your head hasn't led you astray, I hardly think your heart will. Marrying for love is a gift you will give yourself every day for the rest of your lives together. That doesn't seem like a bad decision to me."

"Thank you, Lady Havard," I say. I'm so stunned by her revelations that it comes out in a whisper.

"My dear, I think it's high time you start calling me Aunt Farryn. I have no need of a lady's maid, and I have come to love you as family the way I love Bethea."

We arrive at the jailhouse and Byron opens the carriage door for us to step out. Lady Havard – it's a bit too soon for me to start thinking of her as Aunt Farryn – holds her head up high. The jailhouse isn't exactly a place where people of her ilk are commonly found. Plus, I'm sure she thinks a bit of snoot might earn her what she wants.

"We're here to see Thomas … er …" she starts.

"Freye," I fill in.

"Thomas Freye. We're told he's being held here."

"He is," an officer says, "and who might you be?"

"I am Lady Farryn Havard and this is my niece, Miss Coralyn Perle. She is engaged to be married to Mr. Thomas Freye. You wouldn't keep a young woman from her fiancé, would you?"

"Your niece, eh?" the officer looks speculatively between us. I'm clearly dressed in the garments of a domestic.

"For all intents and purposes," Lady Havard replies, holding up her nose and turning away. "Now where can we find him?"

"This way," the officer relents and takes us down a few dingy hallways. We come to a cell – a cage is more like it – and Thomas jumps up at our arrival.

"Cory!" he cries, and I hurry over to him. On the carriage ride over, I slipped the amber ring onto my finger. He notices it as soon as we've clasped hands through the bars.

"Are you going to let us in then?" Lady Havard calls after the officer walking away.

The officer chuckles, "What, you want *in* the cell?"

Lady Havard's face changes. She's indignant and asserts, "I want this cell opened up so that my niece can …"

"Right, right, right," the officer interrupts her, turning around to stick a fat key into the fatter padlock.

I'm shocked by how rude he's being to a woman like Lady Havard. As soon as he unlocks the door, I step inside and throw my arms around Thomas. The officer locks us both in together.

"What are you doing here?" he asks, pulling my arms down to take me in. "I only meant for Byron to let you know I'm here, not for you to come down to this place yourself. You shouldn't be here."

"You needed an answer to your question, didn't you?"

"I see I have it now," he delights, kissing me, not even caring that Lady Havard stands nearby. "I've been in here since Monday and thought of nothing but you."

"Since Monday! Why didn't you tell me sooner?"

"I thought I'd be out by now. But as I'm not, I've had a lot of time to picture a moment just like this, finally seeing you again. Though we weren't both in here in my imagination."

"I want to be wherever you are. Here or anywhere else."

"Lord Paden's housing for his stable master's family?"

I eagerly nod. I realize I haven't informed Lady Havard of my newly realized plans to move to Lord Paden's estate but when I look around to fill her in, I discover she's disappeared. Probably to give that officer first some discourse on manners and then a pitch to get Thomas released.

"Who would have thought the happiest moment of my life would come in a locked cell after I've been charged with murder?" Thomas says.

"I'll get you out. Whatever I have to do, I know you didn't kill those men."

"Those men …" he says. "It turns out one of them is one of the men that assaulted you. If I'd gotten to him first, I probably would have killed him too."

I shush him, "Don't say that! Not in here."

"But I didn't kill him."

"I know you didn't." It's true. I am certain he didn't. But no one else seems convinced. At least not the people who need to be.

I sit with Thomas in his cell, talking a little about how we can get him out and talking a lot more about the life we plan to create. I tell him I won't leave Lady Havard unattended. He tells me to take as long as I need.

Eventually, Lady Havard returns with the officer, who unlocks the cell, and calls me out.

"Come on, Cory, it's time for us to go home."

I realize that means she has failed to get Thomas released. My heart sinks but my resolve does not. I give him a final hug and kiss, whispering promises to see him soon. I'll stay here all day tomorrow if that's what I must do to see him.

Thomas sends me on my way, putting on a brave face and ardently asserting his love for me.

On the trip home, I've gone through so many emotions, I can't quite figure out what it is I'm feeling most strongly. If I had to guess, seeing what Thomas is up against, I'd say it is fear.

Anselm

PRINCESS GISELLE'S CONFERENCE WITH THE OFFICER DIDN'T get her far in seeking Thomas's release. Veronica's message was that it didn't look good, but Giselle would keep trying. So I come up with a better idea.

The identities of the men I killed were made public. *Petros Wilkes. Leo Marmus.* I'm horrified to find that one of the two men I killed, this Leo fellow, was not Cory's assailant. He was not on the list of names Faizal gave me. He was not in Nyx Notch that night. I took his suspenders and fraternizing with the gold-toothed man to mean he was Ivan Rhomar. As it turns out, Ivan Rhomar still walks the streets at night while Thomas does not.

On my day off, I go to the temple. I pray for Leo. I know nothing about him. I don't know whether he was a good man or just as heinous as his companion. But he did not assault Cory that night. He did not deserve to die. Not for that. Not at my hands. I feel no guilt over Petros Wilkes but Leo Marmus … he'd be alive today if not for my brash initiative. I can only ask for the gods' forgiveness as I drop a coin into the fountain, tap my forehead, and go next to Faizal's.

When I enter the smithy, I ask Faizal for the other dagger of mine he found last week. Faizal warns me against what I intend to do. Leo Marmus was a mistake I can do nothing about but seek the gods' absolution and I've already done that. What they decide on the matter is their perquisite. As for Ivan Rhomar, *his* fate is in *my* hands. "I don't have a choice. I have to get justice for Cory. And now I have to get justice for Thomas too. If there's another death while he's in custody, they'll have to release him," I explain.

"And when does it end? There is always someone to get justice for," he beseeches me.

"It ends tonight. Will you be here?"

Faizal considers for a long moment how to respond. Finally, he nods sadly and mutters, "I'll be here." Before I leave, he hands me one more pair of gloves.

I must be careful tonight. People are on edge. A loner and an unfamiliar face like mine will stick out. I wait until almost midnight before I even approach Nyx Notch. I hide in a short alley cutout, listening to every voice and footfall that passes by, no one the wiser to my lurking presence. Drunken men and women eventually filter out of the taverns and inns as they close up shop. I look for suspenders, but no one wears any.

I'm about to give up as the road has been silent for some time. Then I hear something.

"Ivan," a voice says. "Hey, Ivan, wake up."

There's a groaning from the man. *Ivan Rhomar. It has to be.* He must have passed out drunk, which is why he never walked by me.

"Get out of here," the sober voice tells him. "Get home. Get back to your wife and kids. Don't you have work tomorrow?"

Ivan groans again.

"Lazy bum," the other man says. It sounds like he heaves Ivan to his feet, grumbling, "On your way now."

The man's words echo in my ears. Ivan Rhomar has a wife and kids. I second guess whether or not to kill this man. What would his family do without him? Then again, I suspect that with a man like Ivan Rhomar heading the household, a drunkard who rapes young women, they might be better off without him.

The man named Ivan stumbles past me and I watch him list one way and then the other. He lurches, hits the ground, and lies there for a minute before getting himself back to his feet. Then he starts to sing. Soft at first and then loud, it's clearly the bumbled words to a drinking song.

I trail behind him at a fair distance, keeping to the shadows. I have no idea where Ivan Rhomar lives, but he will not make it home tonight.

A man approaches, crosses the street, and calls, "Night, Ivan!" as they cross paths, and the stranger heads on his way. People seem to know Ivan Rhomar. And they'll know he was alive at 2:00 in the morning. I stow my dagger. I don't think I'll need it considering the state he's in.

When Ivan falters and finds himself on the ground again, I make my move. He's fallen in a spot untouched by moonlight, so I hurry over and grab him by his suspenders.

"Thanks, pal," he slurs out, thinking I'm helping him up.

"Ivan?" I ask, kneeling to the ground and looking him in the eye.

"Yeah …"

"Ivan Rhomar?"

"Yeah … I know you?" He's so drunk he can hardly settle his gaze on me.

I let go of his suspenders and position my body behind his. I place a gloved hand over his nose and mouth. He's too intoxicated to fight. It doesn't take but a minute before his body goes limp.

There are so many ways to kill a man. While I'd love nothing more than to tear him to shreds, he would hardly feel a thing in the state he's in. It's better not to risk the dirty methods. When I'm sure he's dead, I lay him on the cobblestone, pin a note to his shirt, and walk away.

The note reads: *YOU GOT THE WRONG MAN.*

They'll have to let Thomas go now.

Faizal waits for me. He's surprised when I return with the knife unbloodied. "Did you change your mind?"

I shake my head and say, "Just opted for a cleaner method." I take the gloves and toss them into the burning forge. I hand the knife back to Faizal, saying, "Keep it. I won't ask for it again. I promise."

The very next day, Byron comes by to give me the news that Thomas has been released.

Cory

I'VE NEVER BEEN SO HAPPY AS WHEN I SEE THOMAS'S FACE come into view through the front window. I drop the rag I'm cleaning with, fling open the front door before he can waltz to the servant's entrance, and fly into his arms.

"They've let you go!" I cry out.

He smothers me with kisses and then says, "Seems there was another murder last night, and it clearly wasn't me that did that one."

I'm too elated to ask questions. "Let's go inside. Lady Hav—, er, Aunt Farryn will want to know you've been released."

"And I need to thank her for bringing you to me and for doing what she could to try to get me released."

I retrieve Aunt Farryn and we all find places in the sitting room.

"You say there was another murder? Who was it that was killed last night?" Aunt Farryn asks when we've settled.

"A man called Ivan Rhomar," Thomas replies. "It's funny, though. When they first took me in, the officer told me a man by that name was a friend of Petros Wilkes, one of the men killed the first night."

A shiver runs through me at hearing the name. Thomas earlier told me that Petros Wilkes was one of the men I had the misfortune of running across in Nyx Notch.

"When they arrested me, the officer said that this Ivan fellow told them that Petros had assaulted a young girl in Nyx," Thomas goes on. "That's the information that put them onto me, seeing as how I'd been seen there with you a few times."

"And I suppose this Petros fellow went bragging to his lowlife friends about what he did to you," Aunt Farryn concludes, incensed by the very thought. "If he hadn't already been killed, I'd have half a mind to do it myself. It goes to show people get what they deserve."

I'd let Aunt Farryn think I had only one assailant that night. I've never told her otherwise. It would only hurt her more to know the truth. As I consider this new bit of information about Ivan, I can't help but feel that Aunt Farryn's assumption is wrong. I don't believe a man is likely to go bragging about raping a young woman when any other lowlife wanting to blackmail him could take that information to the law. No, if the officers knew of the assault through Ivan – and knew of Petros's involvement in it – I can only assume that means this Ivan Rhomar was the other assailant. And now he's dead, too. Deservedly so, just as Aunt Farryn said. But it can't be a coincidence, can it? That both of my attackers were killed only days apart? I must have some kind of guardian angel. A defender. Despite everything that has happened, maybe the gods are looking out for me after all.

No one says anything else about the men aloud, though I imagine we're all still thinking about them. Thomas is here now, finally free, so I'm just eager to move on with my life. My life with him. I squeeze his hand and smile up at him. He wraps an arm more tightly around me.

"When do you move to Lord Paden's?" Aunt Farryn asks, seeing us pet.

"Anytime. I start work there a week from today."

"I wonder if the stable master at your current post will be able to replace you so quickly," she says.

"Oh, yes," Thomas says. "Byron is taking over in fact, effective today. He'll have to find a new place to live, I'm afraid. Our place is a bit high for him to manage on his own. I've promised to help him look for something. Or find him someone else to move in."

"I have an idea," Aunt Farryn says. "Let's go see your new residence. I have some furniture I don't use that you two are welcome to."

I smile. "That's mighty generous, Aunt Farryn."

"Well, it's just going to waste. May as well get some use out of it," she shrugs.

She doesn't like for her generosity to be pointed out.

"I'll give you two a few minutes alone while I get ready."

When she's gone, Thomas practically leaps at me. "I've missed you so much!" he declares, burying his face in my neck, my hair, anywhere he can nuzzle, and kissing me everywhere. "When will we be married?" he breathes against my skin, his voice muffled. Then he pulls away and looks me in the eye. "I'd marry you this very day."

I laugh and push him off of me, playfully scolding him, "Be serious! I haven't even told my uncle. I shouldn't have even told *you* yes without his approval."

"Then we should pay him a visit."

"I'll write him today to let him know we can come by at week's end. Aunt Farryn will surely let us borrow her carriage."

"The week's end can't come soon enough," he says, and then smothers me with more kisses.

The stable master's residence is much larger than I was expecting. There's a sitting room, a kitchen, a pantry, a bedroom, a washroom, and another spare room on the first floor alone. On the second floor, there are four more bedrooms and another washroom. I spy a well through one window. It isn't too far away. I also see a line out back to hang laundry. I can't imagine what we are going to do with all this space.

"It was probably built to house several stable boys. It looks like they might be housed over there now," she says and, points through another window at a smaller building. "The man in charge gets the grand house now."

"Aye," Thomas agrees, "*there.*" And he points to Lord Paden's enormous estate off in the distance.

There are a few furnishings in the home already, but they're sparse and look rickety at that. A few might be salvageable, but the rest could be broken up for firewood in winter.

"A lot of rooms here," Aunt Farryn says, giving voice to what we've already thought. "I imagine children will be running around here in no time."

"Aunt Farryn!" I admonish. "We're not even married yet."

"Well that's easily arranged," she says, moving to the next room to explore.

"You remember what Pia said?" Thomas asks me when Aunt Farryn is gone. "Married in a year's time. Four kids in four years. We're ahead of schedule by quite a lot," he teases, pinching my side, and I wriggle away from him.

"Not so fast," I tell him.

I cannot imagine what life will look like in a few years' time. I cannot imagine having four children. But I can easily imagine having children with Thomas. I'd give him as many as he wants, just not yet …

"Thomas," I say, "do you think we could bring Uncle Penn to stay with us?"

"Of course," he says, "plenty of room here."

I'm so happy I could cry.

Princess Giselle

I'M COUNTING DOWN THE DAYS, WHICH IS PRECISELY WHAT Veronica told me *not* to do. I miss Devayn terribly. I read and reread his letter to me, the one that arrived just this morning. He tells me about Callinor, describes the peaks and valleys of their mountains, tells me the lake he visited reminds him of me and our perfect final outing when he asked for my hand.

I fold up his letter and put it in my desk drawer where I've kept all the others. I'll write him later today. First, I have a meeting to attend.

My parents wanted me to get involved with the politics of the nation and so I have. I put together a proposal that I plan to present to them today. The idea came to me when I broke open Anselm's letter, the second one after he left, the one saying his mother had already passed. My heart broke for him, and I thought it should never happen again. Never again should a guard be forced to walk a castle wall while his family members suffer, maybe even die, all alone.

Veronica helps me into a raspberry-colored dress. I don a simple tiara, which I've started wearing to all the meetings – and otherwise – now that my official duties as a princess have commenced. When I think I'm ready, I collect my papers and depart, thanking Veronica for her assistance.

My parents are always on time, so I make sure to be early. When my father has called the meeting to order, I launch into my proposal.

"Pursuant to earlier events when an exception was made for a first-term guard to take personal leave, I have drawn up the following proposition.

"I do not believe it is decent or principled that we ask the sons of this nation to forget their obligations to their own families for the period of four years they are required to give us. If they make the daily sacrifice to be of service to us and to this nation, it is only right we show we are willing to do the same for them. Therefore, I propose the following.

"Members of the Royal Guard are to be given up to two weeks leave each year, which does not include days spent traveling to their destination. The cost of traveling may be advanced to them and subsequently taken from their pay. Every request for leave will be evaluated and either approved or denied on the basis of how well it meets certain criteria, including emergency circumstances and health of family members. Members of the Royal Guard will be required to provide documentation evidencing the reasons for their requests. Leave will not be granted on the basis of holiday. A determination will be made for how long a guard shall be allowed to suspend his service. Should circumstances arise that he finds it necessary to be gone longer than two weeks, every additional day will be made up at the end of his term in the amount of two days' extra service.

"Further, the exception that was made for the guard already granted leave will no longer be considered an exception but a gesture of good faith before legislation of this kind was agreed upon and enacted."

When I've finished speaking, no one says anything. I think the council is waiting for my father to make the first move. After all, they are not familiar with the guard I mentioned or the circumstances surrounding his leave. They do not know of my previous relationship with him and the way I bargained with my father on his behalf.

"I see," my father says, "and what of transportation?"

"Each and every guard will be required to obtain it himself, whether acquaintances collect him, he rents a horse, or he finds other means. No horse of the royal house will be available for such travel." I've adopted my father's stipulation for Anselm, that he could not take one of our horses for his journey to Memnon. I hope it engenders his goodwill for my proposal. I do think it's fair.

"I find it interesting you wish to double the days made up beyond two weeks leave," he says, curious.

"There might be another way, but I think it would give guards incentive to return to duty in a timely fashion so that leave is not taken advantage of as though it were a holiday." I can thank Devayn for that bit, seeing as how he's the one who told me what incentive was provided for young men to learn archery in Callinor.

A discussion ensues, weighing the merits of the proposal along with its drawbacks, and finding ways to address them until a final statute is agreed upon.

"Giselle, if you wouldn't mind drafting the final measure?" my father asks.

"Certainly," I reply, gathering my notes on what's been discussed. I'm beaming on the inside, but I work hard not to let it show on my face, nor does my father betray his own feelings on how I performed. Still, he looks at me out of the corner of his eye as the meeting proceeds with other topics that require attention. I think I'm living up to his expectations.

"Your Majesties," a council member says, moving the meeting along, "we've had a heightened number of complaints about the condition of the roads connecting our cities. Carriages and carts are losing wheels with increased frequency, causing travelers to become stranded. Thieves pick off their goods. It has a small impact on trade supply between cities at this time but if left without response, it will only get worse."

My father says something in reply, but I'm only half listening. I think he grumbles about how recently roads have been repaired.

"Um," I interrupt, and all eyes turn to me, "I think I'd like to explore this problem and see if I can come up with a feasible solution. I just need to do a little research." I have the fringes of an idea forming. I hope I can deliver after piping up so impulsively. I shouldn't let the delight at my earlier success get me in over my head.

Both of my parents look somewhat bewildered. I know next to nothing about roads, and they know that as well as I do. But I do know someone who might be able to help. At the end of meeting, I hurry to write him immediately.

In my letter, I tell Devayn how much I miss him and wish he might return to Dionysius soon. I don't know if I can wait these six months. Well, just over five now. Then I ask him about rocks. Jareth told me he studied geology and mineralogy. And the last day we spent together at the lake, he talked about how rocks are formed. I don't know much about roads, but I do know they're made of gravel and gravel is merely crushed up bits of rock. I hope Devayn can tell me what else I need to know.

That evening, Veronica helps me prepare for bed, pulling back my bedsheets and handing me a fresh, soft nightgown. As I slip into it, she says, "I heard Anselm's cousin was released."

"Really!" I reply, thoroughly pleased – and surprised – to hear it. When I spoke with the official on his cousin's behalf, he seemed disinclined to reverse course and let the young man go. He was evidently convinced of Thomas's guilt and my speech on his excellent service in the Royal Guard did little to sway him to leniency.

"It seems there was another murder in the area, a man connected to the first two. A note was left on the body."

"What a strange turn of events, to be so unfortunate for one and yet so fortunate for another."

"Strange indeed," Veronica agrees. "But isn't life just like that? Ambrosia to one is poison to another."

I climb into bed and pick up a book from my nightstand earlier retrieved from the library.

"Well, good night, Your Highness," Veronica says.

"Good night, Veronica." I turn to my book and delve into the dry material awaiting me.

IT'S ONLY A FEW DAYS BEFORE I RECEIVE AN ANSWER FROM Devayn, who expresses his curiosity about my newfound interest in geology. He provides me with suggestions for books to peruse, and I hope I can find them in the library. He also tells me how gravel is formed naturally as rocks break down over time, often due to such weathering effects as streaming water. It then mixes with the sands, silts, and clays of riverbeds. He tells me gravel can also be quarried from rock beds, where workmen break down the rocks rather than waiting for nature to do the job. He says the make-up of the gravel is different depending on where it comes from.

I head to the library to track down the book titles Devayn listed. I also want to find a map of Apollonia that shows our geologic features. I've seen many of the land formations myself in my travels through the nation, but I know very little about how they're formed or the minerals and natural elements that comprise them.

I see from the map that Apollonia has mountains stretching from the southwest end of Dionysius, cutting nearly all the way through to the sea that forms our southern border. There are some stretches of valleys in between the mountain ranges, offering passage from one side of the range to the other. The Nereus River also winds throughout the region, finally spilling into the sea. Various tributaries through the range look like veins to the main artery that is the river. There's an abundance of riverbed to acquire gravel from, and I assume the gravel used to form our roads is already sourced from here.

But I don't just want to pave new roads. I want to pave roads that will last. Roads that won't bend and warp under the pressure of carts, carriages, and horses traversing them. Roads that won't break apart over time as rainwater weathers them, loosening their cohesion and, by extension, their stability.

There's a solution somewhere. I just have to find it. I open the books and soak up as much information as I can.

Cory

EVERY DAY SPENT WITH THOMAS IS BETTER THAN THE LAST. He comes by daily now that he's in between jobs. He has already packed up his few belongings in the apartment he shared with Byron. We plan to take his things to our new home on Sunday. I won't be moving in until we're married of course, and I've told Aunt Farryn I won't leave her without a replacement. That's if I decide to leave at all, though traipsing from Lord Paden's into the city everyday will be quite a hassle. Aunt Farryn knows this too, but we avoid the topic because neither of us want to acknowledge the reality of my impending departure.

Thomas has gone to retrieve the carriage and horses, so Aunt Farryn and I take care of last-minute details before leaving for Perseus. Butterflies work up a storm in my stomach because I'm so anxious to see Uncle Penn and to introduce him to Thomas. I have no doubt Uncle Penn will adore him like I do, but he'll surely be wary considering how quickly this has all transpired.

We busy ourselves for a long time until we find there isn't anything left to do, so we take up seats in the sitting room to wait. We were hoping to be gone by now, but Thomas has not yet returned. If he isn't here soon, we may have to postpone the trip a day to avoid traveling after sunset. I can't imagine what's taking him so long, especially considering he is so eager to take this trip.

I finally see someone approaching, running is more like it, and I rise to open the door. But it isn't Thomas. It's Byron, who works in the stables now.

"Cory!" he cries out by way of greeting. "Come quick!"

"What is it?" I ask, needing some kind of explanation for his harried manner.

"It's Thomas. There's been an accident."

My heart sinks. Aunt Farryn has joined me at the door, drawn by Byron's excited manner. A hand flies to her heart.

"Where?" she asks.

"Corner of Aether and Erebus," Byron says.

"Go on, dear," she says to me, "I'll be along."

Byron and I can move more quickly than she can, so we set out while she gathers herself and locks up.

I move as quickly as my legs will carry me for however many blocks separate me from Thomas. It doesn't take long for my lungs to start aching and a twinge to form in my damaged leg, but I ignore them both, knowing every footfall brings me one step closer to him.

As we approach the corner, I can see him lying on the side of the cobblestone road, a small crowd gathered around him. I rush over, kneel beside him on the ground. I look him up and down, trying to determine what I need to fix.

"Thomas," I cry. It's a plea. *What's wrong? Tell me what to do.* "Can you move at all?" His body lies still but his hand reaches for my face.

Neither Thomas nor Byron has to say anything for me to know what's happened. I see the horse and carriage a short distance away, the horse still restless, snorting and jerking, threatening to rear. The whites of the horse's eyes are wide as he monitors us. I don't know what might have spooked the animal to cause him to bolt, but it's obvious that Thomas was in his path when he did, horse and carriage both tearing over him. I want to pull up Thomas's shirt, to evaluate his injuries, but I'm scared of what I'll see.

"Cory," he wheezes. He tries to smile as he looks me over and wipes away at the tears wetting my cheeks. "My gods, you look like a goddess in this light."

I can't help but let go a convulsive sob seeing him like this, seeing the adoring way he still looks at me, injured as he is. His breaths come in staggered fashion. I'm sure Byron or one of the bystanders in this crowd has summoned a doctor. But if he doesn't arrive soon, which one of these breaths might be Thomas's last?

I grip the hand he holds to my face and wait for help to arrive. It isn't long before a physician pushes through the crowd to look Thomas over. He gently tugs on Thomas's shirt, then cuts it with scissors when Thomas winces too much at the tugging. With his shirt torn away, I see indentations across his chest and stomach, where the horse landed heavily upon him, where the carriage wheel drew a thick line across him. I don't know how many times the horse reared before running off, but the damage is extensive. The bruising is already dark and widespread. I see the uneven rising and falling of his chest as he struggles to breathe, an entire section of ribs crushed and severed from the rest of his rib cage. The doctor is light in his touch, as he evaluates the injuries. Thomas keeps his eyes trained on me, but I keep mine focused on the doctor, trying to read his face for any hint of what he might be concluding. He has a lamentable look when he says, "Flail chest. Must be a ruptured spleen."

Even if I don't know what the words mean, even if his expression weren't already clear enough, his sorrowful tone when he speaks these words tells me all I need to know. His injuries are too severe. Thomas will not survive this.

The doctor returns the scissors to his physician's bag and extracts a bottle instead. "I can give him opium for the pain," he says, and I nod. I don't know how much time he has left, but I don't want Thomas to be in pain. I look at Thomas as the doctor administers the drug. I'm not sure he's really heard a word of anything the doctor has said.

When he's finished, the doctor slips the bottle back in his bag and clasps it shut. He pats Thomas's hand and sighs, shaking his head as if to say he doesn't understand the gods' choices sometimes. *I don't understand either.* I hear the doctor ask if anyone has summoned the temple priest, but I miss the answer over my whimpering cries.

"I love you," Thomas ekes out, his eyes never leaving my face. He wants me to be the last thing he sees before the gods claim him. *How long until then? How much time do we have left?*

"I love you," I say, clasping tightly the hand he has kept to my face. I don't know if I'm trying to savor the warmth of his body while he still has it or feed into him the warmth of mine, as if doing so could somehow save him, could somehow breathe life back into him.

"Grant me … one … small favor," he says between gasps. His breathing has already deteriorated to such uneven wheezes in the mere minutes I've been here, he can no longer utter a full sentence. *Please, gods, no.* "A kiss."

I catch my breath, wipe the tears from my face as best as I can, and lean down to kiss him. His lips are dry while mine are soaked by salty tears. He can muster little pressure and I don't know if bestowing more would hurt him or please him. I kiss him again and again, as my unyielding tears fall upon him.

When I pull back, I can see he holds onto life by inches. A tear of his own has escaped and slides down the outside corner of his eye.

"I love you," I tell him again, once more lowering my face close to his.

Moments later, I realize I can no longer hear breath scraping across his throat. My own breath catches, and I'm terrified of what I might find when I finally dare to look once more at his face. When I finally work up the nerve, I discover that his eyes are glazed over and no air passes through his mouth. I cry out and fall to pieces, wailing in my grief. *Thomas is gone. Please, gods, bring him back!* But they've claimed him and no matter how I plead, it's a prayer the gods will never answer.

On the day we were supposed to be going to Perseus, to share our love and happiness with Uncle Penn, to get his blessing for us to spend our lives together … *how can this be happening?*

At some point, my tears run dry and my cries turn to fitful sobs. I carefully rest my head on Thomas's shoulder in fear that holding him more tightly would hurt him, though I know he is no longer here. Still, I cannot let go of him and no one dares pull me from him. That is, until the temple priest arrives, proffering blessings and prayers, sending Thomas on his way in the afterlife.

I look on without hearing anything. Aunt Farryn finally helps me to my feet and I immediately bury my face into her side. She keeps an arm tight around me. No doubt I would fall to pieces if she were not there to hold me together. I would disintegrate and wither away in the breeze.

I think Aunt Farryn has directed others as to what to do because a pair of men lift Thomas's lifeless body and place it in the carriage. He's to be taken away and prepared for burial. *Where will he be buried?* I wonder. *Where will I visit him?*

Aunt Farryn turns me around and walks me home. I follow along mechanically, unaware of anything going on around me.

Once we're home, she helps me into bed and closes the bedroom door behind her when she goes. I lie there deathly still, beseeching the gods: *If you won't give me Thomas back, then please claim me too!*

Anselm

NEWS OF THOMAS'S DEATH REACHED ME YESTERDAY WHEN Byron paid me another visit at the castle. He tells me Thomas's fiancée and her family will manage the burial arrangements. I had no idea Thomas had even become engaged. Byron didn't say, but I assume Thomas proposed marriage to the young lady's maid I never had the chance to meet. My heart aches for her, whoever she is. She must know the grief I do at losing Thomas.

The only person I want to see right now is Cory, but when I went to call on her, Lady Havard informed me that they will be spending some time in Perseus after Cory suffered another recent tragedy of her own. She provided few details and wouldn't even let me in to say goodbye. The truth is, it's probably best we don't see each other now. She's been through enough. I don't want to pile on with my own losses. My own demons. I'll give her some time and space and check on her again later. I elect to go to Faizal's instead.

"How can this be?" I ask him. "Saved from certain hanging, he's trampled by an unruly horse with carriage not a week later. Where is the justice in that?"

I can't help but wonder if the gods have chosen not to absolve my sin of killing Leo Marmus. And my punishment is that they've taken someone from me in recompense. My cousin. The last close family member I had. A good man who did not deserve his death, just as Leo did not deserve his.

"Human justice is not the gods' justice," Faizal says. "If the gods planned to claim him, who are you to say whether it's by hanging or by any other means? If it was his time, you know the gods will not be denied."

Was it his time, though? I'm consumed by guilt and anger. I want Faizal to tell me I'm right to be angry. That what I've done in Nyx Notch on two separate nights is still justified even if Thomas is gone. *It is, isn't it? For Cory's sake?* I want Faizal to fix everything. To tell me I'm not alone when that's precisely how I feel. But I know Faizal can't fix anything. He cannot bring my mother back – or my cousin, or Leo Marmus.

He does only what he can, which is to hug me and say, "Go see Cory. Let her comfort you."

And I have to tell him she's going to Perseus. As for myself, I have nowhere to go but the castle and here.

"Then today you'll stay here and forge a weapon and tomorrow you'll return to work. And if it isn't this week or even next month, you will eventually find yourself again."

I nod. I'm not sure I trust his words just yet. I take his advice anyway and select a hammer to start pounding a rod of molten steel into shape. It dawns on me that I understand why Giselle summoned me to her room whenever she was desperate. Grief, anger, passion, all of these emotions have to be channeled somehow. The repeated swinging of the hammer helps to relieve the helpless despair bit by bit, one blow at a time.

By the time I get back to the castle, I've let off plenty of steam. I think I'll be able to sleep tonight because I've exhausted myself with the exertion of blade smithing. I go to bed early, wanting nothing more than the oblivion sleep offers.

And just as Faizal has suggested, I go to work the next day, searching for the comfort of routine.

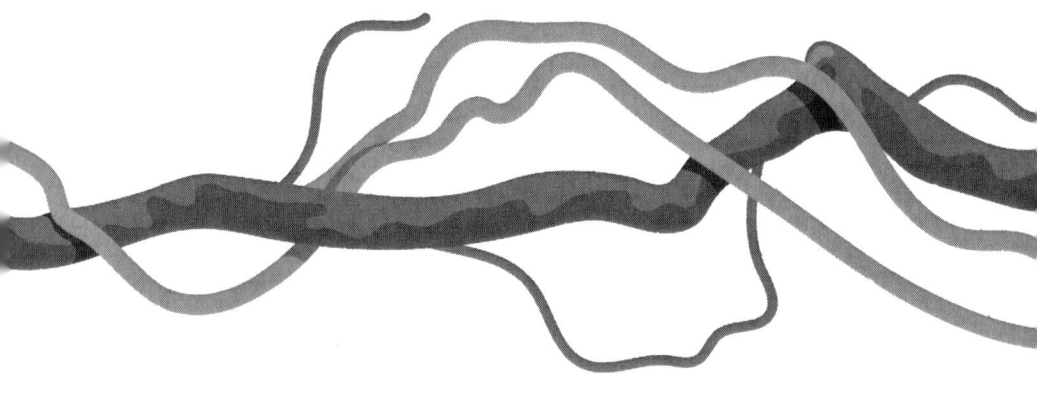

WINTER
five months later

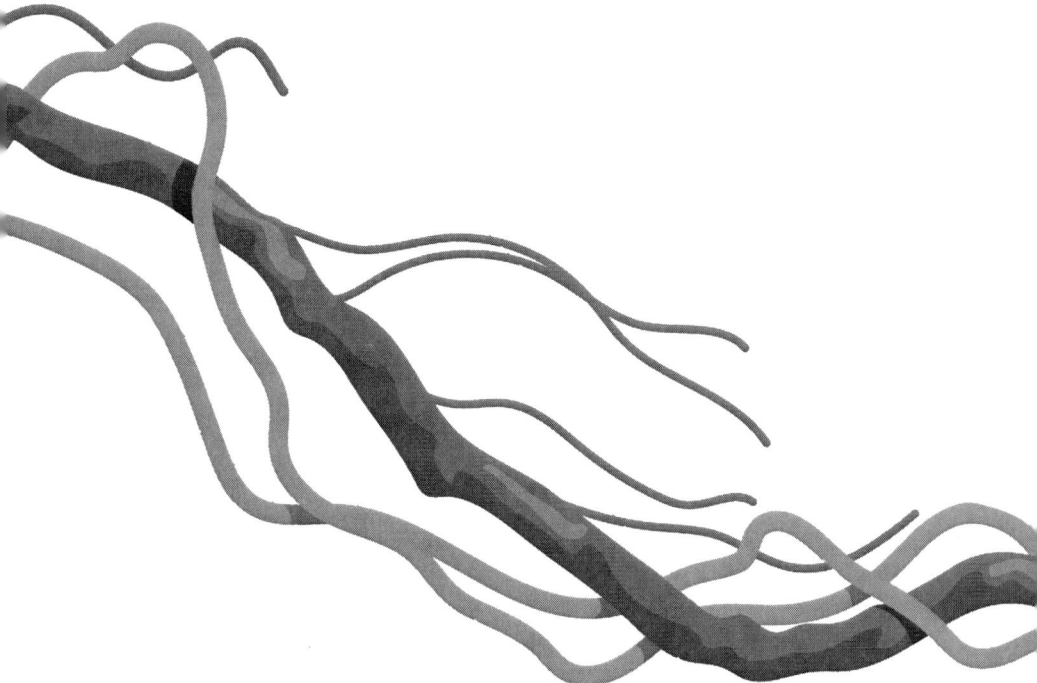

Princess Giselle

DEVAYN'S CARRIAGE ISN'T SET TO ARRIVE FOR ANOTHER TWO hours, but I can't help but keep posted by the front doors, peering out to see if I can catch sight of his approach.

Veronica reminds me I ought to keep busy to make the time pass more quickly, but my elation makes it hard to focus on anything else. I'm thrilled to finally see him and I'm thrilled to share the good news I alluded to in my last letter.

We spent the last five months corresponding with superfluous letter writing. With Devayn's help and with extensive research – which included making a few trips to several places in Apollonia and studying the natural features our nation offers – I made a remarkable discovery. A variety of trials were run to test a few theories, and on the basis of those analyses, I've written up a proposal to present to my parents and the council.

Devayn's carriage finally comes into view in the distance, cavalcade and all, and I run outside to await him, even though he has another five minutes at least before he actually pulls up. Veronica runs after me, cloak in hand.

"It's cold out here," she says, but I don't even notice the winter weather. What is quite noticeable, however, is the bulge in Veronica's stomach. I've told her time and again that she needs to take bed rest before the baby comes because it will surely arrive any day. But she has stubbornly refused.

I take the cloak from her if only to make *her* go back inside where it's warm. However, when the carriage finally stops before me and Devayn steps out, I drop the cloak and throw my arms around him.

He returns my embrace, then lifts me, spinning me in a circle. "Even more beautiful than I remember," he says. "And trust me that I never once stopped picturing you." He starts to kiss me before noticing my parents who have stepped into the doorframe. He elects instead to greet them.

"Your Majesties," he says, "thank you for accommodating me here."

"You're most welcome," my mother replies, "and we're pleased to have you back."

"It will only be until the wedding of course," my father adds, looking conspiratorially at my mother.

"Yes," she agrees, "I hope it isn't too soon to tell you what we plan to give you as your wedding gift." They glance again at one another and my mother continues, "We're electing to bequeath Hera Manor to the two of you to make your home together."

Hera Manor! It's the beautiful château near Lake Harmonia where Devayn asked for my hand, the one we never visit because it's so close to the castle. Still, it's a delightful hideaway that would be a terrific place for us.

"If you'd like, why don't you go appraise it now? I imagine it's in need of some updates and repairs," my mother says. To Devayn, she adds, "That is, unless you'd like to rest first after your long journey. You must be tired."

"I don't think I could rest if I tried," Devayn says.

"We thought as much. We've already sent for a carriage to be prepared for you. Your own carriage will be lodged, and your horses fed and sheltered. Your things will be taken up to your quarters and will be awaiting you when you get back."

"Very generous, Your Majesties," Devayn says, bowing slightly.

When my parents have gone inside, Devayn takes me again in his arms and gives me a deep and passionate kiss. "The rest of our lives starts right now," he tells me. "Are you ready?"

"If it were up to me, it would have started six months ago."

He kisses me again as our carriage pulls up. He spies my cloak on the ground, picks it up, and wraps it around me, advising, "It will only get colder."

"Not right here," I say, folding myself into his warm embrace.

"True. Never right here."

Hera Manor is a bit large for only two people, but part of the bargain struck with my parents was that within five years, children's feet will be padding through and filling out the extra space. Stepping inside, I see why my mother was so eager to urge us to the manor. It's been completely transformed. The furniture, the décor, the drapes, everything is brand new, befitting a young couple like us. It's quite a wedding present, though I'm certain we won't be allowed to move in together until after the wedding. Still, I drag Devayn through the rooms, heading directly for the grand bedroom on the second floor.

"Wow," he says upon seeing the massive bed with blue sheets hanging in canopy fashion overhead, dangling down on either side.

Lake Harmonia can be seen through the window, offering a beautiful view. The site of his proposal can also be seen from our bedroom window where I can gaze upon it every single day if I want to. The lake is nearly frozen over now. In a month's time, we should be able to skate there without fear of the ice cracking.

He turns to me, kisses me. "Beautiful," he says, and I'm not sure if he means the house, the view, or me.

"Let's try it out, shall we?" I say, tilting my head in the direction of the bed.

His eyes narrow at me. I kiss him, guide him to foot of the bed, then reach to remove his clothes.

"Are you serious?" he says. "Now?"

"You weren't going to have me wait until the wedding, were you? That could be months away! I've waited months to see you already!"

He grins, pulls off his jacket, and shoves me lightly onto the bed. I scramble to my knees and kiss him as he stands at the foot of the bed, unfastening the back of my dress. I let my cap sleeves fall to reveal my bare chest where the effect of the chilly air is quite obvious. He takes each breast into a warm hand, massaging heat back into them, leaning over to kiss me at the same time. It's thrilling to have Devayn's hands on me, and I let out a small moan against his lips.

It occurs to me that I'm savoring the moment, in no rush to jump in and be done quickly the way it always was with Anselm. And the reason becomes clear. Anselm was an outlet. Devayn is the love of my life. Anselm served a purpose. Devayn is my everything. I wonder if he's making the same comparison between Maris and me, as he takes his time caressing me.

I've never bothered with much foreplay, but that's precisely what Devayn and I fall into. Our clothes come off slowly, one piece at a time. His hands search every inch of my body. His lips do the same. I had no idea just how exhilarating lovemaking could be when it involves true love.

His hand slides up my thigh, between my legs, and his fingers find a splendid rhythm, lulling me into bliss. I close my eyes, relishing the feeling, and before long, my back arches involuntarily. I grip the bedsheets as a tingling sensation radiates through my body to the very tips of my fingers and toes. He watches my face and my heaving chest as the residuals of climaxing course through me.

I keep my eyes closed to luxuriate in the full effect that has yet to abate. He leans down to me and whispers, "What do you want to bet I can make you do it again?"

I silently thank the gods that this man is mine. My eyes open, find his. Challenge accepted. I reach a hand down and find he has clearly taken pleasure in watching me writhe.

He quickly climbs on top of me. When his hips descend, he takes his time at first, making tempered thrusts. Before long, arousal overtakes him and he can't help but quicken his pace. He keeps his eyes trained on mine, making me feel a kind of vulnerability I've never experienced before, but I crave it nonetheless.

I move my hips to the rhythm he sets. Soon, I have lost the bet as his final, deep thrust, sends him over the top and I quickly follow suit. I'm surprised that the second time matches the thrill of the first, so much so that I release a protracted moan.

Devayn's heart races, and he takes a long moment to collect himself before sliding off of me. He falls onto his back beside me, still gasping for air. "My gods, woman," he mutters.

I turn to my side and nuzzle against him. For the first time ever, I don't feel saddened now that the act of lovemaking is over. I feel elated. Adored. I never want to leave the comfort of his arms.

We spend a few hours exploring the manor. We make love twice more before getting dressed for the last time to return to the castle. As he fastens the final button on his jacket standing in front of a tall mirror, I wrap my arms around him from behind, pressing an ear to his back, and whisper, "I love you."

Satisfied that he looks put together, he turns, cups my face in his hands and says, "You can love me like that any time you want."

I giggle. Then we kiss and leave the manor hand in hand.

"You never told me your good news," he reminds me on the carriage ride back to the castle.

I snuggle into his side, unable to separate myself from him. "Come to our advisory meeting tomorrow and you'll find out," I tease.

Devayn does attend the meeting. He sits beside me as I review my papers and the information I'm about to present. My parents arrive, call the meeting to order, and ask me to start. I take a deep breath and dive in.

"As you are all aware, we've been testing a variety of materials to improve the conditions of our roads because it is not enough to simply rebuild them. We want to construct roads that are durable, long-lasting. We've discovered that roads which are most susceptible to absorbing water suffer destruction more easily, which explains why roads in the worst shape tend to be in areas with the most rainfall.

"We've also discovered that select particles are more prone to breaking apart when significant weight is placed upon them, no matter how compressed they are to begin with. In order to address these issues, we've conducted experiments to blend various resources with three goals in mind. Those goals include increasing compression, supporting traffic weight without bowing over time, and improving capacity to disperse water. I'm very pleased to announce that after extensive research, I believe that we've found an excellent blend of natural resources that achieve all three of these objectives."

I sneak a peek at my father to see how he's receiving my declared success. As I've yet to explain how, his expression tells me nothing. He's stoic, waiting for more information to weigh before revealing his thoughts.

I take a breath before continuing. "The riverbed gravel we already use has proved to be an excellent starting point, but it is insufficient on its own, as it breaks apart too quickly with repeated exposure to heavy loads. As the roads bow, it places undue pressure on carts and carriages and results in wheels breaking apart."

Stop rambling, I chastise myself. *You're telling them what they already know.*

"Therefore, we began to experiment with a variety of soils found throughout Apollonia that might serve to amplify the strength and efficacy of our gravel. We wanted the soil to help fill in the gaps between gravel particles, thereby augmenting compression, reducing particle shift, and improving road durability."

I cast another glance around the room and find impassive faces staring back at me. *Are they bored or simply dispassionate?* My nerves are escalating at the lack of reception I'm receiving, but I do my best to quell the fluster and keep my voice steady.

"In our research, we encountered a problem with soils that are particularly adept at absorbing water. While this is excellent for agriculture, it is equally problematic for road quality, as the absorption of water serves to break apart gravel particles and ultimately the roads themselves. However, there are other soils that are poor candidates for agriculture because their inherent properties restrict infiltration of water needed for crop growth. As a result, these soils demonstrate the most success in improving road quality."

I think I see a couple of them raise their eyebrows. *Is that a hint of interest at last?*

"In our final analysis, we determined that the soil found in Perseus proved most effective when blended with riverbed gravel. This combination of materials should provide the most firm, long-lasting, and water-resistant foundation for roads, reducing undue impact on the carts and carriages that traverse them. With this composite, our roads ought to hold up longer, requiring less money to be poured into fixing them. It is expected that the long-term savings has the potential to be substantial."

I see a few council members jotting down notes; one is even nodding slightly. It gives me a touch of confidence before my final announcement, one I'm particularly eager to report.

"Furthermore, I'm pleased that this has the added benefit of improving the economic conditions of Perseus, one of our poorest cities, as their soil will now be in demand for roads built nationwide. Local laborers can of course be called upon to collect and transport the soil as needed."

When I'm done, no one says anything for a long, drawn out moment. Despite the boost in confidence a moment ago, I'm still nervous they don't like what I've proposed, that I've missed some obvious problem. I'm afraid I'm about to be excoriated for my ineptitude. For taking on a project I knew so little about and failing. And all of this in front of my parents and Devayn. I never should have invited him to witness my humiliation.

Finally, my father speaks. "Remarkable, truly remarkable, Giselle – very well done."

I release a breath I didn't realize I was holding. I want to remain professional, but I can't help but beam in response to his approval.

"You've solved two problems with a single solution."

"Very thorough," a council member adds.

"Impressive work," another tacks on. And throughout the room, more and more members express their endorsement and admiration of my work. I recollect the first meeting I attended when it felt like they gave me fabricated approval to augment my confidence. This feels nothing like that.

I breathe another sigh of relief as the practicalities are next discussed. Things like methods for obtaining the soil and gravel, mixing them, compressing them, hiring laborers, and so on. These are things the rest of the council is adept at sorting out.

As everyone in the room chatters, picking up where I left off, Devayn leans over to me. "If you can solve such grand problems in a matter of months as princess, I can only imagine what you will do with years as Apollonia's queen."

My chest feels as though it will burst with pride and happiness, and I simply cannot contain my broad smile.

Cory

I THINK I NEED TO BE IN DIONYSIUS. IT'S WHAT I TOLD BETHEA and Uncle Penn after staying with them for two months following Thomas's death. Aunt Farryn stayed with me there the entire time too, and when I made the decision to return, we packed up the carriage and headed back to the city. I want to be near him again. Remember him where I knew him. I can't do that in Perseus.

Now that we are back, I only want to sit on Aunt Farryn's backdoor steps where Thomas first kissed me. Where I can picture him pacing, clutching his tattered cap. I want to wander to the Erato Gardens and sit where he gave me the amber ring I now wear on my right hand, a symbol of his love that I don't want to relinquish.

For a few weeks at least, I do little else but despair, often sitting on the steps out back. So when Anselm stops by unexpectedly, Aunt Farryn leaves him at the front door to notify me.

"He seems troubled," she says of Anselm. *Someone else's troubles are the last thing I need.* "He might understand what you're going through. You might be able to help each other."

"I won't talk about Thomas," I say firmly enough that she backs off. I mean it. Thomas is mine. Our memories are mine. I don't want to share them. She nods in understanding, though she clearly doesn't agree with my decision. It wasn't so long ago that Aunt Farryn wanted me to choose Anselm over Thomas. She wouldn't have wanted me to divulge my relationship with Thomas to him then. Now, she's encouraging me to open up to him. But I won't. I can't.

Just as I finish getting ready, I can hear Aunt Farryn whisper to Anselm, *"Don't ask her about what she's gone through. Some things are best kept to oneself."*

I'm grateful she has mentioned something to him so that I don't have to explain my silence on the matter. And I can be assured he won't ask what has me down.

The first day out of the house is the hardest. I take Anselm's arm for a walk and it immediately becomes obvious what Aunt Farryn meant when she said Anselm seems troubled. I'm not so blinded by my own grief to know he's grieving too.

When I ask him if there's anything he wants to talk about, giving him the chance to open up about what troubles him, he simply says, "I've spent quite a lot of time in the temple recently because I felt the very bedrock of my being faltering. The gods claimed my cousin soon after my mother. I had hoped to introduce you to him. When I asked the gods what I should do, they answered my prayers. They told me to go to you anyway. I hope it's not a bother."

"Of course not," I say. "I'm pleased you thought to pay me a visit." I'm surprised that as I speak the words, I find they're true. I *am* pleased to see Anselm and I'm quickly reminded of how safe he makes me feel.

We promptly move onto other topics and do not return to discussing affairs that trouble us, as we both clearly prefer to keep our secrets to ourselves.

WEEKS PASS AND WE SPEND A GREAT DEAL OF TIME TOGETHER. More and more, Anselm's company helps me to reconnect with life. He takes me to Faizal's smithy and shows me the sword he has finally completed, and there is no word to describe it but majestic. I still have the dagger he made for me, and I carry it when we walk, even though I have the protection of daylight and a member of the Royal Guard with me. Still, I feel comforted knowing I am not defenseless, thanks to Anselm.

He has taken me to Erato Gardens several more times. The expanse is often covered in a light sprinkling of snow now that winter is taking over. It's beautiful here in all seasons.

I would initially steer us away from the spot by the lake where I sat with Thomas, where he gave me the amber ring I still wear. But as we venture to the Gardens more often, I let myself walk more freely, edging progressively closer to places I've kept sacred in my memory – still never confessing to Anselm the reason for the sadness in my heart.

But the more time we spend together, I realize that the sadness that has been weighing me down is slowly beginning to lift in increments. It's never far away and always returns at the end of our outings, but there are reprieves that I begin to crave. I think the same might be happening for Anselm. A smile here or a laugh there shifts back into grief at the end of the day when we part company.

"It's all right, dear. You must know," Aunt Farryn says as I await Anselm's arrival for our next jaunt.

"What?" I ask.

"To fall in love again."

But I can't. Not now. It's much too soon. It has only been six months since Thomas was taken from me!

"Don't you think he'd want you to find someone to love and protect you?"

The answer is yes, but I can't bring myself to acknowledge it just yet. It would mean letting him go for good. I remember Aunt Farryn telling me that when her husband died, she gave herself six months. If I do the same, I'm now out of time.

Anselm arrives with a carriage. He has clearly rented it but hasn't said where he's taking me. Aunt Farryn ensures that I have a thick cloak as well as gloves because it's the dead of winter and snow blankets the ground, no longer merely a thin sheet.

Anselm takes my hand and helps me into the carriage where a rectangular box rests on one of the benches, but he does not let me open it just yet. "Where are we going?" I ask.

He smiles. I think it's a genuine smile, which is something neither of us has seemed capable of displaying very often for quite some time. "It's a surprise," he answers.

My only clue is the route we take through the city, eventually traveling toward the mountains to the southwest, but I still have no idea precisely where this path leads or what he has in mind.

"Have you heard how things are in Perseus?"

He's curious about how things are changing since the royal family issued a plan to reinforce the infrastructure of the roads throughout Apollonia using Perseus's soil. It's been a month since the announcement, but I haven't received much correspondence from Bethea or Uncle Penn in a while. Furthermore, I'm assuming the work won't begin until winter has passed. A new layer of snow falls before the first several inches can be plowed away.

"I'm pleased Perseus will see some growth," I tell him. "It will take a lot of laborers to shovel the amount of soil they'll need for the entire nation's roads. Then they'll have to rebuild the local roads as well. Princess Giselle has helped us so much. Even if the economic impact isn't felt just yet, the entire town's spirits are lifted by the prospect."

Anselm smiles again, this time a more wistful smile. He had a relationship with the princess, which has been over for months now, but I know the mere mention of her name brings back memories of their time together. Since then, she's become engaged and set a wedding date for spring. I wonder how he feels about it.

"Will you be a guard at the wedding?" I ask.

"I'm afraid not. I'm still not supposed to be around the princess. Not so long as I'm in the Royal Guard, that is."

"Supposed to be?"

"Well, we corresponded a couple of times." In response to look on my face, Anselm laughs. "Not in the way you're thinking. She is engaged after all. Very happily at that, it seems. The princess and I formed a friendship, and we like to know the other is doing well. In fact, she helped me plan today's outing, though don't let anyone know that."

"My lips are sealed."

It isn't long before we reach our destination. He helps me out of the carriage, and I look around. The landscape is stunningly beautiful, but I can't say I know where we are.

"This is Lake Harmonia," he says. He takes the mysterious box and leads me to the water. Ice is more like it. The lake has frozen over solid. Only a thin, sparse sheet of snow coats the surface, in contrast to the earth where we trudge through a half-foot of it at least. When I wipe a gloved hand over the ice, it's so thick I can't even see the fish swimming underneath.

"How do you know about this place?" I ask.

"I told you," he says, "the princess helped. You see that estate just over the way?" He points into the distance, and I can see a beautiful château there. "That is where Giselle and Devayn will live once they're married."

"How lovely," I respond. Then he opens the box and inside I spy two pairs of beveled wood pieces, one set longer than the other. Blades are inlaid along the bottom of each piece while holes along the top allow for three straps to pass through, spaced evenly apart. "You're not serious …"

"Don't tell me you're scared," he prods.

"Scared! Appropriately cautious is all."

He hands me the smaller pair of blades, and I dangle them by the straps. They're surprisingly heavy. I touch the ice again to test it, just in case.

"I assure you, it's perfectly safe," he laughs, positioning the blades and tying the straps around his boots. When he's done, he helps me with mine, as I sit on the soft snow. He fits the straps snugly around my shoes, tying up the loose ends so they don't drag. Then he pulls me upright, offering a steadying arm as I wobble. I really hope I don't twist an ankle in these.

"Are they tight enough?" he asks, and I nod, testing them. "You've really never ice skated before?"

"Do you remember Perseus having a lake?" I ask.

He laughs again.

"We have a small one in Memnon. The other boys and I would pass around the few sets of blades we had, not enough for all of us. We'd have to take turns on the ice."

He grips my hand at chest level as I take my first step. My foot slides back and forth as I work to find my balance. Once I'm certain I won't slip, and knowing Anselm won't let me fall, I set the other foot on the ice, stabilizing my weight between each foot. "Now what?" I say, bending forward. My feet seem much too far apart.

"Now we glide," he says. He stands beside me, slightly ahead, and pulls me along slowly as I try to propel myself forward without falling face first on the ice. "That's it," he encourages.

I can sense my balance improving, adjusting to the slippery surface. Somehow I'm moving forward, not quite like walking but advancing in a staggered sort of way.

Then Anselm says, "All right, I'm going to let go now."

"Don't you dare!" I cry and clench his hand tighter. He bellows a hearty laugh.

"All right, all right," he reassures and continues pulling me along ever so gently. I don't even notice how far we've gone until I look back and see the edge of the lake behind us. My heart starts to pound, and he comforts me once again, "The ice is thick. You're perfectly safe on the lake. You think I didn't check to be sure before I brought you out on it?"

"You did?"

"Of course. I won't let anything happen to you."

An unexpected sensation kindles from somewhere inside me. It's small but reminiscent of how it felt when Anselm departed for the castle after tending to me for a week. I was desperate for him to stay longer at Lady Havard's, terrified that sense of peril would return without him.

"Oh," is all I can say in reply.

The longer we're on the ice, the easier it becomes, though I do not let Anselm get far. I fall twice, but he helps me to my feet each time and I'm not hurt. The second time I fall, I pull him down with me and he hits the ice with a thud, rubbing at his backside. I can't help but laugh, so he feigns leaving me on the ice alone. He doesn't, of course. Once he's found his feet, he helps me to mine and we glide along again.

I eventually become accustomed to skimming the smooth surface of the ice and feel comfortable testing it out on my own, so I let Anselm release my hand. He stays close, even positions himself ahead of me, skating backward. I'm not sure if he's flaunting his skills or merely reassuring me that he's there. But I don't care. I'm simply moving toward him, and he's ever present, as though he's waiting for me to reach him.

We continue skating for what seems like hours, and he keeps his hand in mine most of the time. I feel a sense of freedom on the ice that I haven't felt in a long time, like the weight that has borne down upon me is lifting little by little, flying off my shoulders in the chilly air I slice through. That we seem to be completely alone out here is equally liberating.

We finally glide back to the bank and collapse on the snowy cushion, falling to our backs. My legs are aching, and I'm sure they'll still be hurting tomorrow, since I've discovered an abundance of muscles I didn't realize I had.

Anselm rolls to his side to face me, propping himself up on an arm. I'm still smiling in delight for the fun we've had. "You know something?" he says, his sober expression a contradiction to my jovial one. "It's been a rough year, but this is the best I've felt in months. I've laughed so much today my cheeks hurt. That ought to tell you how little of that I've been doing lately. This euphoria today, though, I have you to thank for that."

I know exactly how he feels. I've barely smiled let alone laughed except in Anselm's company. Yet I've done quite a lot of both today. There's a twinge of guilt for allowing myself these moments of joy, but I remind myself that Thomas would want me to feel this way, to bask in it, to remember what it's like to *want* to be alive. I need to because the gods failed to deliver on my prayer for them to claim me when they claimed Thomas. Perhaps being alive still isn't so bad after all.

In my head, I hear the words: *Six months have passed.*

Anselm collects the blades we've shed and drops them into the box. I massage my feet before standing. My legs need a minute to figure out how to walk on solid ground again. Then Anselm grabs my hand and says, "Follow me."

We bound through the snow into a thicket of trees, bare but for the moss that still flourishes on their trunks.

"I've always thought trees in winter were more beautiful than when they're full of greenery," I say, grazing one of them with a gloved hand.

"I can't say I disagree."

"It seems stronger somehow," I go on, "standing tall in spite of the harsh conditions that strip it bare."

"Without a doubt," he says so low that I'm not entirely sure he wasn't merely speaking to himself. By his tone and the way he looks at me, I can't tell if he means the tree or me. But I haven't felt strong in a long time. I've forgotten what it feels like.

"Look there," I say, noticing a pair of trees at the edge of a rock ledge. The soil beneath them has fallen away and their thick roots stand exposed, twisted together.

"Did you know the roots of one tree can provide nutrients to the other?" Anselm asks.

I shake my head. I did not know that, but it makes sense, the symbiotic relationship that can form between two entities that find they just might be better off together. I take one last look at the enchanting scenery. It's a winter wonderland unlike any I've seen before. "Thank you for bringing me here," I say, and it comes out in a whisper. "I don't think I realized how much I needed this."

He takes my hand, weaving his fingers between mine, and we amble back to the carriage to go home.

SPRING
four months later

Cory

"ARE YOU READY?" AUNT FARRYN CALLS OUT FROM THE hallway.

"Nearly," I call back.

"Byron will be here with the carriage any minute. I'll just be in the sitting room," she says.

I hear the sound of creaking floorboards as she walks away. In the meantime, I look quickly in the mirror and adjust the dress she's bought me for the occasion. It's a beautiful green and magenta frock and it has a delightful flow from the waist down when I twirl. I partially tie back my hair, which has grown out quite a lot, and pin a flower there. I make sure to allow tendrils of hair to hang alongside my face in the hopes that it will obscure my scar.

Out of the corner of my eye, I see the reflection in the mirror of a box, tucked away into my armoire with the door ajar. I haven't revisited the memories in that box for quite some time. I try to keep the armoire closed, but the broken latch sometimes causes the door to swing open. Maybe it's a sign that I need to put these memories away once and for all. I dig out the box and peer inside to see the contents.

Thomas didn't own much, and Byron kept his clothes. Atop the pile of his personal effects, I see his cap, the one he always either had on his head or clutched nervously in his hands. I take it out, squeeze it as if I could draw him out of it, then set it aside. There are a few knick-knacks, gifts from friends or family I presume. There's even a little money that I leave there. If everything Thomas was could be whittled down to a single box of his belongings, the paucity of contents here would belie the extraordinary impact he had on me.

At the bottom of the box, I extract another item, one I had not noticed before because Thomas packed this box when he was preparing to move to Lord Paden's estate. It's a dagger. I unsheathe it and see it's beautifully constructed, with even weight. The handle is made to look like the trunk of a bare tree, the hilt extending on either side of the blade like leafless branches. When I look closer, I see the initials carved there – AO.

I recall the first time Anselm took me to Faizal's, and he showed me the sword he was working on, now completed. He was unsure about his craftsmanship, but I affirmed that it was remarkable.

"Haven't others you've shown said the same thing?" I had asked.

He replied, *"I haven't shown anyone else. Only Faizal knows about it. Well, and my cousin is aware I've taken up the hobby. I even gave him a knife I made. In fact, he's the only person who owns a blade I've created. But that's the extent of it."*

My journey with Thomas never crossed paths with Anselm, and my journey with Anselm never crossed paths with Thomas. All this time, I had no idea the cousin of which Anselm spoke was my Thomas all along. Anselm's sadness of the past few months and mine have had the same root, though his was amplified by his mother's recent passing and mine was amplified by the fact that Thomas was my fiancé and I lost a future with him.

I pack the box away again. I decide not to tell Anselm what I've discovered. He hasn't talked about his cousin since Thomas was claimed by the gods, and I think he prefers it that way. I don't want to revisit the incident either. And what would he say if he knew I'd planned to marry Thomas? How would it change our relationship now?

"Cory," Aunt Farryn calls, "Byron is here."

"I'm coming," I call back. I hesitate at what I'm about to do, but I do it anyway. I slide the amber ring off the finger of my right hand and place it into the box with the other items. "Goodbye, Thomas," I whisper to the ether. When I reach Aunt Farryn at the door, I say, "I think perhaps the box in my closet should be returned to his family." I can't look her in the eye as I say it. It's hard enough simply to get the words out.

"Oh," she says, wavering a moment, knowing full well which box I mean. Then she says, "Yes. Yes, I think that's probably best."

There's a moment of awkward silence before she turns to her handbag and withdraws a bottle of skin balm. I recall going with Bethea to purchase an identical jar for her my first week in Dionysius.

"I don't know why I hadn't considered it before," she says, "but I'd like you to have this." She opens the container, dabs some of the oil on the side of my face. "It's a remarkable ointment that's made with a mineral they say helps to heal damage to the skin. It may well reduce the appearance of that scar. I know how it bothers you."

I find a mirror and finish rubbing in the balm, examining my face. If I look hard enough, I can imagine the purple and yellow spots from my bruises after that night in Nyx Notch. I can see the handprint that lingered on my neck. Of everything I've been through, it suddenly seems absurd that this scar I've had all my life would dismay me so much. It's really the least of my concerns and no one I know and love has ever cared one whit about it. Only me.

I sigh and tug the loose tendrils of hair away from my face. I sweep them up with the rest of my hair into a bun and secure the flower there instead. I return the bottle to Aunt Farryn, who seems at first surprised and then pleased as she pulls me into a hug.

"You've never looked more beautiful." She smiles, and I beam in return. She extends a hand to the front door, "After you, my dear."

Outside, I step inside the carriage to take my seat. Upon entering, I let out a cry of elation. Uncle Penn is here, alongside Bethea and her husband. I fall into Uncle Penn, eager to embrace him.

"What are you doing here?" I exclaim, as Aunt Farryn climbs in behind me.

"Surprise," he says, "Lady Havard sent for us."

Her formal title sounds so strange to me now.

"Would you stop?" she says. "The name is Farryn. My goodness, I stayed with you for two months in Perseus. I thought we were friends."

Uncle Penn smiles shyly.

I give Bethea a quick hug before the carriage sets off for the town square. The same day she purchased the skin balm, we had also watched as Princess Giselle returned from her nationwide tour. That day seems so long ago now. The princess's subsequent tour was postponed. For one, they decided to wait until the new thoroughfares were constructed. For another, there was a certain wedding in the making, a ceremony taking place on this very day.

It has turned into a sort of festival for the nation to celebrate along with their princess. There are wreaths of flowers, music, dancing, and food everywhere. We haven't walked far before Uncle Penn quickly finds a bench, his lungs and joints bothering him. Aunt Farryn follows and takes a seat beside him.

"Oh, no," he insists, "you go on with the others. I'll just wait and watch from here."

"Nonsense. The younger ones will move much faster without us old folk slowing them down."

Uncle Penn laughs and says, "If it pleases you, it pleases me."

Through the crowd, I hear my name being called, "Cory!" It's Anselm and I hurry to greet him. He hugs me and steps back to admire first my dress and then my hair, which he's never seen pulled back like this. "You look beautiful," he says, leaning in to kiss my cheek.

"Come on," I say, taking his arm, "there are a few people I want you to meet." I drag him back to where Uncle Penn sits and introduce them to each other, then I present Bethea and her husband.

"I thought members of the Royal Guard would be at work for today's events," Uncle Penn says.

"That's right," Anselm replies, "but we're taking shifts so we can each enjoy the festivities as well. I already took my shift this morning."

"So you won't be occupied the rest of the day?" I ask, and he nods. I grin, squeezing his hand in mind.

At around 4:00, the horns sound, signaling for everyone to clear the square. The carriage carrying Giselle and Devayn is set to travel through, coming directly from the temple where they were wed only moments before in a private ceremony. I'm sure Giselle will share the details with Anselm, who will in turn share them with me. Anselm and I find a spot on the side to watch. He stands behind me, a hand pressed firmly to my back. Before long, four elegant horses traipse through, pulling an open-topped carriage.

Giselle and Devayn wave at the cheering crowd. They dazzle in their elegant wedding attire and jubilant smiles. At the crowd's request, they give each other a kiss for all to see. The throng explodes with hurrahs. If I'm not mistaken, I do believe Princess Giselle looks right at me and Anselm and blows us a kiss.

"She looks so happy," I remark.

"I believe she is," Anselm replies, "and so am I."

I spin toward him and declare, "You know something? I am too."

That evening, there are fireworks in the night sky. The mass of people has thinned out, as children and adults alike have tired and opted to trudge home. Even Aunt Farryn, Uncle Penn, Bethea, and her husband have left. Anselm has promised to return me home safely.

As the final fireworks fly into the air and the last few cheers go up, Anselm and I sit on a bench together. He takes my hands in his and says, "Cory, I get out of the Royal Guard in one year's time. I've already arranged with Faizal for me to work there. He's planning to retire soon, says he's already made too much money and wants to travel. He's offered to let me take over his smithy when he does."

I light up. "Anselm! That's amazing. What a wonderful opportunity!"

"It is. I'm planning to design a new line of swords for the Royal Guard. The idea was inspired by you actually. You asked if the sword I made was intended to guard the princess, do you recall? I'm sure I can convince Giselle to present the idea to the advisory council. Stronger, lighter swords for the Guard. I expect they'll accept the offer, if it doesn't cost them too much."

"That sounds like a fine idea."

Anselm hesitates then pulls a folded letter from his pocket. He offers it to me. I unfold it and start to read – I can read much more seamlessly now, thanks to his ongoing tutelage.

"*My dearest, Anselm,*" I begin, then stop immediately. This letter is not written to me. I check the bottom and see it's from his mother. I look at Anselm to be sure he wants me to read this.

"It's the letter she wrote me when she knew her condition would not improve," he says. "I hadn't had the courage to read it until the day we went ice skating on Lake Harmonia. I finally opened it that evening, and I've been waiting for the right time to show you."

I accept his explanation and look back to the letter.

My dearest Anselm,

If you're reading this, my illness has overtaken me, and the gods have claimed me. We both knew the rules of the Royal Guard and that it might come to this when I fell ill. Though I may never again see your beautiful face or draw you once more into a mother's embrace, I will greet you with open arms when we meet in the next world. Do not take it as a slight, but I do hope that day does not come for a very long time. I want you to live a full life, with boundless love, and I will watch over you in joy from the stars for every moment of it.

My son, there isn't much I could say to you that you have not already learned. You had to grow up much too young. I am so proud of the man you've become. My wish for you is that you find light in your life and bask in it. Find happiness in your life and relish it. Let go of darkness, hold onto joy. Life is much too short for anything else. With your father and brother and soon with me, I think you've learned that lesson well enough. I only wanted to remind you.

As for the estate, keep it or sell it. Whatever you do, just make your life your own.

With love,

Your proud mother

When I've finished reading, I fold the letter up again and hand it back to him. He stuffs it into his pocket. "I was scared to read it because I knew it would really be goodbye. I would have nothing left of her. After that day at the lake, I saw your courage. I saw that whatever had been pressing down upon you for so many months, you were finally letting it go. I knew I had to do the same, so I read the letter when I got back and wished I'd read it sooner. I'm not going to make the mistake of waiting too long again.

"Cory, you've been my light where I've been in darkness. You've brought me back from winter to thrive in your summer. My light, my joy, it's all wrapped up in you.

"I've got money from the sale of my mother's estate. I'll get remittance when I leave the Guard in a year's time. I'll have the smithy that will more than provide for us."

Us. I'm smiling from the inside out. I realize what's coming next and my heart races to hear it.

He withdraws a ring and holds it up. The light of the fireworks bounces off the modest ruby flanked on either side by a delicate, golden leaf. They look like petals of a flower and the ruby is the bloom.

"I designed this myself, crafted it on my days off," he says.

I take the ring and marvel at it. The exterior of the band looks like four braided strands. The smooth surface of the interior shows an inscription: *Blossom in the light.*

"I love you," he tells me. "I want to spend every day of my life warmed by your light, working to ensure it never fades but only shines brighter, making you feel the way you make me feel. Coralyn Perle, will you marry me?"

I already know my answer, and I'm sure he knows without a doubt if my smile tells him anything, but I say instead, "I can't say yes without Uncle Penn's blessing."

"Very well. He already gave it."

"What?"

"When you and Bethea left and brought back sugar plums, I asked him, and he said yes. Aunt Farryn, too, for what it's worth."

"Then yes!"

He slips the ring on my finger before kissing me. I immerse myself in the love his kiss exudes. His hickory brown eyes peer into mine before his lips graze my nose with another kiss, then my forehead, and finally the top of my head as he wraps me in his arms. They're strong and solid, and I know with Anselm by my side, he will never let any harm come to me. With Anselm, I am safe. With Anselm, I am loved. And I silently give thanks to the gods for giving me every day I have with him.

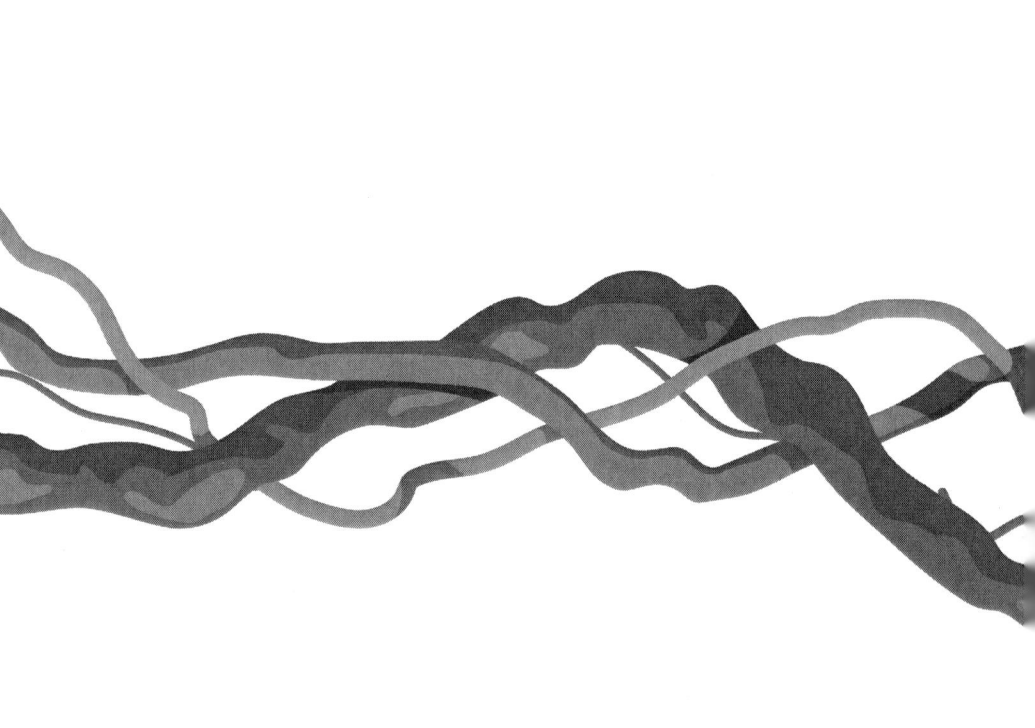

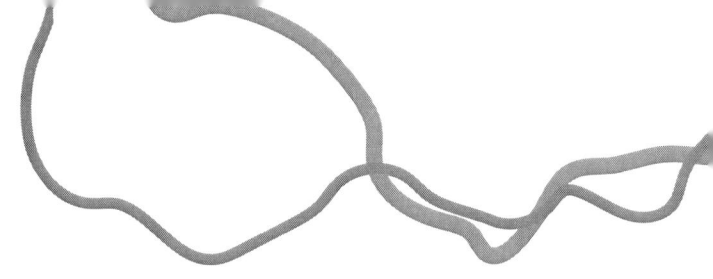

SUMMER

one year later

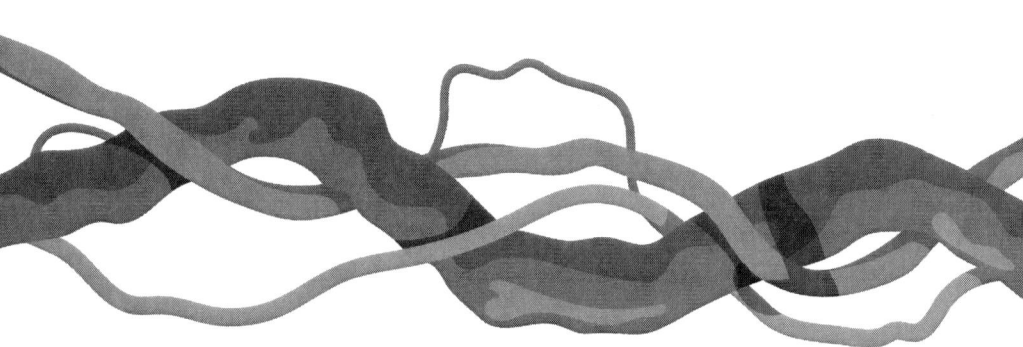

Princess Giselle

MY ONE-YEAR ANNIVERSARY WITH DEVAYN IS MARKED IN celebration in more ways than one. I didn't know it was possible to only become happier with every passing day. The first delight is wrapped in a bundle in my arms, nursing as I sit in a rocking chair looking out over the lake. Devayn arrives and stands beside me, watching our miracle flourish.

"She's perfect," he says. And she is.

Devayn is dressed up for the second delight that will take place in twenty minutes or so. The ceremony is set up outside by the lake and nearly everyone in attendance – a small handful of people – is already down there now.

Anselm talks with the temple priest here to carry out the wedding ceremony. Cory's uncle is already seated. Bethea and her husband are settled there as well. Behind them is the blade smith, Faizal Sarif. Lady Farryn Havard attends to Cory in this very manor, helping her finish dressing and fixing her hair.

Veronica enters the bedroom, her fourteen-month-old son toddling unsteadily behind her. My daughter has taken all the milk she wants and blinks at me before eyeing the other faces before her, her father's and Veronica's.

"Beautiful girl," Veronica says, reaching for my daughter. She'll watch my little one and her own son while Devayn and I go down to attend the wedding. "I think they're ready now," she adds.

I pull the top of my dress back up. When I stand, Devayn helps me to fasten the back. Thank goodness she didn't spit up after I'd already dressed. Of course, she wasn't going to wait for her meal until after the wedding, so I had little choice.

I walk on Devayn's arm down to the lake, where I hug Anselm. He's no longer a member of the Royal Guard, having completed his four years. I'm no longer prohibited from seeing him. And thank the gods for that. He's become much too dear a friend to lose him forever. I think my parents have also seen he's not a threat to my relationship with Devayn, whom I'm certain the gods created just for me. Not to mention, my parents were quite impressed with Anselm's blade-smithing designs and were eager to contract his services for a full set of swords for our Guard.

The other guests courteously bow their heads to me and Devayn as we approach and soon Lady Havard arrives, also nodding respectfully to us before announcing that the bride is on her way. A harpist is the only other guest here, and she starts to play. Anselm stands beside the priest and watches as Coralyn Perle makes her appearance.

She's radiant. I daresay she's more beautiful than I was on my own wedding day. Her white dress has an overlay of lace embroidered in a floral pattern. A white hibiscus adorns her hair, and she carries a small bouquet of white hydrangea. No one can take their eyes off of Cory, but I find myself turning to watch Anselm instead. I've never seen him look so vulnerable. So in love. I squeeze Devayn's hand. I know the feeling.

The temple priest blesses the couple and says prayers to the gods above. We all tap our foreheads in thanks for bringing the two of them together. Anselm and Cory speak their vows, exchange their rings, and share a kiss with such adoration that I think they forget the rest of us are here. We applaud their union, their happiness. Then we dissolve into a cacophony of congratulations as Devayn's valet brings out a tray of champagne chalices.

What a beautiful day, a beautiful year, this has been.

Cory

PRINCESS GISELLE HAS BEEN WONDERFULLY KIND TO ME AND Anselm. She provided us a setting for our small wedding and the use of her manor for me to dress and get ready. Then she presented us with arrangements she made on our behalf. She thought we deserved to spend some time together, just me and Anselm, without the pressure of everyday life, so she presented us with directions to a mountain retreat.

"The stars shine bright up there, up above the clouds," she told me, and I discover that she was right.

It took us three hours to reach the mountain pass and another two to ride our horses to the modest lodge. I hoped we wouldn't get lost, but I wasn't scared, even as dusk came on and daylight slowly left us. I trusted Anselm to find the cabin. He's familiar with the countryside, and he would never let anything happen to me out here. I savored the quiet of dusk, my horse traveling alongside Anselm's until the path became too narrow and I pulled my sweet mare back to follow Anselm's lead.

As the night falls, there's no question that the effort has been well worth the reward of this view, which I've had difficulty pulling myself away from. Since we had dinner, Anselm cleaned things up while I was drawn by the twinkling lights in the night sky.

He approaches me from behind and watches the stars with me. The night air is crisp and cool this high up. I left my shawl inside, in too much of a trance to bother grabbing it. I wonder which star Anselm's mother calls home now. Or Thomas. Or Aunt Trudy or Tobin or anyone else we've known who went to live up there among the gods.

Anselm's hands are warm, but the way he lightly moves them up my arms sends a shiver through me. He tugs at the thin fabric covering my right shoulder, letting it drop down my arm. He replaces the fabric with a kiss on my shoulder. He repeats the motion on my left shoulder and the fabric covering my top half slips to my waist without the support of my shoulders to hold it up. His arms wrap around my stomach as he kisses my neck. I arch my neck to see him, to kiss him.

I have never lain with Anselm. I refused until this night. And though he's ready to embark on this next step, he manages to be slow and loving anyway. He knows the one and only time my body was taken in this way was a moment of torment, and he wants to replace the memory with one of love, letting me ease into it.

I let him move his hands to my bare chest, and I bathe in the comfort of his touch. I love Anselm. I'm safe with Anselm. And we are far removed by time and distance from that awful night in Nyx Notch.

I've never told Anselm what I know about what transpired after that. About the day I sat with Thomas and Aunt Farryn in the sitting room after Thomas's release from jail. I only told two men about the assault that night. Anselm was right about me when he said that I see things as they are, not as I would like them to be. And while I didn't let myself consider it for a long time, it's as clear to me now as the night sky. Anselm figured out who to hunt down. Who to kill. An act he's trained in. The mistake of killing Leo Marmus the first night ended up allowing for Thomas to be released. That there were no more murders after Ivan Rhomar let me know the men who were targeted had been slain. No one else would be killed. The mission laid out was completed. I know Anselm killed my assailants. I know how far he would go to protect me. To take care of me. Which is why I'm not apprehensive about giving him my body tonight.

I turn around in his arms and start unfastening the tie at the neck of his shirt, pulling the fabric over his head. When I reach for his pants and unfasten them, he scoops me up into his arms and I wrap my legs around his waist. I bend down to kiss him and he carries me inside. He finds the bed, kneels upon it and lays me gently down. He slips the rest of my thin shift over my hips and takes in the sight of my body for a moment, fully revealed to him. Then he pulls off his own pants, revealing himself to me. He leans down toward me, nudges my legs gently apart to wrap around him once more.

I knew it would be different from the time this act first made me feel unclean, the time after which Anselm had to tell me he still saw me as pure, even if I felt anything but. Still, I had no idea just how different it would be. My body doesn't resist him. It invites him. It craves him. He doesn't cause me any pain that doesn't also feel like pleasure.

His hickory-hued eyes are trained on me and I now know what *one flesh* meant when we took our vows only hours ago. There is no separation between us. Not as he moves above me and tenderly kisses me. And not after when he lies partly beside and partly atop me, his head on my chest and my legs tangled up with his.

I run my fingers through his hair, which I think relaxes him further. He lies there so long I wonder if he's fallen asleep. Then he mildly stirs, tightens the hold his arms have around me, and he whispers, "I love you, Cory."

I brush the hair from his face, though I can hardly see him given the angle at which he lies. Instead, I gaze out at the star-filled sky, draw a hand along the thick muscle of his arm, and say, "I love you too, Anselm."

It isn't long before I drift off to sleep, safe in the knowledge that when I awake, Anselm will be there. Ever my guardian, ever my angel.